DEATH AT A CROSSROAD

IAN KENNEDY

A NOVEL

IN MEMORIAM IEM

This novel is set in Caribe, an island that does not exist save in my head.

Equally the characters are fictional. You may know someone who is like the saintly Cesar or the ruthless Gaudi - we all do - but my Cesar and Gaudi are made up.

The events are set in the early 1960s, a time without the internet and mobile phones. Younger readers may be bemused, but the world was once like that.

A number of people have commented on drafts, my brother Alan, a veteran writer of fiction, David Paterson, and John Sills, and I am extremely grateful. They bear no responsibility for what remains.

Anna and my son Jack deserve my gratitude for piloting me through technical stuff.

I also thank my family for their support. They have humoured me as, on occasions, I sought to explain this or that bit of plot which, without context, was entirely meaningless to them.

Ian Kennedy lives in London. He spent time in the 1960s in Mexico, Puerto Rico and Cuba. He has written a number of books. This is his first novel.

iankennedyconsulting.com

LIST OF CHARACTERS

At the Globe

  Tony Conway – Journalist

  Harry – Editor

  Zack – Journalist

In Caribe's Government

  Don Basilio Barbosa - President

  Raul Salcedo - Chief of Staff

The Echevarria Family

  Lydia – Writer and Journalist

  Alejandro – Lydia's Father, Professor of Mathematics

  Elena – Lydia's Mother

  Melba – Lydia's Maid

The Morales Family

  Luis – Taxi-Driver

  Josefina – Luis' wife

  Carlos – Son

Police

Alberto Gomes – Captain

At the Sand and Sea

Joe – Barman

Beatriz – Girl from the country

Bud Greenberg – American Businessman

Mike Slavic – American Businessman

In The Network

Cesar Sanchez – Ex-Professor of Classics, now Cane-Cutter

Circe Garcia – part-time waitress

Atilio – Painter

Patricio – Musician

Dolores - Student

Magda Gonzalez – Doctor's Wife

At the British Embassy

Jeremy Brown – Second Secretary

On the Campaign

Jose Gaudi – Union Leader and Commander

Nino – Second-in-Command

Ines Fonseca - Assistant to Gaudi

Emilio – Sergeant

At the Circulo Latino

Mary Baxter – Wife of American Banker

Joyce Lloyd – Wife of American Lawyer

Betty Lloyd – Joyce's Daughter

Soledad Fuentes – Socialite

In the Courts

Saul Noriega – Chair of the Popular Tribunal

Captain Crespo – Prosecutor

Lieutenant Fernando – Prosecutor

Others

Carmen – Barbosa's Wife

Ramon Aguirre – Lydia's Fiance

Jose, Fulgencio, Cristiano, Javier – Police Officers

Teresa – Receptionist at the Circulo

Pablo, Jaime, David, Mario – The Driving Team

Tomas – Circe's Little Brother

Sylvia – Ines' Sister

Ricardo Leon – Lawyer

Chapter 1

The adventure begins

Conway wandered out of the Embassy building and into the garden with studied nonchalance. A reception was being set up so no-one paid him any attention. He found the shed. Inside there was a lawnmower which had a seat which he was happy to rest on. Apart from his fear of spiders, which he imagined lurking in the darker recesses waiting to pounce, he felt fine. He was about to embark on an adventure. He was excited.

As midnight approached, three cars took up station in the streets at the front and side of the Embassy. A fourth car was held back, about three hundred yards from the Embassy along the narrow lane which ran past the garden wall which he would have to climb over. Aware that Raul's men knew that Conway was in the Embassy and that they would aim to prevent any escape, the three cars were to act as decoys. They drove slowly up and down past the Embassy, stopping and starting randomly. Then, as the regular police patrol car drove past the back wall on the hour and turned left, one of the cars swerved towards it causing it to stop suddenly. The police got out, the car driver also got out. There was much shouting and gesticulating. The drivers of the other two cars, one at the front and the other at the side of the Embassy slowed down and pushed open the passenger doors. Raul's watchers, distracted by the altercation with the police, struggled to see what was happening now that the passenger doors of the other two cars had been opened.

Wearing a pair of gloves he'd found, Conway left his shed at midnight. He'd reconnoitred the area and had found the bougainvillea. Now he made his way across to it, thanks to the reflected light from the salon where staff were cleaning up after the reception. He parted the branches and there was the wall as promised. He'd commandeered a step ladder from the shed to help him over the wall and to leave as proof that he had in fact absconded. Peering over the wall to check on the patrol, he saw them go past and then heard the noise of the altercation round the corner.

Now was the moment – there'd be no going back. Conway hovered on the top of the wall and dropped to the ground. A car reversed towards him at speed. The back door was thrown open. He dived in. The driver gunned the engine and they flew down the narrow street and out into the wider Avenida. As they did so, the man in the passenger seat threw a blanket over him. "Don't move or make a sound till we're safely out of the city". The car slowed down and merged inconspicuously with the late night traffic. In half an hour they were out of Puerto Grande and heading for the interior of the island. "I made it", he thought. Then he mumbled, "Oh Christ, what if it all goes pear-shaped?" The question died on his lips as he fell asleep, the blanket serving as a pillow.

Chapter 2

Don Basilio

"Thank you for agreeing to see me, Don Basilio".

"I have read your book, Señor Conway. It is all wrong, full of lies. But of course that will mean you will sell a lot of copies". Don Basilio didn't bother to disguise his disdain.

"I'm sorry you think that, sir. But, I understood you wanted to talk to me."

"Yes. I want to tell you the truth, though I know you will not publish it and it's too late anyway".

It had been Harry's idea. After the success of his book, which the Globe had serialised, ex-President Barbosa's chief of staff, a Señor Raul Salcedo, had contacted Harry.

"Yes, indeed. Don Basilio would be willing to be interviewed. A fee of $50,000 would be acceptable".

Harry liked the idea of a follow-up piece - 'Ex-President bares his soul' or some such. He offered $4000. Salcedo accepted immediately. Barbosa wanted the publicity if he was ever to make a come-back rather than disappear into the history books. And the money wouldn't hurt. So, Harry told Conway to get on a plane to Miami. Then he caught an island hopper and picked up a car from Hertz.

The villa was on Key West. They were on the patio. A breeze was coming off the sea. It was a beautiful morning.

The ex-President seemed to be running out of steam after treating Conway to almost an hour of his spleen. He'd dutifully taken notes which he doubted he'd ever read. During one of the pauses, he moved the conversation on.

"Do you see yourself ever being back in Caribe?"

"Shall I go back", Don Basilio asked rhetorically. "I am always ready, Señor, to do my duty, to serve my country".

A pause, not for any dramatic effect but rather as if tired from delivering this weighty thought. Don Basilio seemed much older. And fatter. He was very fat. His arms and thighs and stomach challenged the ingenuity of his tailor. His face had a yellowy pallor. The gold in his teeth didn't help. But the effort towards beauty, not neatness nor elegance but beauty, still showed.

The hair remained jet black. The suit, spilling over his frame, was of grey silk. A diamond pin fixed the blue silk tie to the white silk shirt. The boots, hanging inches from the floor as he leaned back in the upholstered chair, were of patent leather. Those tiny boots which once tempted a rash correspondent to label him Caribe's Caligula still seemed hopelessly inadequate to the task of supporting him.

It was the first time Conway had seen him since Don Basilio had left Caribe. He preferred to say that he had "left". In fact, he had scrambled onto the plane just ahead of the bullets.

Don Basilio was how he liked to be known now, rather than Presidente, General, Excelencia, or any of the other titles granted to him by a thankful nation. His new role saw him busy living out the second of his two great fantasies, that of being the patron, the fatherly, kind and generous land-owner.

The villa was large. As they sat on the patio, he could see into the living room over Barbosa's shoulder - the tiled floor, the thick rugs, the heavy Spanish furniture, everywhere signs of wealth. The Library had few books. The paintings were arranged to cover the walls, not to be looked at, which was just as well. Pride of place on the wall above the faux fireplace went to photographs which exuded both the bombast of his former power and, with no-one to admire them, the painful loneliness of his exile. Though full of things, the room was soulless, full of emptiness.

In the swimming pool, Carmen his wife, the third beneficiary of his eternal love, swam length after length. Watching her reminded Conway of one of those zoo animals whose only response to the inevitability of captivity was to fall into endless compulsive to-ing and fro-ing. The return to his native Newcastle of George, the latest in a line of rather too good-looking teachers of conversational English, meant that for a time at least she had no-one's attention but Don Basilio's. Hence her determination to stay in the pool for as long as it took till it was time for his nap after lunch. It was difficult not to feel sorry for her. Pretty, young, vivacious and ambitious, the approaches of El Presidente had seemed, if a little unsavoury, worth encouraging. Money and what it could bring were hers for the taking if she played her cards well.

When she had read in the Diario del dia of her impending marriage to "Our Happy Leader", the word was that she'd been shocked, appalled. Then she'd smiled to herself. "Crafty old fox, but I can handle him". The images of power and wealth were strong medicine.

Within months she was scrambling for her life onto the airplane that was to get her out of Caribe and into exile, bullets flying everywhere. She would never forget the picture which greeted her as she scrambled aboard. Don Basilio, aka El Presidente, sprawled across a seat, moaning and shaking with fear. Periodically, he threw up into a pink plastic bucket thoughtfully placed between his tiny feet by Raul. Ave Maria! Was this to be her future?!

"But do you think the people want you back"?

"The people? Do they want me? Señor Conway, you writers always ask such grand questions. I am a modest man, Señor, without education, without culture. How am I to answer philosophical puzzles"?

"Come on, Don Basilio, you can do better than that".

"If you ask me what I want, what my friends want, I can help you – to eat and drink, love and be loved, worship God, and live in peace. Isn't that what everyone wants? The people of Caribe once thought I could provide them with those things. They were persuaded otherwise. If they should decide to turn to me again, I shall be ready to try again".

A pause. The diamond pin flashed as Don Basilio's chest pitched and heaved. Suddenly, the outburst: "But as long as that Communist murderer and his henchmen loot and rape my country, I must remain here, rotting in this beautiful prison".

He waited for Don Basilio to go on.

"Shall we go into lunch, Señor Conway", was all he said.

As they rose, Raul Salcedo appeared and handed Don Basilio his inhaler.

"Ah! The elusive Mr Salcedo. I'd like to talk to you about Lydia, once Don Basilio and I have finished."

But Salcedo was already half out of the door. All that he heard was: "Ah yes! Lydia". Then Raul crossed the patio onto the drive where Vic, one of the bodyguards, who was built like a line-backer because that's what he'd been, was holding the car door open for him.

Chapter 3

Conway goes to Caribe

It was in 1962 that Conway was sent to Caribe. He knew practically nothing about the place. His area was domestic politics. He had left University and said goodbye to the delights of Catullus and Cicero. The next step he'd been told would be the approach from one of the "Top Corporations" which were waiting to snatch up bright young men like him. Of medium height, with blond hair and moderately good looks, he was presentable without exactly standing out.

There was no approach. He was not snatched up. He languished. Ted, his father, had been right. "Wait till you try to get a job, son. Then you'll see what good bloody classics is".

He couldn't get a job. He was even prepared to admit failure and become a teacher, but every school already seemed to have a dozen classics masters, clinging like limpets to their jobs. As for PE, he had nothing special to offer; anybody with two arms and legs can play a fair game of rugby or bowl a decent leg break when the opposition is 4 feet 9 inches tall. True, they were still recruiting teachers for the few remaining colonial outposts, but he preferred the Labour Exchange and his father's scorn.

It was a Yorkshire weekly that finally took him on. The usual apprenticeship of funerals, fetes and football was served. He gradually moved up the ladder and after four years he'd made it. He got a job on the political staff of a national daily, the Globe. Then came the instruction to pack his bags. He was off to Caribe.

He racked his brain to figure out what mistake he'd made, whom he'd offended, but his record was clean. Not inspiring. He wasn't on anyone's fast track, but his performance was steady. Moreover, the Chief's words weren't entirely convincing: "It looks like something's going to happen out there and we want a good man on the spot". It sounded like just the thing an officer might have said as he sent his men over the top.

* * * * *

The first thing that hit him as he got off the plane was the heat. The flight from Mexico City in an old DC3 hadn't helped. It was long, uncomfortable and bumpy. Coming down the steps onto the tarmac, he felt the humidity envelop him. "Christ, it's boiling". He realised that the suit which had seemed very lightweight and Colonial-tropical in the shop in Piccadilly was now heavier and hotter than a blanket. And, it marked him out. He was clearly a foreigner given his inability to make himself understood in his kindergarten Spanish. But, he wasn't an American tourist - he sported neither a natty straw hat nor an oversize shirt with palm trees sprouting from his navel. He must therefore be a person with business in Caribe.

This qualified him for circumspect care. The Customs Officer looked over his tape recorder, camera and typewriter and then, said in heavily accented English,

"Your cases, Señor. Please to open."

What followed was not any detailed search of his luggage. Instead, the Officer observed a quaint ritual. He took out the two pairs of shoes and one pair of sandals and painted each one all over with a clear fluid. Once the ritual was completed, they were put into separate plastic bags and handed back to Conway. The reason, he gleaned, was to prevent the import of some nasty bug or bacterium which might attack the tobacco or the sugar cane which were Caribe's only way of surviving. The shoes he was wearing, however, escaped attention. Was this an oversight by a tired official, laziness, or Latin hospitality whereby it was more important that he did not have to walk around in wet shoes than that the harvest be protected?

Given the press of humanity around him, Conway considered himself fortunate to get through so quickly. He chose one of the several taxi drivers, each of whom was trying to wrestle his suitcases from him.

"Hotel Valencia, por favor", in his best Spanish.

The drive into the centre gave him his first impressions of Caribe and its principal town, Puerto Grande. The taxi was an old 1954 black Chevrolet with one headlight and no rear lights. There was no taximeter. Clearly the cost of the trip was going to be haggled over when they arrived. He made a mental note to try to agree the price beforehand in future. Luis, the driver that first evening, was a slim black man with tired, pinched features. He sported a thin pencil moustache and short hair, balding on top. His blue cotton short-sleeved shirt was well pressed as were the fawn cotton slacks. His black pointed shoes were worn down at the heels and spattered with mud. Around his wrist a heavy, gold-looking bracelet told the world that he was Luis. Throughout the trip he sucked on a pipe into which he'd stuffed a half-smoked cigar.

As they drove down the long avenue lined with jacaranda and dusty palm trees which connected the airport with the main coast road, Conway looked back. The sun had not quite set. Mountainous dark clouds signalled the onset of night even as the sky was lit as if by some enormous furnace out there in the sea. It was spectacular. It reminded him of when he was growing up in the industrial wastelands of the Black Country. When the furnaces in the steel mills were opened in the evening, the light softened the harsh industrial landscape and, for a moment, it was almost beautiful.

The airport, by contrast, receding into the distance, looked mean and ugly. Its history had been chaotic. The New York/New Jersey axis had offered a growing tourist trade in the early 50s which inevitably led to demands to increase capacity. No sooner had work started than one of the cyclical political upheavals which were Caribe's lot persuaded the tourists to take their dollars elsewhere. As a consequence, runways ran nowhere and roads slowly surrendered to potholes and weeds in the warm alchemy of a tropical island.

Then, Don Basilio, or Colonel Barbosa as he then was, emerged. His mission to save Caribe included building a fine airport to 'attract foreign capital' to 'our island paradise'. He had been President now for five years and progress had not been rapid. Tired, faded signs still welcomed the unwary to roofless deserted sheds and pilots regularly complained about the runways and the disconcerting presence of goats on the tarmac.

Luis said nothing as they drove. From the back seat, Conway looked around into the approaching dark. Colleagues in London had told him that it was a twenty minute drive, "give or take ten minutes depending on how sober the driver is". He registered the lazy caricature. In fact, Luis drove well. He didn't speed, as if aware that Conway would want to see as much as possible. And this stretch of road was in good repair. It ran through a flat coastal plain. For someone unused to the tropics, the sticky heat, the incredibly verdant countryside and the evening sounds of cicadas and frogs were at the same time strange yet familiar. This, he thought, was what it was supposed to be like.

They passed small wooden cabins thatched with palm fronds, clustered together or standing alone. Children, their bellies hanging over their torn and grimy underpants, squatted outside watched over by grey-haired old ancients. Fat but formless in sun-bleached cotton frocks, they sat on porches or on the ground. They didn't seem to mind the mosquitos swarming around. Younger women, harassed and thin-faced, came and went, stooping to enter the dark shacks. The only light came from oil lamps which drew a steady flow of moths to a fiery death.

"The Happy Rooster", "The Singing Donkey" and other such titles announced the presence of bars. They were usually set on the side of the road near a large group of shacks and seemed to serve also as shops and meeting places. This is where the men were, standing with machetes in leather scabbards at their sides. Some sat at metal tables or crouched on their haunches. Occasionally a beer was passed from hand to hand. A few nursed small glasses of rum. They sucked on their dominoes with massive concentration before slamming one down.

Suddenly, street lamps appeared. They'd reached the outskirts of Puerto Grande. The squalid shacks gave way to single-storey houses, each with its patch of garden. The sharp, metallic lighting sucked the colour out of the surroundings. Everywhere seemed lifeless and indeed there were few signs of life. Cars pulled into driveways or parked on the streets - city workers coming home. Then, another change: the bright neon lights of stores, bars and restaurants lit up the interior of the taxi. They were now part of the loud, harsh throb of downtown. There were people and traffic everywhere, lurching and cursing, shouting and laughing. It was as if they had suddenly come upon a giant stage after the gloom and stillness of the rest of the journey.

"Hotel Valencia, Señor".

Luis had stopped in front of a double set of glass doors, which were being pushed open by an alert porter. From inside the taxi, Conway couldn't make out anything else about the hotel except that it was on a busy street but appeared OK if the badges on the door were anything to go by. He suddenly realised that he had no currency. He'd made sure to buy some pesos in London, but they were in the jacket which he'd taken off at the airport and put in one of the cases which were now being carried inside. Embarrassing! How was he going to pay Luis and then tip the porter? The porter was holding the car door open and looking at him quizzically. He haltingly embarked on what he hoped would be understood by Luis as an explanation. Pathetically, he pressed an English pound note into Luis' hand. Luis examined it and smiled.

"It's OK, Señor, you can pay me later. I work from the hotel", spoken in English with a heavy American accent

Conway's embarrassment was compounded. Why didn't the fellow tell me he spoke English?

He stammered out, "Gracias, gracias. Oh Yes. Thank you. That's fine. That's excellent then. Of course. Yes. Gracias." Then he ran for cover into the hotel and made for the desk.

"Good evening, Señor. May I help you?" The man behind the desk spoke English without prompting. His lapel badge said that he was Bernardo.

"Yes I have a reservation. The name is Conway".

"A reservation? Let us see, Mr, er ..."

"Conway."

"I'm sorry, Mr. Conway. No, Señor, we have no reservation in that name."

Good old Daily Globe, he reflected. They can print a million copies a day, but can't book a hotel room. "There must be some mistake," he urged in time-worn fashion. "In London, I was assured ... ."

"Oh. You are from London. My favourite city. One day I hope to go there. All that beautiful fog and rain, and the people – so polite. Tell me, Señor, is it true that no-one speaks to anyone else without a formal introduction?"

"Well, not quite. But" ... he was anxious to get the priorities right, "more important, if I may say so, is whether I can get a room here".

"A room? Let's see, Señor. I will get back to you in a moment, Señor." Even though there was no-one else at the reception desk, Bernardo gave the impression of being very busy. "Perhaps you would like to step into the Bar for a moment while I check whether we can find a room for you".

Tired and frustrated he wanted a room and a shower He didn't want to 'step into the Bar'. But Bernardo was going through a file index and wasn't to be disturbed.

The Bar was empty and about as inviting as a church hall in Wolverhampton on a wet Monday. He dragged his suitcases with him. At least it would give him time to find his cash. He opened the first case but the jacket with his money in was not there. So, having had to lay out everything in the case on the floor, he then had to re-pack it and go through the other one. With almost all of his clothes and everything else on the floor, he still couldn't find the money. He picked up the jacket and went through all the pockets again. No money. With blasphemy a millisecond from his lips he found what he was looking for. His money was in a shoe – it had fallen out of the jacket pocket. Once he'd packed everything away again and regained a semblance of dignity, he approached the barman, whose name apparently according to his badge was Cyrano. He mused that he would probably have killed his parents if they'd wished that name on him. Cyrano had been watching him with a look of puzzled amusement.

In halting Spanish, Conway asked for a beer, proffering a ten peso note.

Cyrano replied in heavily-accented English, "We don't take cash, Señor. We put it on your room bill. What is your Room Number, please Señor?"

"I wish I'd known before I put all my underwear on display", he muttered. Then, more loudly, in English, "Room Number? I don't have a Room Number yet. Your man Bernardo is sorting it out".

"Sorry, Señor. I cannot serve you without a Room Number. The Bar is for patrons only."

"Oh Christ" was all that he could manage. "Is it alright if I sit in one of your chairs, or do I need a Room Number for that as well?"

"Make yourself at home, Señor" Cyrano replied equably and went back to polishing glasses.

Time passed and he found himself dozing off. He got up and went back to the desk.

"Ah, Señor, I wondered where you had got to", Bernardo greeted him.

"I was in the Bar where you sent me", he snapped. Then remembering the unequal bargaining power as between him and Bernardo, tried the more conciliatory, "Have you been able to find a room for me?"

"Yes, we have, Señor. There was a mix-up but I have sorted it out. The reservation we received from London was for a Miss Cromwell and", he asked, too archly for Conway's liking, "you are not Miss Cromwell, I take it, Señor."

"No. I'm not". To himself, "I'll kill that Tracey in accounts – she must have thought that was funny". Then, to Bernardo, "Thank you, Bernardo, for sorting it out".

"That's no problem. Now, Señor, all of our rooms have a bath and shower and some also have sitting rooms."

"Oh. Just a small room will be fine. Perhaps," he added hopefully, "with a view".

"A view? Of course, Señor. Do you want a view of the city or of the harbour?"

"The harbour would be nice".

"Nice. That word. So English. Perhaps you could sign here, Señor Conway. And, your passport".

At the door to room 611, he pressed the retrieved ten peso note into the porter's hand. He couldn't now remember the exchange rate but hoped it was enough. The look on the porter's face told him the bad news – it wasn't. He reflected that he hadn't done a great deal to advance Anglo-Caribe relations in the hour since his arrival.

A shower, clean comfortable clothes, a drink, some dinner and perhaps a stroll, then bed. These were his thoughts as he sat on the edge of the King size double bed and looked over the balcony at the moon riding on the swell in the harbour. A cockroach scuttled across the bathroom floor. He imagined he saw "Welcome to the Tropics" etched on its shiny black back.

Chapter 4

Lydia

"But you don't really believe all that nonsense, surely", Conway said, smiling.

Lydia was dressed casually in blue jeans with a patterned belt and a white blouse. On her feet she wore a pair of flat-heeled pumps. What little make-up she wore emphasised her high cheekbones and dark eyes. Her hair was that shade of black that shone like a raven's feathers. They were having lunch in Casa Juaquin, a quiet little restaurant near the big Supermercado on the Paseo Lincoln at the edge of the Convento district. They were the only patrons that lunchtime.

"Of course I do, Tony. And it's not nonsense. You are so obviously a Virgo. I knew it before you told me. So fussy, and precise and analytical", she replied.

"And boring," he added.

"Sometimes," Lydia conceded. "And me? What am I"?

"I don't have any idea. I don't even know all the signs. Is there a sign for people who are charming, intelligent, witty, good-looking and helpful to stray foreigners", he replied, mildly embarrassed at his attempt at sophistication.

"I'm Gemini", she replied, ignoring the question.

"What are they supposed to be like?"

"We are an air sign. We love to talk, we love to write. As you can see, Tony, we love to make contact and communicate." Then the tone of her voice changed, her eyes looking down at her hands which had suddenly become agitated. She began to twist a lock of hair round and round her finger. "We are passionate, Tony, and because we are born under the sign of twins, we can be social chameleons – we can be two people. But, enough of that. What would you like to know?"

Conway parked the momentary revelation, feeling he'd just caught a glimpse of some mystery which had vanished as quickly as it appeared. He'd come back to it later, he thought.

"I don't know", he replied. "My head is already stuffed with so much information. You are a good teacher but I'm afraid I'm rather a slow learner. Tell me. Why do you spend so much time telling me about things here? You must have a million and one other more interesting things to do".

"Oh. It passes the time. I enjoy it", she replied light-heartedly, as if half-embarrassed by the question.

"No, tell me seriously, please", he insisted.

"There's nothing to tell. You are an interesting and intelligent man with an open mind who works for an internationally known newspaper." Looking around and confirming that they were alone in the restaurant, "You are a Virgo. I know I can trust you if I talk in a way that my friends might not understand. Of course, you must not attribute anything to me. It wouldn't do for me to be heard expressing my real views. After all", she laughed, mocking herself, "I have a position to maintain. As you are presumably here to write about Caribe and as I love my little island, I want you to get to know it, as you say, warts and all".

"Well, at the risk of offending you, Lydia, from what I've seen in the two or three months I've been here and from what you've told me, there seem to be quite a lot of warts".

"We have our difficulties, you are right. Remember, we are not Britain or France, far less the United States of America. You have had your industrial revolution and your massive material prosperity. All we can do is grow a few crops and catch a few fish and hope to sell them at ever-lower prices to buy the goods we need to raise ourselves a little. And, of course, these goods cost more every day. We are like a little garden on a rich man's estate. He has lots of gardens and can let us lie fallow and ignore us for a while. He won't notice, but we do. What can we do?"

"But, you have tourism now. Doesn't President Barbosa hope to make tourism a major industry"?

"Yes, tourists are coming back again. Our people once more can take up their jobs as cleaners, bar tenders and prostitutes", Lydia shot back, smiling as if to offset the bitterness of what she was saying.

Conway reached for his glass and took a few nervous sips of beer. Was he being too intrusive? After all, he saw Lydia as a friend. It wasn't some interview for the paper. She stared back at him, still smiling. As if divining his thoughts, she said quietly, "Don't worry. You haven't offended me. Please go on."

"Thank you. You're very patient with me. I can see what you are saying, but surely there are things to be pleased about. The President has brought some stability and that's the first step towards some kind of progress, isn't it? And the people seem to be behind him".

He'd been introduced to the President at a reception held at the Embassy not long after his arrival. Apart from the unprepossessing looks - small and very fat - Conway had found him anxious to leave a favourable impression of himself and Caribe.

"Welcome to Caribe, Señor. You are from England", turning to the Ambassador, who nodded. "I will see to it that doors are open to you. I want you to be able to tell your readers all about the wonderful progress we are making here".

"Thank you, sir", he'd replied as the Ambassador moved the President on to more important guests.

Lydia picked up on his remark. "The people are behind him, you say? My dear Tony, have you asked 'the people'", barely concealing the sarcasm dripping from her voice. "And you the experienced political commentator! Caray! Forgive me, but God save us from experts".

"Well don't they", he persisted, his pride a little hurt. "I know there's some poverty and unemployment and what have you, but it seems to me that most people I've seen look content despite the warts".

"You sound like a travel brochure. To answer your question, not that it really deserves an answer, I would say this. Some obviously support El Presidente. Otherwise he wouldn't be in the Palace. They do so because it suits them. Some do not support him, but they have no power and can do nothing.

"One day, there will be change. There will be a government that is not interested in power just for what the leaders can stash away in foreign banks, but cares for all and is supported by all - is committed to the common good. But I'm preaching. I'm so sorry".

"Not at all. Tell me. When do you foresee this second coming?"

"You mustn't mock me, Tony. It is I who should mock you for your naivety".

A small black curl fell across her wide forehead. She twisted it round and round her finger; the only indication that Lydia was agitated. Throughout lunch and the conversation she had remained outwardly calm. It was as if there was a curious contradiction in her, a deep-seated ambivalence. Her composure lent authority to her words but at the same time detracted from them. He was trying to draw her out and to some extent he had succeeded. Yet he was not convinced that she wouldn't take a different point of view in a moment if the circumstances warranted it. He simply couldn't fathom her. Through her kind and careful tuition, he was learning much about her island, but very little about her. Nor could he figure out why she gave him so much of her time.

She interrupted his reverie. "Ay! Look at the time. I shall have to fly. Thank you for lunch, Tony. I enjoyed it. Sorry if I sounded cross. I wasn't. I'll call you tomorrow. In the morning, OK? Around 9.30?"

"That would be great, thanks, Lydia," getting up to see her to the door.

"Oh! I almost forgot," she said, turning around. "What's the date today? Is it the 12th?" He nodded. "How careless of me. You're invited to a party tonight, at my place. Please say you can come. I planned it a week ago but forgot to tell you. You'll meet Raul."

"Well. Tonight was to be my induction into the sacred rituals of the Embassy bridge evenings. So thank God I have an excuse not to go. I'd love to come. What time? What should I wear? Who's Raul?"

"I'm so glad", Lydia purred. "About 9.00. Wear something casual. Raul? Raul is an aide to El Presidente and an old friend. You'll see". And off she went, climbing into her red Buick before the doorman could open the door for her.

Conway paid the bill. Once outside, it dawned on him that the conversation he'd just had with the waiter about whether the Tigers would beat the Creoles that evening had been in Spanish. "I'm almost bilingual already", he thought, choosing to overlook the fact that a good half of the conversation had involved actions, signs and grunts rather than actual words. He nodded to the tall, gaunt, grey-faced man at the corner of Calle Formosa. He had seen him before but he couldn't quite remember when or where. It seemed as if he knew his face quite well yet couldn't remember meeting him.

The walk back to the hotel took Conway along the Malecon, the curving road which skirted the sea. In the old days it was said that political opponents would regularly be pitched over the sea wall for the sharks. He'd already learned not to walk on the sunny side like the tourists and get burned to a crisp in the brutal heat of the sun. He crossed to the side opposite the sea, a colonnaded walk where the sun never penetrated. The shade was a plus. The dank smell which hovered like a barrier to be breached was the price to be paid.

His thoughts were about Lydia. What a stroke of luck that he had met her. It was the only sensible thing the chinless wonder, Jeremy Brown, the Second Secretary at the Embassy, had done for him. It compensated for the attempts to recruit him for the annual cricket match against the West Indians, the bridge club, the choir and the suggestion that he might like to do a bit of lecturing for the "Understanding Britain" fortnight.

Jeremy had mentioned Lydia to him as someone worth contacting. She was a writer and occasional journalist, spoke perfect English courtesy of school and University in Boston, and was a friend of people in high places. When he had called her, she was friendly and helpful. She was clearly intelligent and well-informed and being a journalist knew the sort of things he would want and need to know. Add to this the fact that she was young and very attractive and, yes, he was able to overlook Jeremy's shortcomings.

The party she'd invited him to sounded interesting. It would be his first exposure to Caribino society. He was looking forward to it. So far, he and Lydia had only met a few times. They had lunched together, talked a lot and walked all over the city. But they had never been out together in the sense of a non-business, social engagement. He found himself wondering who this Raul was and his connection with Lydia. He put together a sort of mental image of him, deciding that he was a happily married, ageing, bald man with lots of children. He found this image comforting. "Good Lord", he thought, "I'm jealous." Of course, Lydia had given him absolutely no reason to believe that she led a celibate, nun-like existence, just waiting till the right foreign correspondent showed up to awake the dormant passion within her. She had always treated him as a fellow-spirit, another journalist keen to know the ropes. True, she had been very diligent in doing so, but, as she had said, she just liked doing it.

"Come on, Conway", he mused. "Snap out of it. Grow up. You've been away for a month and you already think every woman who smiles at you has designs on your irresistible manly qualities. Still", he thought, "I hope this Raul does turn out to be bald, with maybe the occasional tooth missing and the bad breath to go with it". Further variations on the theme of Raul's shortcomings occupied him till he reached the hotel. By then Raul had also fallen victim to eczema, the scars of juvenile acne and, of course, impotence.

Once in his room, with the breeze from the sea offering some respite from the clammy heat, Conway filed another report for the Globe. It was a fairly boring affair and in his note to the Chief, he half apologised for this, while at the same time pointing out it was the Chief who had sent him there. He described the problems with the sugar harvest and the impact a shortage would have on the world price. He went into some detail about the hurricane – this one had been called Gilberto – and the damage it had caused. In fact, he had spent a day and a half holed up in his hotel room watching the sea boiling over the road and had been scared stiff. Given the average English reader's ignorance of hurricanes, he went to town a bit, remarking on 'Nature's elemental force'. He knew much of it would not survive Harry's editorial eye, but what the hell, it had been pretty sensational.

Conway glanced at his watch. Only 3.00pm. Plenty of time to get over to the Post Office, file the report and check for any messages, and then have a drink at the Hilton. He didn't like the hotel nor the kind of people it attracted, but the air conditioning worked and it was a good place to pick up gossip.

The lift was still being repaired. He trotted down to the Lobby, jumping from the bottom step to head the goal that would win West Brom the FA Cup. This may have gone unnoticed if he hadn't shouted "Goal!" and punched the air. A startled maid shuffled aside muttering under her breath. He looked around for one of the taxi-drivers who used the hotel as their base. Luis was among them and greeted him pleasantly.

"Muy buenas tardes, Good Afternoon, Señor", he smiled, dextrously removing the ever-present pipe with its half-smoked cigar. He was opening the door and herding him into the old Chevy before the other drivers realised that they'd just lost a fare.

Chapter 5

A car crash

"And, where to this afternoon, Señor", he asked, relaxing now that his quarry was safely in the back seat.

"The Hilton, please".

After some grumbling, the Chevy started off, leaving a trail of black smoke. Luis observed his usual silence, answering deferentially any query made of him but otherwise keeping to what he saw as his place. Luis had driven the Englishman around quite a bit since his arrival and it was always an effort not to try to practice his English. If he got rusty, he'd lose his edge with the American tourists at the hotel who provided his principal income. But Luis' sense of what was proper prevailed, so he occupied himself with his driving.

Conway noticed that Luis would occasionally stir himself sufficiently to mutter at some pedestrian who was taking too much time reaching the safety of the sidewalk or at a too-aggressive bus driver, then lapse back into silence. He assumed that, though muttered, the words used were particularly offensive if the reaction they provoked was anything to go by. Consequently, like a schoolboy, he strained to catch them so as to embellish his limited vocabulary of "bad words", but he could never quite get them.

The only other distraction Luis allowed himself was the proper appreciation of the female form. An ample bosom or backside seemed to beckon from its tight cotton prison. Luis would slow down and proclaim "Guapa" to the owner through the open window. Conway had soon learned the word and recognised it as meaning pretty but in a kind of leering way. He even found himself spotting a possible trophy and pointing her out to Luis. Luis did not, however, approve of the Englishman's taste; he seemed to like his women half-starved. But more important and without the slightest sense of irony, Luis disapproved of the

Englishman's ogling at 'our women'. But, of course, he said nothing. Instead, he made a mental note of 'Señor Conway's type' so as to be ready to earn a little extra cash if the circumstance ever presented itself that the Señor needed a woman.

The taxi was now sweeping along the Malecon. At the end of each block, narrow streets which wound down from the old part of the city fed into it. At the junction of one of these, the Calle Hermosa, he saw a large black car suddenly swing out of control into their path. It was going far too fast and the driver had not even slowed down before entering the busy thoroughfare. Luis braked and swerved, but it was impossible to avoid the car which slammed into the front of the taxi. Conway was flung sideways against the door and then fell back again onto the seat. Apart from the shock, he wasn't hurt. He looked up to see Luis clutching his head. Blood was seeping out of a gash in his Luis' forehead from when his face had hit the steering wheel.

Someone was shouting outside. The door on the driver's side was pulled open and Luis was hauled out. Conway got out as well. The sound of glass under his feet told him that the one remaining headlight on the taxi had been shattered. A wing had also been badly dented. A short stocky man was screaming at Luis. He wore the uniform of an air force officer. His dark aviator sun glasses accentuated the white, clean-shaven face and his gun-metal grey crew cut.

Conway couldn't follow what the officer was saying in detail but it seemed clear that he was blaming Luis for the crash.

"You fucking blacks" he heard. "You shouldn't be allowed near a car. You're too stupid to drive", was followed by the officer taking a swing at Luis. Luis avoided the blow but said nothing. Incensed at what he saw, Conway walked up to the officer. His anger caused him to stumble over his words.

He got no further than, "What do you think you ..." before he was pushed out of the way and told to "Shut your mouth".

He fell back against the taxi. Furious, he launched himself at the officer, this time settling for English. "Hey! What the hell do you think you're doing, mate?"

Withdrawing a pace, the officer, in a fluent movement, drew the pistol from its holster on his waist and aimed it at him. Conway stopped in his tracks.

"Get back in the car, Señor", the officer snarled, in heavily accented English. "And you", he continued in Spanish to Luis, "Get out of my way. If I see you again, you'll be sorry".

With that the officer strode to his car, crashed the gears into reverse, backed up a few feet, then with his tyres squealing, roared away making Luis jump for his life.

"God! Jesus Christ! Who in hell is that. I'll get him. I'll report him as soon as I get to the Hilton." Conway was livid with anger and frustration.

"It's nothing Señor. Just an unfortunate accident. I'm sorry. I should forget it".

"Nothing? Nothing?" he repeated incredulously. "You're out of you mind, Luis. What do you mean, nothing?"

"He is a very important officer. He had been called to the Palace. It was my fault for not looking out for him".

Conway's mouth fell open in disbelief. Some lunatic driving too fast out of a side-street had smashed into Luis' car, bloodied his head, pulled him out of his car, called him a 'fucking black', hit him, pulled a gun on both of them and driven off, and here was Luis saying it was his fault.

"Well, I'm damned sure I'm going to do something", Conway said, after a pause. "And, who's going to pay for repairing the taxi?" Remembering the time he'd had a minor accident on the A1 outside London, he asked, "Did that madman leave his insurance details or whatever you do here?"

"Oh, the damage is nothing really. I can fix it. It's best forgotten. An unfortunate accident. And, if I were you, Señor, I'd forget it also."

"We'll see about that. I just don't understand, Luis, how you can accept this so calmly. You are in the right and I'm a witness. We'll sue the bastard and make him pay for the repairs."

"As I said, Señor Conway, I should forget the whole thing". Luis' voice had acquired an edge to it. "An accident caused by my carelessness in not looking out for someone engaged in important business for our country".

The finality with which this last sentence was delivered indicated that the conversation was over. Luis got back into the taxi, still mopping the blood on his brow and started the engine. Conway climbed into the back seat, fuming inside at the way Luis had supinely tolerated an obvious wrong. Neither spoke till they reached the Hilton. As he got out, Conway made one last try to engage with Luis.

"Are you really going to let that bastard get away with it?"

"I have already given you my view," Luis replied coldly and drove off. At every bump in the road, the battered wing threatened to separate itself completely from the car.

Chapter 6

A match

Conway made his way to the Hilton's bar. He was anxious to get some advice on what to do. To his surprise, none of the usual faces was in evidence. And, he belatedly realised that he hadn't a clue who the officer was, nor, as the super-efficient journalist that he was, had he taken the number of the car. He nursed his rum and Coke while with his other hand he drummed out his annoyance.

Lydia would know what to do. She would find out who the bastard was. He decided to call her, then remembering he was going to her party that evening, decided to ask her then. He ordered another drink and stared angrily into space.

Still frustrated though less agitated, Conway decided to take a stroll along the hotel's terrace and into the beautifully manicured gardens. The warm air and the alcohol softened his mood as he wandered among the palm trees. He found a patch of the kind of grass that shrinks up into a tight ball if touched, and teased it with his shoe. Life was not so bad after all, he thought, on this tropical island with the setting sun on his back and the sound of the waves breaking on the sea wall beyond the lawns. If only The George, his local pub on Haverstock Hill, could be moved out here so that he could have a decent pint of beer instead of all that bloody coffee.

A tap on his shoulder broke into his thoughts. "Do you have a match, Señor?"

Conway turned to see the same gaunt, grey-faced man he'd seen at lunchtime, holding a cigarette. Was he being followed he wondered, half-heartedly? He didn't smoke himself but often carried a book of matches.

"I think I have some. Just a minute. By the way, haven't I met you somewhere?"

All this was said as Conway was turning out his pockets looking for matches. He didn't see the fist which smashed into the side of his face. He felt it. At first, shock and a surprising numbness. Then pain. He staggered back. A knee crashed into his groin. He fell onto the hard path, gasping and retching. Air couldn't find its way into his lungs. He just curled up on the ground wanting to breathe and shout for help but could do neither. Eventually, he was able to breathe in short bursts. He opened his eyes, one of which was throbbing badly, and raised himself onto one knee. There was no-one to be seen nearby. In the distance, a bell-boy from the hotel was running towards him. Edging himself onto the grass, he sat there bemused. He hadn't a clue what had just happened. Someone had worked him over. And his head and body ached. But more? He didn't begin to understand.

"You OK, Señor?" The bell-boy was bending over him.

"No".

The bell-boy was helping him to his feet. "I see you fall, Señor. You hurt?"

"I didn't fall. Somebody hit me. Didn't you see?"

"Hit you? Oh, no, Señor. I din see no-one hit you. I see you fall. The heat, Señor, or maybe the rum? The rum do funny things, Señor."

"Somebody hit me! Oh, what the hell. Nobody sees things it seems. Everybody's playing at being one of the three monkeys".

"Monkeys, Señor? I din see no monkeys".

"See no evil, hear no – Oh, forget it."

Leaning heavily on the bell-boy, Conway made his way back towards the hotel. The bell-boy sat him on a bench and came back in a moment with a large glass of iced water. He took a couple of sips then poured the rest over his head, hoping to dampen the drill which was boring through his temples. He probed his aching lower abdomen. "You can put all thoughts of that out of your mind for a week or two", he joked to himself, though he didn't find the joke very funny.

He hailed the bell-boy, "Can you get me a taxi, please. Oh, and thanks for the water".

"De nada, Señor. You welcome. Right away, Señor".

Conway sat there till the taxi arrived, He was confused and in pain. He needed to work out what had happened: who the man was; why he'd suddenly hit him; what it was all about. But he didn't have the energy right then. Leaning again on the bell-boy he made his way to the taxi. He was guided through the back of the gardens into a quiet side-street, whether to save him or the hotel from embarrassment he wasn't sure.

"Hotel Valencia", he mumbled. He found a relatively clean handkerchief in his pocket, spit on it and held it to his head. At the hotel, he put on a good show as far as the lift, using the handkerchief to cover the fast-growing swelling around his left eye. Thank Heavens the lift was working. He pressed the button for the sixth floor and sagged against the side, groaning quietly. The lift pitched him out and he staggered weakly towards the door to his room.

No key! The realisation almost brought tears to his eyes. In his dash for the sanctuary of the lift he'd forgotten to pick it up from the desk.

"Forgotten your key, Señor?" It was the maid turning down the beds on that floor who was just emerging from the room opposite. At first, he didn't understand the rapid, high-pitched Spanish. When she repeated what she said, he was so relieved that he let out a huge sigh and threw his arms around her. First jumping up and down the stairs shouting to himself, then staggering about, and now this. The maid made a mental note to keep her distance. She extricated herself from his embrace which by then had become for Conway a matter of support and quickly opened his door. Then, with her most business-like "buenas tardes", she moved on down the corridor.

Conway closed the door behind him and arranged himself carefully on the bed. This time he would definitely call Lydia. He had to do something. He was asleep before his hand reached the phone.

Chapter 7

Luis goes home

Luis realised that there was nothing he could do except nurse the old car back home and then see whether he could fix it up yet again.

"That damned lunatic! He could have killed me," he muttered to himself. He carefully picked his way through the busy streets, trying to avoid the ubiquitous pot-holes and hoping that the police would not spot him and his clanking taxi dragging its tired and broken body home.

"And he called me a 'fucking black', the fat bastard. The English was right. I should have done something. Just wait. Next time one of them tries to get tough I'll ....". Luis mused for a while on what he would do. He already knew that he wouldn't do anything, but allowed himself to go through the reasoning process which hundreds of times and countless insults had led him to that conclusion. It was as if it reassured him that he was right. He had a good job, didn't he? And a place to live and food on the table. And he could still think what he liked, couldn't he? Nobody could tell him what to think. So let the big-mouth officer call him names. So what?

But, where was he going to get the money to repair the taxi? Yes, that was the problem. That was where it hurt. His calculus didn't seem to deal with that. He couldn't see a way of balancing it out. Just then Luis spotted a little girl, blonde and smart in her convent uniform, waiting to cross the road. He slowed down as if to allow her to cross. As she set off, he accelerated, causing her to jump back and fall over. As she lay there, her legs in the air, her little black pants defiled by his eyes, he yelled the most vulgar epithet he could summon from his not inconsiderable collection. Pausing only to watch the red blush begin to transform her pretty white face and the tears begin to well up in her eyes, he drove off. It was supposed to make him feel better. All it did was to make him feel ashamed.

Soon Luis was crossing the bridge out of the Convento section of the city. After another bridge he turned right off the main Avenida and took the narrow Calle de Los Puentes that followed one of the canals feeding into the harbour. The neighbourhood changed quickly. Elegant colonial villas with their high walls and wrought-iron gates gave way to small stuccoed two-storey houses, interspersed with bars and shops. He turned left onto Calle Florida. The neighbourhood changed again. He was now running parallel to the harbour in what looked like a shanty town along a dirt and gravel track, rutted and pitted through the attentions of the weather and traffic. Old cars and trucks, some with no wheels, others with no insides, lay at the side of the track or shipwrecked on the narrow patches of dirt in front of houses. The houses were no longer of stone. They were shacks, some made of good, sound wood with zinc roofs, others a combination in varying proportions of wood, tin and cardboard, the last of these ransacked from the advertising hoardings on the main Avenida. They sat along the side of the track which sloped down towards the water. Dark alleys smelling of rot ran away between them down to the edge of the water.

As the poor had migrated to the city, more and more had sought a place in this filthy back yard. Living in other parts of the city was not an option. Here they lived and died with rats as company - the rats lived rent-free. Yet even in this blighted spot, there were rank, privilege and status. The shacks abutting the track were on solid foundations and were mostly well-constructed. They were close to the four large water taps which served the whole neighbourhood. These taps had been installed with great ceremony (and some haste) on the occasion of an election some years earlier and usually provided water even if it was brown when it rained. These shacks also often boasted electricity from the city's system to which they were connected, albeit illegally. The further down the slope, the meaner the shacks. Only when the sun was overhead did light intrude into the dank gloom. Their one or two rooms were raised on fragile wooden piles, gradually eroding from the attention of the termites and the water in which they stood. The city's refuse spilled and swilled under the floors. When the waters rose it lapped against the doors.

Luis Morales parked the taxi alongside a large weathered shack. The Barrio went by the name of La Joya - someone's idea of a joke when districts were named. It would have been difficult to imagine anything less jewel-like. He was one of the Barrio's elite. He had a house directly on the street and opposite one of the water taps. It was late afternoon. The smells cultured by the day-long sunshine rose to meet him.

"Ay! Que tal. Estabas borracho, chico?"

He ignored the question and the interrogating look of the neighbour who was running his hands over the taxi's wounds. Josefina, his wife of eighteen years off and on, had seen him arrive. She was a small, heavy-set woman of indeterminate middle-age, her greying hair tied back with a bandana. Her all-enveloping muumuu had been washed so many times that all the colours had long faded.

"Well" she asked, from the doorway, "like he says, was you drunk?"

"Caray. What the hell you mean? I don drink when I'm working, woman! Some damn fool air force officer came out of Hermosa downtown too fast. He smack right into me. Get me some water will you. My head's explodin".

Josefina saw the gash on his forehead for the first time and told him to go inside so she could bathe it. As she went for the water, he made for the rocking chair and flopped into it, resting his head against the darkened pillow fastened to the top. He shut his eyes and rocked himself slowly, just using his toes. In this room, in this chair, in this position, with his pipe and cigar, gently rocking backwards and forwards, he was secure.

The room served as kitchen, living room and, at night, bedroom for Carlos, their son. Across from Luis there was a table which Josefina's scrubbing had long since robbed of its cheap white paint, and three chairs, one of which leaned against the wall to compensate for a missing leg. An electric cooker that he had found abandoned on the Avenida, a shelf and a row of nails for crockery, cans of food and pots, a battered couch which served as Carlos' bed, and a television set on a crate which had once held bananas, completed the furnishings. Tacked to the wall above the television was a picture of the Virgin in a gilt frame. Next to it was a photograph of President Kennedy, much prized by Luis. It was a matter of constant regret that JFK was now surrounded by pictures cut from magazines of people Carlos preferred to look at from his couch. They were an eclectic bunch including Elizabeth Taylor, Emiliano Zapata and Jose Marti. Luis had forbidden the iconic photograph of Che Guevara.

He and Josefina slept in the other room at the back of the house which overlooked a side-alley. It got very little sunlight and the shutters were kept closed to keep out the smells, the noise and the cats. It had a dank, oppressive air. Two nails and a narrow tallboy accommodated their clothes. A double bed, sagging in the middle almost to the floor, received their tired limbs. Another Virgin, strictly speaking the same Virgin in another aspect, looked down with what Josefina believed was compassion.

"Here". Josefina pressed a wet cloth onto his head. "Hold it. Can't stand here nursing and get food on the table".

"Alright. Alright," he murmured. Clearly, his wife was not minded to indulge him in his suffering. "Coffee?"

"Well. If you has it now, there's none for after dinner."

"Alright. A cup of water?"

"Cup and tap's in the usual place. An you got two legs last time I looked."

"Miserable, hard, wrinkled old bitch" he muttered to himself, careful to make sure that Josefina didn't hear. He stirred himself, fetched the water and sat down again.

"What you gonna do about the car", Josefina asked as she sat down at the table to prepare the plantains she was going to fry for dinner. Carlos liked them with his rice and he was a growing young man who needed his food.

Josefina rehearsed these arguments just in case Luis complained about the expense.

"Roberto'll fix it. He owe me a favour".

"He been paying that back the last three times he fix the car".

"Well. You got any bright ideas? What I do? Take it downtown and have it fixed up and resprayed, all nice and pretty. Service as well, while I there."

Josefina sighed. "Make him pay who did it. Who was it?"

"I dunno. Happened so quick. Drove off before I could do anything. Anyway, he wouldn't pay, would he? Those bastards - all alike. He say it's my fault and get police on me. We can't afford that."

Josefina sighed again. Her husband's acceptance of things hurt her. What hurt her even more was the fact that she knew he was right. He kept out of trouble. He avoided problems. And he also kept his taxi permit. He'd had it for fifteen years and thank God for that. They would never have had this house, let alone food to eat and school for Carlos without that permit.

"I talk to Roberto after dinner", Josefina suggested, bravely putting on a smile. She gave Luis a brazen wink. "He can't refuse me!"

"Hey! Careful what you offer. I want him under the car not under you", Luis protested, but he was also smiling.

"Go lie down, viejo, my old man. I do dinner. Carlos'll be home soon. Maybe we watch television tonight with you at home for a change".

"Maybe I will". He patted her shoulder as he went through to the bedroom.

It was almost dark when Carlos got home. Josefina thought to herself that he looked older than his eighteen years, in his white shirt and dark trousers. Serious and thoughtful, he was different from most of the other boys in the neighbourhood. This pleased her and worried her. He smoked but he didn't drink. He liked girls but he had no girl-friend. He played baseball with his friends but he seemed to prefer to go to the big library downtown. And he was mad about politics. The result was something she was not familiar with. She wanted to be proud of him and defended him when others, especially his father, mocked him for his love of books or his lack of a girl. But she had to admit that she did not understand him, and this politics business, it was just crazy. But, he would grow out of it, she told herself, rather unconvincingly. She longed for him to settle down, with a little place in La Joya. They would help him get one. And grandchildren; wouldn't that be lovely? He was her only child. She had nearly died when he was born. God in His mercy had given her Carlos but taken away the chance of having another child.

She thought to herself that she'd stop by and see Eva on her way back from Roberto's. Eva was so right for Carlos; good around the house, sweet-tempered, and pretty too. But Carlos barely noticed her. She'd think of a reason for bringing her back to the house.

"Hola Mama".

"Que Dios te bendiga", Josefina replied, returning Carlos' kiss.

"God bless you too, Mama".

"How was work?"

"Same as ever. Terrible! What happened to Dad's car?"

"Some crazy air force man – not your father's fault. Tell me about your day."

"These damned officers. They drive around as if they own the place. Course, in fact, they do own the place. Did Dad get a name? Is he going to get him to pay for the damage?"

"No. No point. Roberto'll fix it. I gonna go down there after dinner. I'll say hello to Eva on my way back." Josefina bit her tongue. She hadn't intended to mention Eva. It was going to be a surprise. "Sell a lot of shoes, did you, querido? I bet you did. Who'd refuse you?"

Carlos wasn't listening. "Why wouldn't there be any point. He hit the car. It was his fault. He should pay for it."

"You don understand – it not as simple as that. Many people in the shop today?"

"Oh, to hell with the shop".

"Carlos!"

"I'm sick of the shop. I hate it and all the people in it. And when I come home I find my father being his usual spineless self, turning one of his many cheeks."

"Hey. Don speak about your father like that. Show respect. He feed you, put clothes on you back and send you to school? What's the matter with you, eh? You need a nice girl. Settle down and learn something about life."

"I know, I know. Where's my gratitude? I go to bed every night praising the Lord that I can sleep on a smelly, beaten-up old couch in this rotten slum and can afford meat twice a week while my father sells his soul to earn the privilege of driving rich people round the block because they're too fat and lazy to walk."

"Enough! You father hear you talkin like that, I don't know what he do." She busied herself with the rice. No. She did not understand that boy.

An air of disagreeable unease prevailed. Carlos could get no sense out of his mother. Women of her generation just didn't understand. But his father would have to listen.

Josefina felt powerless. She knew Carlos was going to fight with his father. These days, any pretext seemed sufficient and this problem with the car, their lifeline, was better than most. Carlos seemed so angry all the time. He seemed to be obsessed with fighting people. Standing up for your rights he called it but she had another word for it when the only possible outcome was to land on your backside! When was the boy going to learn what life was really about rather than just bury his head in books? Yes, Luis could be a bit sharp, but basically he was right: you don't bite the hand that feeds you.

In her heart, she knew, or thought she knew, that Carlos would grow out of it. It was just a stage. They all go through it when they want to prove themselves. She'd said this often enough to Luis but he seemed to have lost patience recently. He said Carlos was pig-headed (the word she herself had used but never said out loud). He'd even gone so far as to tell her that if Carlos didn't mend his ways and remember how to show proper respect, he'd have to find somewhere else to live. Of course, Luis couldn't really mean it, but it terrified her nonetheless. Carlos was all she had. But what could she do?

"Carlos, see what we got for dinner", she said at length, showing him the plantains she'd prepared. "You father said fry some for you. He know you like them."

Carlos looked up from his magazine. Didn't she realise how obvious she was? He didn't respond.

"We'll all watch television after dinner before I go over to Roberto's. Nice to have all three of us here for a change?"

"Wonderful."

"You tired, Carlitos? You work hard today?" Josefina persisted doggedly.

"Mother, can't you see I'm trying to read?"

"Carlos don fight with your father – let's have some peace in the family, eh? Forget the car. We'll get it fixed." She couldn't contain the flood of worries on her mind.

"Who says I'm going to fight? I don't give a damn about the car. If he wants to let people push him around that's his business."

"Carlos, enough! Don speak like that. Read you magazine if you got nothing better to say."

Quiet again.

At length, Josefina dropped the slices of plantain into the oil and, as this was the last thing to do before dinner was ready, quickly went to the bedroom door and called Luis. He emerged, slopping along sleepily in his slippers, wearing only a pair of trousers, hair tangled and his back and chest glistening with sweat. He glanced at Carlos and then sniffed. The smell of frying plantains offended his nose.

"Caray, woman. Why you cook those things? They stink an I don eat them," he snorted as he went outside to the tap. Carlos contented himself with a knowing smile.

Dinner proceeded quietly. Each of them was hungry. They had little interest in using their mouths for anything other than to receive the next spoonful of rice and beans and, in Carlos' case, plantains. Afterwards, Luis took his chair and coffee outside to try to catch whatever movement of air there was. Carlos lay on the couch reading. It was Josefina who brought the subject up.

"What'll I say to Roberto, Luis", she asked as she hung the frying pan on its nail to dry.

"Eh?"

"Roberto. What I say to him? I'm going down now."

"Oh, I dunno," Luis replied. "You'll think of something".

'Yes, but what you want him to do? Shall I tell him you pay him when you see him?"

"What I going to pay him with – beans? Just ask him to repair it for a favour."

"Luis, I don like keep asking favours. We not beggars yet."

"God, woman. An hour ago, he couldn't resist you. You lost you charm all of a sudden? If you don wanna go, don bother. I do it myself, like I do everything else round here."

"Alright. I'll go. I just thought you'd tell me what to say."

Carlos had followed this exchange from behind his magazine. He cleared his throat as if readying himself for action. "Mama, tell Roberto that Don Luis had his car damaged and while he reflects on the appropriate legal action to take against the member of the Republic's Air Force, he would be grateful if Roberto would carry out all necessary and appropriate repairs and charge the cost to his account."

Josefina behaved as if Carlos wasn't there. "Won't be long," she said, forcing her feet into her street shoes. "Alright if I bring Evita back to watch television?"

Luis shrugged. "I'll probably be asleep." Then as Josefina passed him, he beckoned her with his head and asked in a whisper, "What's bitten him," nodding in the direction of the living room.

"Oh, he just tired. He work so hard. He like the job and they like him. He a good boy." All of this she whispered back to Luis, half-apologetic, half-pleading. "You two watch television, eh?" she said, raising her voice. Then she left, hoping that she had mended the fragile peace but knowing that she hadn't.

Luis went through into the living room and turned television on. A troop of British soldiers were defending a fort on the North West Frontier, each urging the others (in dubbed Spanish) to keep their chins up, while the Afghans attacked. Luis dragged his rocking chair towards the set and placed himself two feet from the action.

'Can you turn it down? I'm trying to read."

Luis ignored him.

"Hey! Papa. You deaf? Can you turn it down?"

After a further request met the same response, or non-response, Carlos got up from the couch, walked over to the set and turned the sound down, just as the British bugler was shaking the Virgin on the wall.

"What you think you doing," Luis demanded.

"What's it look like? I'm turning the noise down so I can read".

"Who told you to?"

"Nobody. I don't need to be told."

"In this house, Señorito, you ask first and do what you told. And you respect your parents. If you wanna read, go somewhere else. I listen to the television how I like." Luis had said all this calmly but pointedly. He was tired after his dinner and wasn't up to playing games with Carlos.

"Yeah. You're the boss here. Big deal!"

"Watch you tongue, young man", Luis replied, feeling the bile rising in his throat.

"You're the boss. Does that make you feel good, to be boss of a two room shack where you can lord it over Mama and me while everybody outside pushes you about?"

"Anything more like that and you'll be sorry – I'm warning you". Sweat stood out on Luis' forehead and the veins showed like livid weals on his forearms. He clenched his fists in angry knots of desperation. "What the hell's got into you? Why can't we have a bit of peace round here without you opening you mouth every five minutes to cause trouble. I tell you before, if you don like it here, go somewhere else. You mother break her back for you, God knows why, and you about as grateful as a mosquito. What's the matter? Why don you find a girl and drive her mad instead?"

"That's right. Find a girl. Settle down in suburban La Joya. Raise another generation of waiters and boot blacks. Maybe one of them will even get to be a taxi driver."

Luis held his temper. The Afghans were planning another attack and he didn't want to get himself into a situation where he'd miss it.

"So, I'm a taxi-driver. So what? You refuse the food I buy, eh? That's the trouble with you and your kind. You got a thing about hard work. Standing around in air-conditioned shops a few hours a week's more your style while you decide on you 'career'. You read you books - then wave you magic wand and you have a nice house and plenty of food, while you sit around scratching you backside. Wake up. In this world, if you don work, you don eat."

"And you don't eat if you do work. Can't you see how exploited you are?"

"Oh! Here we go. Don bring any of that revolutionary claptrap in my house. Exploited! Caray! Now, I'm exploited am I? And what'r you gonna do – un-exploit me? Listen, son. One day you grow up and see that the world's a certain way. You live with it - make the best of it. You mother and I give you a decent home. If you uncomfortable among the exploited, go find a nice cave in the hills and run around free till you starve. Now, shut up will you so I can watch the film."

"OK. If you're not exploited, how come you haven't done anything about that fool who smashed your car?"

"I said shut up, didn't I?" Luis was getting angry again, banging his fist against the arm of the chair.

"Just answer and I'll shut up."

Luis weighed the alternatives. If he got up he would have to threaten Carlos and since his threats were apparently futile, he might have to strike his son. He hadn't done so for a very long time – not since Carlos was a child - and he wasn't sure what the outcome might be. If he responded, he would be giving way and he would miss the unfolding battle on the television.

He decided to give it one last go. "I suppose God gave me a son so I could make him a man, so, if you wanna be educated, I give you an answer. Life, Carlos, isn't simple like in you books. It's complicated. It's messy. It's shitty. It's full of problems. You get through by learning when to give and when to take. That officer this afternoon – he could've made trouble for me if I report him. I don't wanna lose my licence, so I let him get away with it. Maybe I have a chance to get my own back another day. Sure, I din like doing it, but it was the only thing to do. OK?" This last said in a conciliatory tone.

"But, don't you think it's wrong that he should get away with it?"

Luis shrugged. "Sure it wrong. Lots of things wrong. And there are things that'r right. I can't change the wrongs. They always be there."

"They needn't always be there," Carlos protested. "Some people want to change them. The Alianza will, one day."

"The Alianza! Don go messing about with them or you end up in jail or breakfast for the sharks. They change things, eh? Yes. They shoot everybody they don like and teach the kids to speak Russian. You keep away from that riff-raff or you not welcome here. Listen, son," Luis went on, suddenly anxious and concerned to build a bridge, "our little island's going along OK. Presidente Barbosa ..."

"That crook," Carlos broke in.

"Carlos. Careful what you say. You don understand these things. Presidente Barbosa trying to do things for us. It take time, but you see. We don need a bunch of wild people trying to take over the place."

"If your Barbosa is so great, how is it that we blacks always end up at the wrong end of town?"

Luis winced and passed his hand wearily over his face. "It takes time, son," was all he could find to say. He leaned forward and turned up the volume of the television. The Afghans were retreating; the battle was almost over.

Carlos grunted and took a chair out to the street where he buried his head in his book.

Chapter 8

Lydia's gets ready for her party

Lydia's apartment was in Roosevelt Tower, the new, sparkling white block on the Avenida Central. On the edge of downtown and just before you reached the neat pavements and high walls which signalled the beginning of the Convento district, it had caused quite a stir when it was built. To those who lived nearby in the Convento, it was ugly and vulgar and would ruin the quality of the neighbourhood, not to mention lower the property prices. They had tried to stop its construction in the courts, hoping a friendly judge would see things their way. When that failed, they hurled abuse at the construction workers and did everything they could to impede progress. Now, faced with the fact that it was here to stay, they contented themselves with sounding their horns and making rude gestures as they drove home from their offices, making no secret of their hope that it would soon collapse.

Presidente Barbosa, by contrast, had eagerly supported its construction and had personally signed the permission. It was, he had said in his speech at the signing, a fine symbol of Caribe's future. If Puerto Grande was to become a modern city, a capital city to take its place alongside Mexico City, Paris and New York (his geography did not always keep pace with his rhetoric), then it had to have modern buildings. They would bring prosperity to his people, providing work for some and homes for others. He had not thought it necessary to mention the prosperity it would bring to him, courtesy of the Hackensack Real Estate Company of New Jersey which owned and operated the block. The "commission" was now sitting comfortably with the others in an account just across the water in the British Virgin Islands.

Many of the apartments were empty, not so surprising when the monthly rent of the smallest apartment was twice the annual income of the average Caribino. Of the tenants, most were American business executives. The rest were an assortment of Caribe's government and business leaders together with the mistresses of these and other similar worthies.

Lydia lived on the fourteenth floor. The view from every room was spectacular, sweeping from the sea front and the old Spanish ramparts across the city to the soft hills of the coastal range. She was sitting in her dressing room. For some time she had stood at the window staring out, first at the eternal wonder of the sunset and then at the flickering and twinkling lights of the city and the sky which met each other and merged in the still, black sea. Finally, she couldn't bear any longer the melancholy this induced and began to prepare for the evening. Would she wear her hair up or leave it as it was? The dress she had decided on was cut very low, so she decided to wear it up so that she could show off her neck and shoulders. She knew how attractive her soft white skin was, particularly when set against her dark hair and the red dress. She wanted to look extra-specially good tonight though she wasn't quite sure why. She brushed her hair with long sweeping movements, then carefully began to pin it into place, humming an accompaniment to Roberto Yanes' *Enamorada* that she'd been playing for the past hour.

The sound of the doorbell startled her. "Oh Heavens! Is it that late?" She found her wristwatch under the pile of pins, tissues, coins and jewellery on her dressing table and saw that it was still only eight-thirty. "Thank goodness", she sighed. "But who can that be?"

There was a knock on her bedroom door. Without waiting for a reply, Melba came in.

"Señor Salcedo has arrived, Madam. What shall I do with him? I haven't finished getting things ready yet."

"Don't worry, Melba. It's not a hurricane. Just give him a drink and tell him I'm dressing and will be out in a while."

"Yes, Madam. What about the things?"

"What things, chica?"

"The things I have to get ready."

"Oh, those things. Well, ask Señor Salcedo if he will be so kind as to excuse you while you finish preparing the food and getting the drinks ready and whatever else you have to do."

"Yes, Madam."

As Melba turned to leave, Lydia said, "Let's have a look at you, Melba". A quick appraisal. "Yes, you look very smart. Perhaps you could do something with your hair - if you have time, of course, and try to get those seams straight. I don't know why you wear those old-fashioned stockings. They're impossible."

Melba ran a hand involuntarily through her hair. "Yes, Madam. Thank you, Madam. I'll get Señor Salcedo his drink now. Will you want me for anything more?"

"I'll need you to zip me up when I put my dress on. Come back in five minutes, perhaps."

Melba went out, the seams in her dark brown stockings snaking haphazardly down her calves.

Her hair finally arranged to her satisfaction, her make-up double checked, Lydia had just put on her dress and was easing her feet into her pumps when there was a second knock on the door. "Perfect timing," she thought. "Come in. I'm ready to be imprisoned".

It was not Melba. It was Raul.

"Raul. It's you. I thought it was Melba. Give me a few more minutes. I'm not quite ready." She said all this to the mirror in which she could see Raul's reflection as he stood in the doorway. She held her dress up under her armpits but it fell away at the sides to reveal the long white slope of her back. She sat down at the dressing table.

"That's alright. It's only me. I've come to say hello." Raul crossed to where she was.

"Please, Raul. I'm trying to hurry. Be an angel and wait for me. Didn't Melba get you a drink?"

Raul waved the drink which was in his hand and said, "Yes, she was very kind". He put his drink down on the edge of the table. "Alberto tells me you had lunch with the English again today."

She half turned to him. "Raul, you haven't been spying on me, have you", half in anger and half in despair. "What on earth for? I don't do anything you don't know about. Can't I even have lunch without you suspecting me of Heaven knows what?"

"I know all about him," Raul replied, a smile dying before it was born.

"Then why do you bother to spy on me?"

"Just taking care of you, my dove", he replied, this time letting the smile show itself. "Don't forget, Lydia, you belong to me."

As he said this, Raul slowly ran his hand up her back, across her shoulders and onto her breasts. She shuddered momentarily but did not move. She sat immobile, staring at Raul's shirt in the mirror without seeing anything, feeling her heart beat against his hand.

"You look beautiful this evening. Such trouble you take to look your best for me. I'm unworthy of it. A toast to you," and Raul raised his glass.

In doing so, his eyes fell on something barely discernible in the partly open drawer of the dressing table. Slowly, he put down his glass and pulled open the drawer. She watched, fearful yet detached, as if watching a scene she was not part of. In the corner of the drawer, almost covered by a pile of silk scarves, there was a photograph. It was a small reproduction of the kind taken at College Graduation ceremonies. It showed a young, intelligent-looking man, whom some would call handsome, with dark laughing eyes and a warm sensuous mouth. Equally slowly, Raul took out the photograph. He tore it systematically into pieces. Without saying anything, he crushed the pieces in his hand until his knuckles were white, then threw the crumpled mass onto the floor. Turning to her, his face drained, the pulsing veins on his neck betraying his fury, he struck her hard across the mouth. Her stifled scream brought Melba running.

Lydia waved her away. "No, there's nothing the matter". Melba shrugged. This was not the first time she had seen Señor Raul standing over her mistress.

Raul, without a word, followed her out of the bedroom. "Melba," he said, barely controlling his voice, "Señorita Lydia is not feeling well but I'm sure she'll be alright in a short while. She wants you to go and zip her up in a few minutes. Perhaps you could take her a drink. Could you get me another now, please. I seem to have left my glass somewhere."

"Yes, Sir," was all that Melba allowed herself, though there was much more that she wanted to say.

Lydia looked at herself in the mirror. She didn't cry. She showed no emotion as she sat there. She just twisted a strand of hair round her finger, again and again. Then she stooped to pick up the pieces of the photograph and tried to put them back together. After a moment, she slipped them into an envelope which she put carefully between the mattresses of her bed; to hide it or to straighten out the pieces? She wasn't sure. With a shrug, she turned again to the mirror. The ring on Raul's finger had cut the corner of her mouth. She could patch it up as long as it didn't swell. She was quite ready by the time Melba knocked and came in.

Chapter 9

Conway makes an entrance

It was ten-o-clock when Conway rang the doorbell. He had had little difficulty in finding Lydia's apartment - the strains of the pachanga and merengue were echoing down the street. The noise of the music almost knocked him off his feet as Melba opened the door. There were twenty or so people in what appeared to be the main living room, some dancing, others apparently conversing as he could see their mouths moving and their hands waving, though God knows how they could hear anything.

"Oh Christ", he groaned inwardly. "They're all in evening dress".

Conway looked at himself in the mirror hanging in the hallway and felt rather silly. Lydia had said casual dress. He had accordingly dressed in the best traditions of the Englishman on holiday: short-sleeved shirt with palm tree motif and white slacks, baggy at the seat. As a gesture to raffishness he had dispensed with socks. His slightly hairy, very white ankles protruded from what looked like orthopaedic open-toed sandals. It was too late to back out of the door and flee. Melba had closed the door behind him. Already several guests were looking at him with what he recognised as a combination of amusement and astonishment.

Lydia had spotted him. She came over, smiling and taking his hands in hers.

"Tony, I'm so glad you could come" she said, or rather mouthed. "Let me get you a drink and introduce you to some of my friends. And, I'll turn the music down a bit."

She looked stunning. It was the first time Conway had seen her dressed up and he approved. Yes, he really approved. It only served to make him feel worse and he pulled back as Lydia went to lead him into the room.

"Lydia," he whispered, then realising that she couldn't hear, he shouted, "Lydia. You said dress casually. I look like a bloody clown."

It was as he was saying this that the needle on the record reached the centre and the music stopped. A sudden quiet had descended. His last sentence, bellowed at the top of his voice, bombulated around the room. All eyes turned to him. There was a ripple of laughter. "Great," he thought to himself, "they must think I'm the entertainment for the evening. All I need now is to throw up and my evening will be complete."

"Nonsense," Lydia was saying, her eyes shining and her smile unwavering. "You look fine. We Latins love to dress up. You mustn't mind us. Relax. Enjoy yourself. Melba, can you get Señor Conway a nice big whisky, please. Come on Tony, come and meet Eddie and Alice. They're neighbours. They're from New York."

He sidled apprehensively into the room. He felt that all eyes were still on him, though he preferred not to check in case it was true. The introductions over, he found himself trying to hear what Alice was asking him and then explaining to her the functions of the Beefeaters at the Tower of London. She had seen them on a trip and thought them just darling. At least it meant that he had a chance to retreat to a corner and let the party regain momentum after his entrance.

After a while, out of the corner of his eye, he caught sight of Lydia coming towards him. He had escaped Alice and the dreadful Eddie and occupied himself with studying the covers of the records. The light in that particular corner of the room was dim - he was able to stand behind a low table so that the offending ankles were not quite so conspicuous. He looked up, his eyes brightening at the prospect of Lydia's company.

"Tony, I want you to meet Raul."

An "Oh!" of disappointment escaped before Conway could check it.

"Oh ... how nice to meet you. I've heard such a lot about you", he blustered, hoping the elision of the two "Ohs" had been successful.

"The pleasure is mine, Señor Conway." Raul's reply, in perfect American-accented English, had all the sincerity of someone meeting their proctologist. "You may leave us, Lydia," he said, this time in Spanish.

"Oh but I thought I'd stay and be entertained by you two charming men," Lydia replied in English.

Raul, in Spanish, "Don't be coquettish, Lydia. It doesn't become you. You may leave us to talk."

"But," Lydia insisted in English, "I haven't spoken to Tony yet at all. I feel I'm neglecting him."

"I'm sure Señor Conway doesn't feel neglected," Raul replied in English. He took Lydia's arm above her elbow. "Go and talk to Augusto will you, beloved."

This exchange had been conducted as if Conway were not there. He decided to assert himself. "Yes, stay, of course, Lydia. I'm sure Mr, erm Raul, doesn't mind. I must say she's better looking company than you are," he added, nudging Raul in the ribs and smiling.

Raul did not appear to be amused. "That is undeniable, Señor. She is indeed beautiful. Now, Lydia," switching to Spanish, "Leave us," this last in a voice that was suddenly cold and hard. And as Raul spoke, Conway saw his fingers tighten on Lydia's arm. She winced involuntarily.

Then, she smiled, though her eyes betrayed her. "Thank you for the compliment, Tony, if it was one. Raul is right. I really must say hello to Augusto. I'll see you later." And she left them.

Conway was angry. He thought to ask Raul "What else do you do besides bully women", but hadn't time to speak before Raul got in first,

"So, what have you learned of our island since you arrived, Señor Conway? I hope you have formed a favourable impression of our progress." Raul was smiling at Conway earnestly as if the uncomfortable scene they had just been part of existed only in his imagination. Without giving him an opportunity to respond, Raul continued, "I see that you have already taken a liking to the beautiful Lydia. She really is delightful company, is she not? It is sad but you will have to take your place at the back of a very long line of admirers, Señor. Now, the sugar harvest. Tell me. I read the report you filed with very great interest".

With this conversational gambit, Raul had skilfully and effortlessly prevented Conway from commenting on what had passed between them and Lydia, had been left in no doubt where he stood in the pecking order for Lydia's attentions, and had it made clear that that he was an open book to Raul.

He took this in as he exclaimed angrily, "What do you mean, you read my report? It's private – for my newspaper, not for you."

"We like to know what others think of us. It helps us to improve," Raul replied smoothly, ignoring as if it were not there the accusation behind the question. Raul, his smile confident, had defeated him and Conway knew it. He searched for words, a rare phenomenon for him. But then he had had little exposure to the subtleties of psychological warfare and domination as practised so expertly by Raul.

Raul then guided the conversation wherever he wished. Conway found himself discussing all manner of things without understanding why. As he did, the reporter in him, as if that part of him was still functioning properly, made mental notes on Raul.

First, physically, what was Raul like? The dinner jacket and trousers were well made, very well made. There were studs down the front of the whiter than white shirt, scorning the ruffles and nylon obscenities that had begun to pass as dress shirts. The studs were gold, inlaid with mother of pearl, with a tiny pearl in the centre. The cufflinks were the same. Raul had clearly tied his own bow tie with a cultivated sense of what Latins called "sweet disorder", anticipating the prospect of several women straightening it for him, affording the opportunity for physical contact and attention. It was clear that Raul was a dandy and the highly polished patent shoes were further proof. But, on further reflection, the impression created was not of a dandy but of someone who was too fastidious, too neat, too conscious of his appearance. The effect was vaguely unwholesome, though it was not easy to explain why.

Raul could have been forty but could have been fifty-five. Of average height and slimly built, his hair was a shiny jet black, parted on one side and so organised as to minimise the effect of the receding widow's peaks. His skin was an olive brown which seemed somehow sallow. But it was the eyes and mouth that were the features that most commanded attention. The eyes were dead. There was no other way to describe them. There was the usual combination of iris, pupil and the rest, but although the relevant parts were all there, the whole added up to nothing – an emptiness. They had seen too much and too much that wasn't nice. They had given up seeing, though Raul still looked out through them. There was no lustre, no brightness, no sparkle, no feeling, no recognition. As for the mouth, it boasted a small black moustache on its upper lip and a fine set of white teeth. But it was the line of the mouth which he noticed. There was barely a sign of lips. It seemed as if Raul had a gash in his face, a gash in the shape of an arc, sweeping down at each end. The effect was a snarl, heavy with malevolence. When Raul smiled, which always looked as if it needed effort, the gash opened a little and the corners jerked upwards. But the knowledge that the gash would snap shut again and that the corners would collapse downwards when the smile was over made the mouth, even at its best, sinister and disquieting.

Conway took all of this in. For reasons which were not clear to him, he realised that he needed to watch this man, get a sense of what he did. Raul, he thought, was important in understanding what a portrait of power but also of cruelty looked like.

Meanwhile, he found himself chattering away, experiencing that uncomfortable sensation of listening to himself and wondering what on earth he was talking about. Eventually, a chance came for him to escape from Raul's suffocating charm.

"Raul, you son-of-a-bitch, where've ya been. I haven't seen ya in hell-knows-how-long". A burly American had lurched between the two of them and now was leaning on Raul, in the guise of putting his arm round his shoulder. The smile jerked upwards and, with all muscles straining, stayed up.

What he expected was some variation on, "Get lost, you fat slug and show me some respect." What Raul actually said was, "Mort, how good to see you." In his easy mastery of his exchanges with Conway, Raul had shown he was nobody's fool in the cocktail catch-as-catch-can. But, with Mort, he saw another side to Raul; a tolerance, almost obsequiousness in the face of this man's boorishness. Such a change of character quite startled him in its rapidity and completeness. Mort was now full-steam-ahead in a monologue delivered inches from Raul's face as he bent over him. The rictus smile stayed in place as Raul linked arms with Mort.

Conway backed away and for the first time edged towards the middle of the room. Things looked different from there and now that he wasn't trying to hide, no-one seemed to be staring at him or even noticing him. As luck would have it, Lydia was at that very moment disengaging herself from Augusto. She stood there, slightly to one side, enjoying her party yet embarrassed by the sensation that she was on her own with no-one to talk to. He moved quickly to join her.

"Lydia, I never thought we'd get a chance to talk. There's such a lot I want to talk to you about. Is there anywhere we can sit for a few minutes?"

"Not now, Tony dear. I really must say hello to everyone"

He followed her eyes as she spoke and saw Raul watching them over Mort's shoulder. "Come on, Lydia. I've got to talk to you. Forget Raul for a second. He seems like a nasty piece of work anyway."

"Tony, not now," Lydia insisted. There was an edge to her voice, though he couldn't work out whether it was anger or desperation, or both. The fact that, as she spoke, she broke into a beautiful smile, confused him even more. A casual observer might think she was greatly amused by this strange Englishman.

She broke away and walked purposefully over to a group of well-dressed young things animatedly discussing the merits of Acapulco Gold. This left Conway in the position that Lydia had been in moments ago; suddenly alone in a noisy party. By contrast, however, no-one beat a rapid path to his side. For what seemed ages he just stood there, frozen in the half-step he had taken to follow Lydia. He convinced himself that everyone was looking at him - pityingly, perhaps.

The doorbell sounded in another lull in the music. "Saved by the bell, to quote a well-known cliché," he muttered to himself, "and never was a cliché more welcome".

Melba hurried past him, smoothing down her dress and fussing with her hair. "Funny stockings", he thought as she went past. "Never seen them with zig-zag seams before."

The new arrival was being greeted warmly by those nearest the door. There were shouts of "Alberto, Hola. Alberto, you old son-of-a-gun", and there was much backslapping. He couldn't see Alberto's face, just a tall figure with greying, close-cropped hair and a long neck. Then the figure turned round and faced the room.

Conway went cold. "It's him. It's that bastard who hit me this afternoon. Jesus Christ! It's him." So far, he had kept this shock of recognition to himself. But as he repeated, "It's him," he began to say it out loud until he suddenly heard himself shouting across the room, "Hey, Lydia. It's him. He's the one I wanted to talk to you about."

Alberto had seen him as he had looked across the room but had not given the slightest hint of recognition, greeting Lydia with grave courtesy and then making his way over to Raul, lighting a Camel from the ever-present pack. Conway's sudden shouting caused the guests nearest to him to stop dancing and look at him quizzically. Lydia looked over, a startled expression on her face. Raul was at Conway's side, his hand on his arm before he could repeat himself.

"Señor Conway, what is it? You are not well?" The question was asked while Raul nodded to those nearby, as if to say, "It's alright. I'll take care of things. The man's not used to our rum, yet". As he spoke, Raul tried to draw him towards the kitchen.

Conway felt the pressure on his arm. "What the hell are you doing", shaking his arm free. "Who's that over there because ... ."

"Señor Conway," Raul interrupted smoothly and without raising his voice. "Señor Conway. You don't want to make a scene and spoil the beautiful Lydia's party, do you? She is looking most upset. Come, come. Why don't you cool down a little and tell me calmly what's the matter".

Again he found himself outplayed. No, he didn't want to spoil Lydia's party, but neither did he want Raul's firm grip or synthetic charm to prevent him from confronting the man called Alberto. He let himself be guided into the kitchen. Once there he gestured angrily at Raul.

"Listen, I've come in here because of Lydia, not you. You'd better watch whose arm you grab. You're not big enough or young enough to throw your weight around, so don't try it again." He was breathing rapidly, his pupils so enlarged they almost filled his eyes. "Now, I want to meet this chap Alberto. I have a private little matter I want to discuss with him."

"Señor Conway," the voice was as smooth as ever, "this is a party. Everyone is happy. Everyone is enjoying themselves." Raul stopped as Lydia came in.

"What's happening, Raul? Tony?" she asked. "What's the matter?"

"Querida, I don't know. Señor Conway seemed to get a bit excited when he saw Alberto. I don't know why, so I thought we'd come in here and cool off a little."

"A bit excited. That's putting it mildly. Look Lydia. I've been trying to tell you all evening that someone beat me up this afternoon in the park near the Hilton - hence the somewhat swollen eye - and that very same someone just walked through your door - your good friend Alberto." Conway paused, then suddenly slapped his palm to his forehead and nodded to Raul. "Ah! I get it. He works for you doesn't he", pointing at Raul, "and you thought I was pestering Lydia, so you set your attack dog on me. Was I bothering you Lydia? Was I?"

Lydia said nothing.

"Beat you up? Alberto? Señor Conway, really! What nonsense is this?" Raul had interrupted him again. "Really, Señor Conway, what can you be thinking of. You must control yourself." Turning to Lydia, he asked "What has he been drinking," in a tone of resigned tolerance of the bad manners of others.

While he was listening to what Raul was saying and getting ever angrier at what he heard, Conway's attention was more and more drawn to Lydia. She was standing quietly to one side. She seemed to be taking it all in her stride, but on her face was an expression which he was to remember and wrestle to understand for a long time. It was an expression of pain, almost horror, and of incredulity. It was directed at Raul who had stopped talking. Lydia just stood there. Conway was mesmerized. A tense calm prevailed.

Raul had seen Lydia's expression and reacted first. "Lydia, my dear, there is no reason for you to be here. You can see it's just some misunderstanding. I will deal with it. Why don't you go back to your guests before they miss you and begin to think something is the matter?" As he was saying this he took Lydia's arm and led her to the door.

Now it was Conway's turn to react. "Hey, wait a minute. Aren't we forgetting something?" Turning to Lydia, "Despite what he says", nodding towards Raul, "I'm not making a mistake. I was beaten up this afternoon and the tall ghoul you call Alberto did the beating. Now I don't want to make a scene, you know that, so perhaps Alberto could be persuaded to come in here and explain what the hell he thinks he's up to. Raul, you like the strong-arm stuff. Why don't you go and fetch him."

Raul looked over at Conway and sighed. "Ah, Señor Conway. And I always thought the English were so well-mannered ... ."

Conway shouted him down. "Look, Raul, I've heard enough of your views on manners and seen them in action. Are you going to get Alberto or do I go straight to the police?"

Raul smiled and shrugged his shoulders. It was Lydia who spoke, her voice flat and expressionless. "Tony, Alberto is a policeman. He is one of the senior police captains in the city. That's why you are so obviously mistaken."

"A police captain! He can't be. He ... ". Conway was completely dumbfounded, lost for words, poleaxed. He knew he was right. It had been Alberto. But this latest piece of information had sent his mind reeling.

"You see now, Señor Conway, why I was so anxious to avoid what would have been a very unpleasant scene. Now, we'll all forget it, shall we? I bear you no ill-feelings, Señor Conway. You were obviously upset. We have forgotten it already, haven't we, querida?"

Lydia nodded woodenly. Her fingers sought out a strand of hair. "I think it would be better if you go home now, Tony. You look tired."

Conway was stung by Lydia's remark. Even she had turned against him, as he saw it, and she was the one he thought he could trust and confide in. He allowed himself to be led quietly to the door by Raul and Lydia. No-one seemed to notice his leaving: the music and dancing and drinking and singing went on unabated. Alberto noticed. He turned his expressionless eyes onto him, looked at him for a second or two, then looked away. There was no triumph, nor satisfaction in the look, far less hostility, just a sense of taking note of what had happened. At the door, Conway made a last effort to talk to Lydia, to try to explain.

"Lydia, I wish you would believe me." He held her hand which she had offered for a parting handshake. He pulled her slightly towards him so as to say something out of earshot of Raul. "When can I call you? We've got to ... ."

"Bye, bye, Tony," Lydia was saying as she pulled her hand free. She was watching Raul who had moved closer the moment he'd tried to whisper. She put her hand on Raul's arm and turned to go back inside.

"You did well, my little Lydia," Raul said as he patted her hand. He was smiling one of his smiles, the corners of his mouth threatening to fall back into place at any moment.

"You can be so despicable," was all that Lydia said as she re-entered her party, smiling and ready for the next dance.

Seething and mystified, Conway made his way back to the hotel.

Chapter 10

The Sand and Sea

It was half-past three in the morning when Raul left the party. With him was the tall figure of Alberto.

"I think I'm going to go home and sleep," Alberto said, yawning loudly.

"Not before we've had a drink or two. I feel like some company."

Alberto shrugged. "OK. Where to, Boss?" He lit another Camel. It might be a long night.

"Let's go to one of the tourist bars for a change. What about The Sand and The Sea?"

"It's OK by me," Alberto said. "One place is as good as another."

"The Sand and The Sea," Raul shouted to his driver as they climbed into the car.

They drove through the deserted streets without talking. It had rained briefly around midnight. The humidity was oppressive and made worse by the smells it engendered. Vegetation, refuse, the odd rat or cat and who knows what else rotted at the sides of the road with renewed energy after the rain. Raul pressed the switch in the panel at his side and the windows of the Cadillac closed. Soon they were out on the Malecon sweeping alongside the sea. The lights of the old part of the city were still burning.

Many of the bars were still open. The noise of music and people bounced across and up and down the narrow, sticky streets. These days, locals having a night out and sailors from the ships in port made up the bulk of the clientele. Tourism, while not the great success hoped for, nonetheless still provided a steady supply of customers. Some, though not many, came from the cruise ships which were beginning to come to Caribe for what the brochure called "6 hours ashore in magical Puerto Grande where the native throb of the samba can be enjoyed in sophisticated olde-worlde surroundings – every night a fiesta!" That the samba, a Brazilian dance, was not a rhythm often heard in Caribe did not concern whoever wrote this immortal prose. In any event, the cruise passengers were mostly of an age which made dancing of any kind something that their surgeon back home would advise against. For the rest, samba, pachanga, pasa doble, Navajo War Dance, it was all the same to them; a chance to bump and grind and "have a ball." Those who were not from the cruise ships were on "economy" or "$10-a-day" breaks organised by their local Kiwani or Lions group from Newark or Pittsburgh. For them, it was a chance to swim, get loaded on cheap booze, gamble and feel superior to the natives, even perhaps make out and do all the other things denied them back home.

The Sand and The Sea was on the Calle Luna which ran down steeply from the Plaza Central towards the port. Many of the houses in this particular part of the old town had been restored to their splendid eighteenth and nineteenth century Colonial best. Some had become smart shops on the ground floor, dispensing antiques made to order in the nearby workshops in the Calle San Agustin. Most of the apartments above had been bought by American businessmen and were resplendent with tiled patios, fountains and 15 dollar Boston ferns.

"Hey Joe. Como estas? Dos rones y soda".

"Yessir, Rool. Coming right up." Joe was wearing a T-shirt emblazoned with the heads of the four Beach Boys and khaki shorts. The T shirt was tight, showing off his pecs and was cut off at the shoulders so that his biceps got air-time too. He was huge. He'd played football for the Packers; a pretty good offensive lineman people said, but who could trust bar talk? He'd been in Puerto Grande since the ACL injury had forced him to retire; since, in fact, he discovered that the two things he enjoyed most, weed and boys, could be had much more readily than in Green Bay and without the irksome interference of the law.

'You two guys been partying again," Joe asked him.

Raul nodded. "Simply out of duty, you understand."

"Yeah, Yeah. I understand. Jeez, you dagos don't seem to do nothing except screw and dance. And the way most of you dance, there ain't much difference".

Joe set the two rum and sodas on the bar. Raul smiled thinly at Joe's tasteless banter and pulled a note from his wallet. Joe shook his head. "Ya think I'd take money from you poor underdeveloped bastards? I've got some principles." This was delivered in Joe's best stage whisper, thereby ensuring that the tourists at the bar could hear and laugh along with him. Alberto smiled obligingly but his eyes were not smiling.

Coming from anyone else, comments such as these would have guaranteed a fairly nasty encounter with a truck as he was crossing the road. Barmen knew who Raul was. After all they spied for him. When he came in, they made the drinks, rustled up a dish of olives, hoped the last piece of information was appreciated, and prayed that the boss had paid whatever was due. But Joe was different. Joe was Raul's own special private eyes and ears. Contacts between tourists and members of Don Basilio's government were his particular brief. So, he encouraged Joe's apparently eccentric even dangerous behaviour.

When others whispered warnings, Joe would say," Hey, Rool's OK. These bastards need me. We got the best booze and there's no better ass in town. And who's gonna tell the sorry s.o.b what point spread to choose when the Cowboys play the Bears at Soldier Field and it's ten below?"

Raul sipped his drink at the bar while Alberto checked with Joe and returned with the news that there were a couple of new girls from out of town in one of the booths. Raul perked up. "What are they drinking, Joe?"

"Tom Collins."

"OK. Give me two big ones and a refill for me. Alberto's not drinking". Alberto was not paid to drink. He was paid to be alert at all times in the service of his master. A drunken bodyguard would never do.

Raul picked his way through the dancers to the booth. The two girls were fending off a couple of locals who had caught the whiff of fresh meat. He slid into the booth by the side of the prettier girl. Any complaint from the locals died in their throats as Alberto appeared and indicated that the show was over. The girls were much impressed by this display of forceful charm. They were even more impressed when Joe materialised at the merest nod bearing the drinks and two red roses.

"Mind if we join you? I'm Raul and this is Alberto. Say hello, Alberto."

Alberto managed half a smile and sat down.

"How long you girls been in town? I don't remember seeing you here before. If I had, I'd remember. It's a good job we're here. Two beautiful girls like you need protection in the big city." All of this was said with what those unfamiliar with it would have described as old world charm.

The girls smiled and were duly flattered. They were country girls - from San Felipe, they said - Circe and Beatriz. They didn't recognise Raul or Alberto. Why should they? They didn't follow the news and both men were too old to feature in stories about the latest pop stars.

"We're looking for work", Circe said. "You know, modelling, and taking art classes." She looked like the serious one. Beatriz chipped in, "I'm not particular. I'll do anything. As long as it's legal", she added. They all laughed. He could see that at least one of them would be turning tricks at the big hotels within a few weeks. And they'd do well for a time till the features hardened and the eyes died.

"Who are you, then? You look very smart, all dressed up." This was Circe. She wanted to know what to expect before she could relax with her drink. Beatriz seemed to be having fewer qualms. She was plain and on the plump side, wearing a dress with a neck line which was too low. She modelled her rose between her teeth, behind her ear, and "wherever else you like" she seemed to be saying to a less than entranced Alberto. She didn't know, and why should she, that his only real enjoyment was to be found in hitting people and hurting them.

"I already told you. I'm Raul and the strong silent one is Alberto. We've just come from a boring party."

"No. I mean what do you do? You the owner or something?"

"Why do you say that?"

"Well, I dunno. You seem to know your way around and you've got people running round waiting on you. We were here half an hour before he'd get round to serving us a drink", indicating Joe.

Joe had just brought over another order of drinks with some olives and flat bread with salsa. A couple of tight-trousered would-be toughs had made as if to take some of the food as Joe passed, but a sharp word and a glance in Alberto's direction had been enough to dissuade them. Their hands faltered and then returned to their natural habitat, shaping their hair and adjusting their Y-fronts, as they retreated to join friends who were just leaving.

Raul saw that Circe had noticed. "Sharp girl", he thought, ever on the lookout for recruits. She didn't look like the usual country girl. He could see why she wanted to be a model. She was tall, slim yet shapely, and pretty to look at, with her auburn hair and green eyes, as if there had been some wandering Irishman somewhere in her genealogical past.

"Oh. They just know us in here," Raul replied. "But, hey, why are we all talking so much? Let's show these country girls how to really dance." And he was on his feet, taking Beatriz's hand with all the style of old Vienna. The crowd parted and regrouped and they were soon entwined in the slow three-four of a bolero. Beatriz did a bit of exploring with her thigh to see if there was any life in this one still. If there was, she couldn't tell. Circe stared ahead glumly, absent-mindedly playing with the swizzle-stick in her drink. Alberto picked his teeth and watched the door, toying with his packet of Camels.

Raul brought Beatriz back to the table, flustered and glistening, but trying not to look too pleased with herself out of sympathy for Circe. More drinks arrived and soon Raul was turning his attention to Circe, so she felt she belonged, even if it made Beatriz pout. The locals saw Beatriz disengage and turn her chair but they kept their distance once they saw who was buying the drinks. Meanwhile, Raul was busy thinking ahead. What did he want to do next? There were several options, each exciting in its own way and most involved wearing clothes that he'd bought for Lydia but never given her, while the girls played.

Then he caught sight of Joe out of the corner of his eye. Joe had picked up the local habit of pointing out or signalling something by puckering his lips and nodding towards the object in question. It looked for all the world as if he was blowing a kiss, which, given Joe's preferences, was always a possibility. Certainly Joe was often misunderstood and explanations had to be made (or Joe got lucky!). But Raul was a native. He followed Joe's glance and saw the two tourists who'd just come in.

Bud Greenberg was thirty-six and running to fat. His buddy, Mike Slavik was five years older and had given up the struggle. Both were bored and fed up and ready to get back to San Diego. They had been in Caribe for six days now, courtesy of the Dental Tools Manufacturing Association, scouting out the possibility of holding next year's Conference there. "Make a change from St Louis or Phoenix," the new dynamic Chairman, Ted Powell, had said.

In private he had put it differently, "Next year, it's gotta be cheap. The Japs are screwing us. And the krauts. Jesus, who won the war? So, cheap all the way: cheap hotels, cheap booze, cheap hookers. The guys will love it. Just tell 'em it's gonna be exotic. They'll join the dots."

In their six days, Bud and Mike had lurched from disappointment to disillusionment. The hotels were not cheap, though some were nasty (they had tried three). The staff who were not terminally idle were thieves. Some were both. Conference facilities were a bad joke. "These guys are about as useful as the Pope's balls," was Mike's way of putting it. And as for girls, so far their ignorance of Spanish, reluctance to spend good bucks, and fear of the clap had restricted their reconnaissance to the hotels. None of the shabby tarts who patrolled the lobbies, more in hope than expectation, had inspired them. One night, Mike had been taken with a young one in a yellow halter top and cut-off jeans but Bud had noticed the foundation covering the seven-o-clock shadow just in time. Mike had retreated deeply troubled and promised to kill Bud if he breathed a word.

Once dinner was over that evening, Mike and Bud had found themselves, as usual, reluctant to call it a day and go back to the hotel. The unwelcoming tawdriness of their rooms was only one reason. They were on the lam, free, in Caribe "famed for fun, friendship and freedom" as the posters had it, leaving no doubt that a fourth word in the alliterative list was also there for the asking. To go back to their rooms would be un-American. It was to admit defeat; to admit that the mere sight of a red-blooded (and red-faced) American waving greenbacks was not enough to persuade these poor underdeveloped natives to roll over and cry uncle.

"Weren't they supposed to go ape and beg us to take their daughters back to the States, or something," Mike lamented.

Disillusioned and bored, and completely lacking imagination, like a couple of old-timers they had gone for a walk, ashamed of themselves for being so sad and praying that the other wouldn't tell anyone. They had stopped outside The Sand and The Sea. They couldn't see much but they could hear music. Nodding to each other, they decided to give it a try and get a beer. Mike was the first to realise it; the barman was talking to *them*. He was speaking American and telling them that the two rum and cokes were a gift from the guy over there. The guy, named Rool or Roll or something, wanted to know whether they wanted to join him.

Mike, all suspicion after six days in the city, looked at Bud, "Come again", he asked Joe.

"Rool, over there, says have a drink on him and would you two gentlemen like to join him at his table."

"What's his angle?" This was Bud, no less suspicious, already imagining the headline in the San Diego Tribune - "Local businessmen drugged - kidnap feared".

"Come on you guys. What angle? The guy doesn't need an angle. That's Rool. He's just being nice to tourists. Say thank you. There may be more where that came from."

"Didn't you used to play football," Mike threw in. "Defensive End? Vikings?"

"Not bad. Lineman. Packers," Joe replied smiling.

"How about that! Hey, Bud, this guy's a pro. I saw you when you played in San Diego. Not bad. How about that?" For Mike things had changed dramatically. This was really living. This was what travelling was all about - the chance to meet a guy like Joe.

"So, should we join your friend," Bud asked, less reverentially. His Los Angeles Blades T-shirt advertised that he was an ice-hockey man himself but at least he was now prepared to trust the reply.

"Yeah, course. He'll show you a good time, if you're lucky." Joe winked. Both Mike and Bud felt a familiar tightening in the throat and trousers and picked up their drinks without more ado.

"Hi! How nice of you to join us. You must be from the great U S of A. Let me guess. California, perhaps", pointing to Bud's shirt. "Let me introduce you. This is Circe. This is Beatrix. I am Raul and the ugly one is Alberto. And you?" All this was delivered with great aplomb as he guided them to two seats which Joe had pushed up to the end of the booth.

Within no time, Mike and Bud were having fun. Mike caught Bud's eye and Bud could read the signal, "Hey, this is alright. This is what it's about.

Stay tuned." Such was Raul's prowess as a host that soon Mike was talking about himself, a sure sign, as with all Americans, that he felt really at home. Another round of drinks caught Mike describing his time under fire at the Incheon River. He had thought that this might have some effect on the girls who, he had to admit, were looking pretty bored. It certainly was having an effect on Bud, who'd looked away. Bud knew that the closest Mike had got to Korea was Hawaii, but he wasn't about to say anything. Not now, anyway! Later it should be worth a few drinks to buy his silence.

While Mike talked and Bud drank, Raul was watching the girls. They were smiling and nodding but he could see that they were not exactly entranced. It was hardly surprising. Mike assumed, and why not, that everyone spoke American, his only concession to foreigners being to speak more loudly.

But Raul realised that, being country girls, neither spoke more than half a dozen words of English. They had exhausted their vocabulary by the end of the introductions. Since then they had laughed when others laughed and generally tried to go along with the flow. But, they were beyond bored. And still Mike was trying to reach his sergeant who'd taken a gut-shot and was screaming like a stuck pig.

Alberto was watching his boss like a hawk. No-one could know what Raul might do, not least because he didn't know himself. Alberto knew that he could do anything. He could get some more girls. He could take against the gringos and get them thrown out on their necks. He could get rid of the girls and come on to the guys just to see their faces.

So, Alberto was on high alert. It came with the territory when your boss was, how to put it politely, unpredictable. Joe caught Alberto's eye - holding the phone and pointing. Alberto leaned across - they were still in Nam - and, touching Raul's arm, pointed to Joe. Raul flashed them a smile. "Excuse me. I'll be back in a moment". As he came back, he said "Sorry guys and girls. We gotta go. Business", quickly rendered again in Spanish for the girls. "Enjoy yourselves".

Alberto caught up with him, wondering what had happened. He looked back to see Joe taking more drinks over to the table "courtesy of Rool" and two very disappointed young women plotting their escape.

"Anything up" Alberto asked.

"No. Just Barbosa- couldn't sleep. And I was getting bored. You know, Alberto, there was a time when I worked the bars pimping for the gringos ..."

"Yes, I know, boss", Alberto cut in, hoping to head off the impending tale, heard many times, of Raul's life before and after Barbosa.

Raul ploughed on. "Then old Don Basilio made his move and yours truly got on board. He needed a fixer and that was me. I fix things. I fix people. All for the greater good of Caribe and our beautiful island's bright future. Not forgetting, of course, my percentage of everything, a great apartment, a driver, and you, Alberto, my personal enforcer. What more could a pimp want than to pimp for a President?!"

He smiled his smile.

"Check with Joe later", he added. "See if he gets anything interesting from those two losers. And find out more about that girl, Circe was it? We might be able to use her."

Alberto nodded and opened the car door, dropping his half-smoked Camel on the sidewalk. They headed home.

Chapter 11

Suetonius

Conway didn't sleep well after he got back to the hotel. However many times he replayed the evening's events in his head, he still couldn't make sense of them. Raul's hold over Lydia, Alberto a policeman, himself being shown the door, his deep sense of anger. They all swirled round. He tried to tell himself that he'd feel and think better if he got some sleep, but sleep wouldn't come. The brandy did nothing. In the end, he drew open the curtains and stood at the window of his room staring out at the sea.

Next morning, he decided he had to find out more about Raul. A talk with young Jeremy Brown at the Embassy might be a good way to start. 20 minutes under the shower, slowly going from hot to as cold as he could bear, well and truly woke him up. Down in the restaurant he tried to get some tea with his huevos rancheros, but they brought him coffee anyway. He filled up on orange juice. Partially restored, he put in a call to Jeremy. Delighted to hear from him in the expectation that he had changed his mind about the cricket team or the bridge evening, Brown hid his disappointment when Conway asked if he could give him some background on someone.

"Of course, my dear chap. Always ready to help members of the fourth estate. Come on over. I'll get some coffee organised".

"Got anything other than coffee? They drink it so strong here and, forgive the blasphemy, I don't much like it anyway."

"A cup of good old English tea suit you?"

Conway made his way to the Embassy, a colonial style villa which had seen better days. A shield announced that it was Her Britannic Majesty's Embassy, but the stuccoed walls were showing their age and the aura was one of genteel dilapidation. Brown was waiting for him at the door and took him through the security check, presided over by an elderly West

Indian member of staff. Dressed in an off-white cotton suit, light blue shirt and the ever-present College tie, Brown looked every bit the junior diplomat, an image enhanced further by the boyish blond curls and the horn-rimmed glasses. Conway let himself be guided by Brown to a small room on the ground floor. There was a round coffee table, a couple of armchairs and a stained rug. The decoration was a standard issue photograph of Her Majesty atop a horse taking the salute at Trooping the Colour in Horse-Guards' Parade. A pot of tea, two cups, milk and sugar were on the table.

The usual stiff awkwardness that attends meetings between Englishmen who don't know each other hung over them.

"Well, Mr Conway, how can I help?" Brown poured him a cup of tea. "Help yourself to milk and sugar"."

"No. Black is fine". Conway took a sip and then offered, "Call me Tony and I'll call you Jeremy, if I may".

Not completely thawed, but willing to engage, Brown inclined his head and nodded.

"I'll come straight to the point, Jeremy. I know how busy you must be. What can you tell me about someone I met last night, name of Raul Salcedo."

"Ah! Our Mr Salcedo. Big beast in the Caribe jungle. Very close to the President. Came from nowhere. Not too savoury – was a small-time crook, I hear, but backed the right horse. Knows nothing about politics and doesn't give a fig for principles, doing the right thing, democracy and all that stuff. Becoming very rich in the service of El Presidente is what matters."

All of this was rolled out like a well-rehearsed speech. "Salcedo fixes things: connections, contracts, people. It's best to stay on the right side of him. We have to deal with him as he's the only way through to the President, but, I can tell you, it's not easy – he always wants to make sure he gets his slice of the pie. Not exactly Queensbury rules", Brown added, adjusting his glasses as if to make some things go out of focus.

"He looks like someone I should find out more about" - half a statement, half a question.

"Well, you journalists have your own ways of working, but if it were me, I'd be very careful and watch my back".

Conway decided not to mention the incident in the park and the subsequent exchanges at Lydia's party. "How do mean?"

"Well," said Brown, "the police seem to do his bidding, especially one rather nasty looking captain, and the police on this island, Tony, don't have the greatest of reputations in terms of upholding the rule of law. Indeed, since the current President came along, they behave more like his personal Praetorian Guard with Señor Salcedo calling the tune. People in the way get knocked over or knocked off!"

Brown paused then went on, "As you know, he's got the beautiful Señorita Echevarria set up in Roosevelt Tower. He rarely sees her, I'm told, but controls her. She may be beautiful, well-educated and charming company but no-one else can go near her. You'll remember I referred you to her. I've met her a couple of times at receptions and been bowled over, but I felt her minder - the said police captain - was never far away".

Conway wanted more. "I've met her a few times since you suggested I contact her. She's been great. What's going on between her and Salcedo? Why's she allowed herself to be his plaything?"

"I'm not sure 'plaything' is quite the right word, Tony. 'Captive' might be better. But, listen, I really must go. Duty calls and all that. Keep in touch and tread carefully as regards Salcedo. And if you change your mind about the cricket or bridge or the occasional lecture do let me know. It would be lovely to have you on the team."

Conway thanked him for his time and assured him that he would, of course, keep all those various options in mind.

He needed to think. Wandering into the heat of the street, he found a bar where the air-conditioning was working and ordered a Coca Cola with plenty of ice.

What was the story about Lydia and Raul? Was there a story? He doubted that the folks back at the Globe in London would be greatly interested in the affairs of a Presidential adviser and a beautiful local socialite. They wanted stuff about the economy and the state of geo-political to-ings and fro-ings in the region. But, if he could claim that looking into Raul was a way of getting a handle on the economy and the politics of Caribe, he could do both. And, he felt in his waters that there was something not quite right. He couldn't forget the hold over Lydia that Raul exerted, the tightened grip on her arm, her submission, her belittling dismissal of him which he wanted to believe was not what she really wanted to do.

The bar had a phone on the wall. He searched his notebook for Lydia's number. He'd call her and see if she could explain what was going on - what had happened the previous evening. After a couple of rings a voice answered. It was Melba.

In his best Spanish, he introduced himself and asked whether he could speak to Lydia.

"Just a moment, Señor Conway". She put the phone down. He could hear music in the background, one of those melancholy songs about lost love that the Latins seem to thrive on. "Madam says that she is very busy and can't come to the phone right now", Melba told him and broke the connection. He began to redial then realised it wouldn't achieve anything. Lydia was not taking his calls.

So, what about the police? He hadn't formally reported yesterday's attack on him. So, why not do so and, in the process, see what he might find out about the man called Alberto and, if possible, something about Raul?

He spoke to a young policeman at the front desk of the central police station. His name tag announced that he was named Arias, Gilberto. Arias noted down his story in his notebook. When he appeared to have finished, Arias drew a line in the notebook and turned to a fresh page. The symbolism was not lost on Conway.

"I'm very sorry to hear what happened to you, Señor Conway. Puerto Grande is a peaceful city. Such events are unusual. We will look into it carefully, of course, Señor, but since you have only just informed us and it happened yesterday, you say, and since you have no description of the person who you say attacked you, though you say he looked like Captain Gomes - a coincidence, of course - and since you did not seek medical help, you will appreciate that we have very little to go on. We will do our best, but....".

The "but" was left hanging. He realised he was wasting his time. He moved to leave. "I look forward to hearing from you", was the best he could manage. "Of course, Señor", Arias smiled in reply.

So far, so useless, Conway thought.

What about that public meeting he'd been told about? It might be worth going to see what it was all about.

It was June 26. There were posters and flyers tacked to trees and stuck on lampposts announcing that there would be a rally at noon in the open air in a little square, the Plaza Garibaldi, in a poor part of the city, not far from the Calle Florida. By the time he got there, there was quite a crowd milling around. A young man with wild jet black hair and a scraggly beard, wearing faded overalls covered in paint, was standing holding a megaphone, trying to get attention. Leaflets were being handed out. On them was a picture of a young, handsome man under which appeared -

"Ramon Aguirre 1934-61". Some in the crowd waved banners exhorting in Spanish 'Justice for Ramon' and 'Down with the Yanqui bosses'. The speaker finally got his audience's attention. It was not easy to hear above the noise of the crowd and the sporadic malfunctioning of the megaphone, but, from what Conway could grasp, the crowd was being urged to march on the sugar factory on the outskirts of the city and join the strikers there in a show of solidarity.

To cries of "Somos con Ramon", "Abajo los Yanquis", the crowd moved off, led by the megaphone man like some tropical Pied Piper. Conway went along with them, keen to see what would happen. He hadn't paid much attention to the strike which had been called a few days earlier. It was just a few agitators according to a stringer for the Washington Post. As the crowd made its way towards the edge of town, however, it was clear that it was more than that. More and more people, mostly young, joined the march. As they got nearer to the factory, he saw the police. They were standing on either side of the road, watching through their reflecting aviator sunglasses, one hand on their gun holsters.

The marching crowd was greeted with cheers by those outside the factory. As they mingled together, megaphone man, who he had learned was an artist named Atilio, raised the loudhailer and began to chant. The crowd soon took it up. "Justice for Ramon", "Strike for your rights". As the sun beat down and tempers rose, some began to throw bottles and rocks at the guards at the factory gates.

This was the signal the police were waiting (and hoping) for. Shooting into the air initially, they rushed the crowd. A detachment of the Guardia Rural (Rurales to the locals) who must have been secretly deployed in a back street joined them. Swinging clubs, they beat anyone within range. Those who slipped or fell were kicked mercilessly. Soon people were running for their lives as gunfire broke out. Conway was at a corner of the square and took cover in a doorway. A small, frail-looking, middle-aged man who had been watching from the edge of the crowd was suddenly knocked over as the police charged. Picking himself up, he dusted himself off and limped painfully away.

As the police moved across the square, the reporter in Conway kicked in. He went over and asked the man if he was alright. The man ignored him. Seeing that he was now limping badly, Conway persisted. He offered to get him home, hailing a taxi on the taxi rank nearby which seemed unaffected by the mayhem taking place just a hundred yards or so away. Reluctantly, the man allowed himself to be helped into the back seat and slumped in the back, resting his head on the back of the driver's seat. Conway got in beside him.

"Hi. I'm Tony Conway. I hope you aren't hurt."

The man nodded as if to say no. "I'm OK, Señor. My name is Cesar Sanchez".

"Where do you need to go, Señor Sanchez?"

"San Rafael".

"Is that OK, Señor", the driver interrupted. "It's outside the city".

"Yes, that's OK," he replied.

"Thank you, Señor Conway", Cesar said quietly, massaging his leg.

It was nearly half an hour before they reached San Rafael on the outskirts of the city. It had sprung up around a sugar mill, one of several that fed the factory in Puerto Grande. Cesar lived in a shack on the edge of the small town Once there, Cesar, with an old-world courtesy, invited him to come in and have a cup of coffee. Conway groaned inside – more coffee!

He was in two minds. If he accepted the invitation, how would he get back to the city? If he didn't, he would miss out on hearing more about what he'd just witnessed. He decided to stay.

"Is there any way to contact you or another taxi to get me back to the city?"

The driver sucked his teeth a moment, "You could try the bar at the end of the lane, Señor. Someone will look after you". Then he drove off.

The shack was neat and clean. Conway looked around while Cesar limped over to a little stove to prepare coffee. There were 2 rooms; one for sleeping and one for everything else. Books and magazines everywhere - on shelves, on the only table, and carefully stacked in piles on the floor. Cesar handed him a cup of coffee; bitter-smelling and scaldingly hot. He'd have to drink it, come what may.

Cesar sat down heavily in one of the two elderly armchairs and invited him to take the other.

"You seem surprised that I read, Señor".

"Well, let's say I was curious. Such a collection of books is not so common".

"It is more common than you might imagine, Señor. We poor people are not just hungry for food".

"Can I ask what you do, Cesar? Why were you at the demonstration?"

Cesar looked at him carefully. "Can I ask you what you do, Señor? Asking questions may get you into trouble round here. You are an outsider, a foreigner, so you're not a policeman".

"I'm a journalist. I work for a newspaper in London, England. I've been sent to see what's happening in Caribe. I have to admit that the demonstration has livened things up. The police weren't messing about were they? I thought you might be able to fill me in a bit."

"Señor, I cut cane during the day and read at night. That's about it".

To keep things going, Conway pointed to his cup and asked if there was more of "this delicious coffee". Cesar obliged then sat down again. An uneasy silence followed.

He wasn't sure how to play this. He felt that there was something he needed to hear but Cesar, for whatever reason, wasn't inclined to be forthcoming. Offering him money would be disastrous. Cesar was clearly a proud man who would be insulted: he'd show him the door, politely but firmly. Then he noticed a copy of Suetonius' *The Twelve Caesars* on one of the shelves and seized on it as a lifeline.

He walked over and asked, "Do you mind?" Cesar nodded. Conway picked it off the shelf. "Gosh. One of my favourites when I was at University", he lied. "What drew you to it?"

"I was a teacher a long time ago, Señor. I taught Latin". Then silence. But, Conway had the opening he needed.

"What happened, Cesar? Why aren't you still a teacher?" He left unsaid the second part of the question – "but instead are living in this shack in the middle of nowhere". It didn't need to be said.

Cesar appraised him. The man was a classicist (or said he was - he knew who Suetonius was). Perhaps he was someone whom he could talk to. But he was a journalist and that meant danger.

"Listen, señor, I'm not sure it's wise for me to talk to you, nor for you to hear. The police and Rurales are everywhere. You don't always see them but they see you. They'll know you got a taxi for me. And they will suspect that we talked."

Conway nodded. He'd stumbled on something, but what? "Look Cesar, if I'm asked I'll just say that I stayed with you just so as to get you settled in bed with a drink of water. You were obviously in pain. You didn't say anything because it hurt you to speak – you'd hurt your chest as well as your leg. Now", he went on, "can we talk a bit?"

"Yes, Señor Conway, we can talk but you must promise not to reveal where you heard it. Do you promise?"

"Of course, and thank you for trusting me. Do you want more coffee?"

"No thank you. I only drink the stuff on the rare occasions that people visit. As you know, it tastes vile".

They both smiled, complicit in his earlier attempt at flattery.

"Yes, and, in truth, I don't like coffee anyway", he added and they smiled again.

Cesar began. "What you saw today, Señor, was the simmering discontent that occasionally spills over into some kind of action, always to be met by a reaction, and an increasingly violent reaction. The catalyst this time was the first anniversary of the death of a young man named Ramon Aguirre. He had been a student leader and then a trade union activist. He believed in such things as elections, democracy, the rule of law. He was from Caguey, a small town in the interior. It's known to the locals as Salsipuedes ("get out if you can!"). Both of his parents died when he was young, so he came to Puerto Grande and did whatever job he could find. By studying hard he got into University and studied classics and philosophy. He was one of my brightest students, Señor. He was inspired by the likes of Pericles and Cicero and, in our age, Nelson Mandela, and George Jackson."

"Obviously, Señor Conway, he wasn't to Barbosa's taste. He became a target. The police and Rurales harassed him. He spent quite a few unpleasant nights in prison cells. Eventually, he had to go into hiding. It was obvious that they were going to solve the problem of Ramon one way or another.

"He was betrayed and shot dead 'while attempting to escape'", using his index fingers to suggest the quotation marks. "He was just 27".

Cesar paused. "Ramon was just another victim of Barbosa's rule. All of those who believe in a different kind of world are victims.

"I was myself forced out of the University when I complained about the continued presence of the police in lectures. They were there, they said, to make sure that young minds were not exposed to anything subversive. I pointed out that education is subversive, but people didn't understand nor care. I was just fired."

"Now I am a seasonal worker, cutting cane and trying to survive. I'm not brave enough to join a political party such as the socialists or, even more dangerous, the communists. I support them but from the side-lines. To do anything more would mean no work, and no work would mean no food. And the Rurales know about my past. So they make their presence known. I decided to go to the demonstration to honour Ramon but I knew it was a risk. Now I've been seen with you, Señor, and some explaining will be needed."

It was clear that Cesar was torn. He wanted to talk. But he was growing noticeably more anxious, concerned that an outsider had spent too long in his house and that there would be repercussions. Conway got up and, without thinking, embraced his frail host.

"Thank you Cesar, for the awful coffee and for the excellent conversation. You've given me a lot to chew on. I'd like to talk more".

Cesar nodded. "It is not safe here Señor, but I will send a message. Where are you living?" Conway gave him the name of his hotel. The silence of conspirators hung over them briefly. Then Cesar broke the mood and made to open the door and show him out. Putting his hand on Cesar's chest, Conway said, "You're ill, remember. That's the cover story. So I'll let myself out". As he did so, he shouted back into the shack, "Take care of yourself Señor, and stay in bed". Then he set off to find the bar and a way of getting back to his hotel.

Cesar sat back in his chair with a cup of water and reflected on the past half hour or so. The Englishman seemed honourable and could be useful to the cause. But could he be trusted? Cesar went through all the details of their encounter, checking at every point for some tell-tale sign that he might be a plant, or just someone looking for a story to write with a bit of human interest which would fill a column or two for the Englishman but could put him in danger. Since he kept his distance from the union people, he could not call on them for help to check him out. He had to trust his judgement. He felt the weight of responsibility and the loneliness which went with it.

It hadn't always been like that. Cesar's mind wandered back to his former life when any responsibilities he might have he could share with Ana. They were a celebrated couple; he the scholar, she the artist. Cesar was an only child. His father had been a judge but had keeled over one day and died of a heart attack at the age of forty. His mother had buried herself in the countryside with her cats and slowly drifted off into a benign form of madness. Fending for himself, he had shone at the University of Puerto Grande and won a scholarship to Princeton in the United States to continue his study of the classics. He returned to the island he loved to become the UPG's youngest Professor.

Cesar had met Ana at one of her exhibitions. She was already a fixture in Puerto Grande's higher society, the talented daughter of a well-known physician whose wife was a contralto in the city's opera group. Cesar had courted Ana assiduously. She was flattered but not sure that this skinny young man who loved nothing more than sitting in a corner with some book by Livy or Catullus was for her. But his persistence prevailed and to the surprise of many, including Ana herself, they fell in love. They were 'the odd couple' in the society pages of the Diario – she the vivacious, outgoing sculptor, he the quiet thinker who only came alive, it seemed, when entrancing his students with his love of classics. In time, they were married and set up house in a run-down old Spanish style villa in the Convento. Ana soon bore them twin girls, Tatiana and Rosalind, and the future could not have looked brighter. Then everything changed.

The ascent to power of President Barbosa signalled the beginning of pressure on those in charge of the University. Not only was it made clear that they should be teaching 'relevant' subjects which would further the economic development of the island, but they were told very clearly that the 'commie' teachers must be got rid of. No definition was offered of 'commie' but Cesar was an obvious target, given that he made no secret of his contempt for the anti-intellectual pronouncements of the government, quite apart from the fact that what he taught was never going to pass the 'relevant' test. His lectures were disrupted by a group calling themselves the 'Students for Freedom', drawn from the US-affiliated Fraternities on campus. He was jostled as he walked to his office and called 'The Red Professor" and "Traitor". Finally, he was called in by the University's Dean who, while seeking to disassociate himself from what he was about to say, told him that he would be fired if he did not mend his ways. Cesar had nodded and said, "I understand the position you are in, my friend. Don't worry".

He resigned within days so as not to give the University the satisfaction of firing him. He had no plans, but Ana was increasingly successful. They would have enough to get by till they could re-group.

Then it happened. Ana was driving the girls back from visiting a friend one night. A car came up behind them very fast with its horn blaring and headlights on full beam. Ana, distracted by the noise and the cries of the girls, was blinded by the lights. She failed to negotiate a corner and the car crashed into the side of a shop and turned over. She was crushed against the steering wheel and the girls were thrown against the front seats. Ana and Tatiana died at the scene, Rosalind died in hospital later that night.

No-one knew who was driving the other car. The police told Cesar that they had no clues and there were no witnesses. The prevailing view was that it was a stunt organised by the 'Students for Freedom' which had got out of hand.

Cesar had lost his family, his job and his income. Friends tried to rally him, but he was inconsolable. He sold their house and moved to the shack in San Rafael. When he ran out of money, he became a cane-cutter. And he resolved that he would not rest till those who had brought him and his family down were themselves brought down. He was not interested in revenge. He knew that it was a corrosive emotion that ate away at you and never gave satisfaction. No, his concern was for the young people of Caribe. They were currently condemned to suffer under a regime which was not only corrupt but, perhaps even more unforgivable, uneducated and proud of it. They did not deserve this for their future. He made a silent oath to himself to make sure it did not happen.

Chapter 12

Ramon

It was still that time when Lydia could dream. She was with her Ramon. The world in those days was a different place.

They had fallen headlong in love. She had met him when she interviewed him for a story after he had spoken at a rally. He was tall, with dark hair and dark eyes. There was something of the gypsy about him. If opposites do indeed attract, they were proof: she from a background of wealth and privilege, he from nothing. They found they enjoyed the same things; poetry, literature, music. They talked non-stop about politics and loved to dance. Ramon could dance. Oh Yes, this country boy could dance. Half the time she was dancing with him she wanted to stop and just watch him, he moved so well. Of course, all the other women in her group also wanted a bit of the action, but Ramon only had eyes for her. She felt privileged and blessed.

But now she felt scared. Things were changing fast, too fast. Ramon was moving from house to house. Lydia was the only person he could trust. She had to protect him from the police and the Rurales. She was sure that they would do something bad, even kill him, if they caught him. And then her life would also be over. It was a Tuesday evening when he rang. Two rings and then the call was broken. Then three rings and it stopped. Then the telephone rang again. This was their code. It was Ramon. Knowing, even though it was her parents' home, that someone could well be listening in because she was Ramon's woman, she simply said "Sorry. Mama's out". This too was the agreed code. She'd meet him at his latest hideout and tell him the next place she'd arranged.

Lydia put on an old pair of jeans and a blouse and her tennis shoes and left on her bicycle about 15 minutes later. She hung a string shopping bag on the handlebars, looking like someone who needed to get some onions which the housekeeper had forgotten for tonight's meal.

At first it had all been exciting, a bit of a game. Now, after 4 weeks, it was serious and scary. She cycled to the market in Plaza San Jacinto and pushed her bike through the stalls till she was in the middle, then rested it against a post. There was the little café a few yards away. She darted into it and, waving to Paco, the waiter who worshipped her from afar, she went out through the back door into a narrow street, the Calle de Limones. Ramon was in the fourth house along on the left, in a back room. The house belonged to one of her mother's friends who was away and had left the key so that her mother could keep an eye on it. She would have to get the key back to its place in the kitchen before her mother noticed.

Ramon threw his arms around her and kissed her.

"No time for that, Señor. We have to move you on", she scolded. "But perhaps we do have time for just one more kiss", she said through smiling lips.

Then it was time to go. Lydia told Ramon the address of his next hideout: a disused warehouse with an office. He could sleep in the office and there was a bathroom attached. It belonged to one of her father's friends who was trying to sell it. She had scouted it and found that the rear door did not lock completely. He'd have to climb over the wall but then with a shove the door would give way. Ramon could get in and then he'd be safe. She'd put some food in the old fridge and there was plenty of water.

She kissed him again and turned to leave. "Leave here when it gets dark, my darling, and take care. I'm doing my best through Papa's contacts to try to sort something out for you with that bastard Barbosa and his thugs. Trust me". And she was gone.

To keep up the appearance, Lydia stopped at some of the stalls, inspecting the guavas and the sweet little oranges known as chinas. She bought some onions and a couple of heads of garlic and headed back to her bike, putting them in the bag she'd brought. Then she set off for home, still savouring the taste of Ramon's mouth on her lips.

Suddenly a car pulled across her. She fell off her bike which went skidding along the road and was winded as she landed on her side. As she sat up, she saw two men getting out of the car. A few passers-by had started to run to her aid, but seeing the car and the men, they had stopped.

"Can you help me up, please, and get my bike," she said, still a bit dazed and not yet focussed.

"Of course, Princess", one of them said.

Lydia looked up and her blood turned to ice. This was no accident. These were police. And she was their target. The one who had spoken took her arm, none too gently, and lifted her up. "We'll give you a ride home, shall we, Princess?"

"No, thank you. And let go of me".

"Now just get in the car, like a good Princess and everything will be fine. We'll get someone to look after your bike".

She decided that she would start shouting. That might deter them. "Get off me, you big goon. Leave me alone". She didn't see the hand but felt the force of the slap on the side of her face. She staggered and cried out. Some of the onlookers gasped and put their hands to their mouths, but no-one made a move. Giving up the pretence of offering assistance, the two men simply picked her up and threw her onto the back seat of the car. They drove off at high speed. The wheels of the bike were still spinning as someone picked it up and leant it against the side of a building.

When she started to scream in the car, one of the men leaned over and smacked her hard across the face. "Shut up or you'll get more".

"You'd better believe him, Princess. He enjoys it", added the other.

Lydia subsided, terrified. Her head was ringing from the blows. What was happening?

The car pulled up at the side entrance of a building. She was bundled inside and taken down some stairs and put in a room. She had no idea where she was. It was not a police station because there were no police, except for her two captors. There was no window in the room which was lit by one bare bulb in the ceiling. There was a mattress on the floor and a bucket. Nothing else.

She sat in the corner against the wall with her arms round her knees. She was terrified. From time to time she twisted and re-twisted a strand of hair round her fingers. No-one would know where she was. Huge sobs of tears welled up. What was going to happen to her? It must be about Ramon. "Oh, my darling", she thought. "I promise I won't let them hurt you".

* * * * *

It was Police Captain Alberto Gomes who had taken the call.

"Captain. We have her in the old office on the Avenida. What do you want us to do?"

Alberto grunted a "Well done. Keep her there", he added. "Leave her to stew. I'll be over in a while".

Alberto had reached for another phone. "Boss. We have her. Do you want to do the business or shall I?" The inflection in his voice betrayed the fact that *he* wanted 'to do the business'.

"We'll do it together, Alberto. Pick me up in twenty minutes"

Lydia froze when the door to the room was unlocked. Her heart was practically jumping out of her chest. She had dried her tears with the back of her hand and was determined to be strong. But her resolve faltered when she saw the two men come in. She'd seen Raul at some reception or other and knew that he was someone important. She didn't know the other. He had a cigarette in the corner of his mouth and exuded menace. They each carried a chair which they placed in the middle of the room and sat down.

"Good afternoon, Señorita Echevarria, or shall I call you Lydia, or Ramon's girl?" It was Raul.

Her worst fears realised in his first words.

"Why am I here, Señor? This is an outrage", she blustered.

"Well, Ramon's girl ..."

"Call me Señorita Echevarria", she shouted. "That's my name, as you obviously know. And answer my question".

"You've got it the wrong way round, Señorita", Raul replied evenly. "I ask the questions and you answer them. She *is* Ramon's girl, isn't she Alberto", he added, turning to the captain.

Lydia broke in. "As you clearly know, I was 'Ramon's girl' as you put it, so romantically. But what you obviously don't know is that we broke up some weeks ago. He was always off on some political stuff. We ended up never seeing each other and it was all too boring". A brave speech, delivered to convey the impression that she was just another spoiled brat grown tired of her rough country boy, evinced a nod from Raul.

"Mmm", he replied. "We know otherwise, don't we, Alberto?"

Alberto nodded. She realised that protesting was not going to get anywhere. The less she said the better. Raul let the silence weigh on her.

Eventually, Raul leaned forward and put his hand on her knee.

"We were very much hoping that you could help us Señorita, weren't we, Alberto? And, just to be clear, we're not playing games. Alberto here specialises in hurting people. It would give him very great pleasure to hurt you. But he won't do anything unless I tell him to. So, if you don't want me to give the order, may I suggest you talk to me. In fact I've only got one question for you. Then you can go back to your lovely home in the Convento and all of this will be just a bad dream. You can't talk about it, of course. It will be our secret. But it will be over and you can carry on with your comfortable life. Now, the question: where is Ramon?"

She tried to keep her voice steady. "I've told you, Señor. Ramon and I broke up some weeks ago. I don't know where he is or what he's doing. Something crazy, I imagine" she added, as if the role she was playing called for it.

Alberto made as if to slap her. She flinched and tried to shrink even more into her corner. Raul put his hand up and said calmly, "It's not necessary, Alberto. Just let her see who is outside".

Her eyes widened in fear. Alberto went over to the door and opened it. Standing outside, flanked by two policemen, was her father.

"Ay, Papi, Papi, Papi, Papi", she wailed as she ran to him. She was no longer the sophisticated society woman. She was the little girl clinging to her beloved father who always made things right. Not this time.

Raul and Alberto didn't move. Her father hugged her, then held her at arms' length. He looked both mystified and horrified.

"Que te pasa, hija? What's happening?" As if noticing for the first time the two men in the room, he recognised one of them immediately. Aware of Raul's reputation, he tried to keep his tone as respectful as he could. "Señor Salcedo. What are you doing here with my daughter? What is this place?"

Raul turned to face him. Over Lydia's continued whimpers, he addressed her father.

"You know who I am, Señor, and this is Police Captain Gomes. It was his idea to use this old office building. We brought your daughter here out of respect for you and your family. It would not look good for an Echevarria to be seen being brought to the central police station, would it? We want your daughter to tell us something. You may be able to help. Then you can both go home.

"Now, please, Señorita", he continued, turning to her, "please sit down where you were and answer the question I asked you".

"What question? How can I help" her father demanded, rather too aggressively.

"It's alright, Papa", Lydia told him through her tears. "It doesn't concern you". She sat down again in her corner.

Raul smiled his smile and shook his head.

"Ah, but it does concern him, Señorita. Let me explain. There is a room next door. The walls are not thick. These two gentlemen escorting your father are going to take him into that room. Alberto here is going to join them. If you don't answer my question, just the one simple question, they will begin to beat your father. You will be able to hear the blows and his cries, perhaps screams as time goes on. After a while, you will tell me what I want to know, preferably before your father has sustained any lasting injury".

She screamed. Her father's legs gave way and he had to be held up.

"For God's sake, Lydia. Tell them what they want to know", he shouted.

"I don't know anything", she pleaded, half addressed to her father and half to Raul.

Raul inclined his head and the two guards part lifted, part dragged her father away from the door and down the corridor. Alberto got up. He smiled and idly cracked his knuckles. She watched mesmerised as he left the room.

"Please, Señor, please don't hurt my father. I don't know where Ramon is. Hurting Papa will not make me know".

"Mmmm. I think you do know. So, choose", he added, with a smile, "Papa or Ramon".

She said nothing. Suddenly, there was a heavy thud followed by a cry of pain. Then silence. Then another thud and another cry of pain, this one louder and more drawn out.

"Your father is a tough man, Señorita, but Alberto has a special gift. Your father will soon be suffering badly".

Still she said nothing. What could she say - that Ramon was hiding in a warehouse on San Jacinto Street? And then what? They would arrest him and throw him in jail. Would they kill him? She thought of bargaining – I'll tell you where he is if you promise not to hurt him. But what good were the promises of a man like Salcedo, once he had got what he wanted?

Her reverie was broken by a sharp crack and a scream of pain. She was slowly being broken herself. She sought out a strand of hair which she twisted round and round her finger as if it might bring some solace. She couldn't choose between the two men in her life. Yet she must if she was going to save her father. She had to believe that though they would capture Ramon they wouldn't hurt him. Then she could begin the fight to free him and expose Salcedo and his henchmen. This was the logic she persuaded herself of.

Lydia fixed Raul with a look of hatred.

"Ramon is in the back of the warehouse on the corner of San Jacinto Street. Please don't harm him. And, now, please release my father and me".

Raul smiled.

"Thank you Señorita. That wasn't hard, was it? We always betray those we love, don't we? We'll send your father back in a while. He'll be fine. I'm afraid you'll have to stay for a little longer. We don't want you sending messages, do we?"

She got up slowly. She had just crossed a line into another world – a world in which she had betrayed her lover. She clutched her stomach to avoid vomiting. Then she threw up in the bucket.

Raul made his way to the other room, closing the door on her. He was delighted and amused by the scene which greeted him. Señor Echevarria was sitting tied at the ankles and arms to a straight-backed chair. A gag was tied across his face. The two policemen were convulsed with laughter, pushing and shoving at each other and shouting out with exaggerated cries.

"Well done, boys. It was very realistic. Even I thought he was being beaten up. Who did the noise and who did the shouting – we might use you again?"

Jose said he did the thuds, banging the palm of his hand on the bottom of a chair. "And I supplied the noise" added Fulgencio. "My mother always wanted me to be an actor".

There were smiles all round except for Alberto. "I don't see why we couldn't do it properly," he said. "It would give him something to remember," pointing at Señor Echevarria.

"Alberto, Alberto, you are very good at what you do, but you lack a certain subtlety. We are going to release the Señor, but if he complains to his important friends that he was abducted and manhandled, where are the marks, the scars, the broken bones? There are none. Should he unwisely try to make something of this little interlude, we will simply say that we found his daughter nearby, having clearly had too heavy a lunch, and, to save his embarrassment, asked him to come and look after her. But I don't think we will hear anything from him. We won't, will we, Señor", Raul added with just enough menace.

Raul nodded to the police who removed the gag and untied him. "Out you go, Señor". As he staggered out, the curses Señor Echevarria had promised himself to hurl at them died on his lips. It was too dangerous and they still had his daughter.

"And, Alberto, there is a further subtlety", Raul continued. "When the Señorita learns from her father what really happened, she will realise that she gave up her man for nothing. It will destroy her. We will know her guilty secret. She will be ours. It will be good to have her dancing on our string among her high society friends. Our beloved Presidente will be most grateful and", lowering his voice, "most generous".

"Oh, and, Jose", he added. "Take the Señorita to the bathroom. We want her to look her best when we send her home. Stay with her, but outside, please. I don't want you misbehaving!" That smile again. "And get something for her to eat and drink. And, Jose, lock her in or I'll have your balls!" Another smile.

* * * * *

The operation was planned for just before dawn the next day. There were eight men, led by Alberto. Raul was in contact by walkie-talkie from an office in police headquarters. Two cars approached the warehouse from opposite directions and did a drive past. All was darkness except for the solitary street lamp on the corner which cast a small circle of light onto the sidewalk. Two men were dropped off to check the back. There was a wall about six feet high. Beyond that they could see the rear of the building. Again, everything was in darkness. There were no sounds and nothing to see.

Alberto had obtained the keys from the somewhat startled owner. The police needed to check something (not explained) and he could pick the keys up at the police station the following day. He said he was only too happy to assist the police and then spent anxious hours trying to remember whether there was anything in the warehouse that shouldn't be there.

Alberto went in first followed by three of his men. Two stayed out front with the cars and the other two stayed at the back. Using his torch sparingly in flashes, Alberto made his way across the empty warehouse. He saw the staircase in the right-hand far corner leading up to what he'd been briefed was an office. Signalling his men to stay at the foot of the stairs, he made his way up, stepping on the two ends of the steps where there was likely to be less give and so less chance of them creaking. He reached the top and, crouching down, inched his way forward until he was underneath the window looking into the office. Raising his head at the corner of the window he looked in. He could barely see anything but there looked like some shape stretched out on what appeared to be a camp bed.

He'd seen enough. Standing up, he went over to the door and kicked it in. He shone his torch on the shape. It was Ramon wrapped in a blanket. The noise had awoken him but he was blinded by the torchlight.

"Who's there", he shouted.

"Your worst nightmare", were the last words Ramon would ever hear. Alberto shot him in the chest and the temple. He then called to his men. "Take him out. Throw the blanket on the bed. Then throw him down the stairs. He was shot avoiding arrest. We feared for our lives. It was dark and it looked like he had a weapon. That all clear, boys?"

"Yes", they replied and did what they'd been told. Alberto called Raul. "All done, Boss".

"Well done. Call it in. Get the ambulance. And write it up. I'll let the guy from the Diario have the scoop - 'Dangerous revolutionary killed avoiding arrest. Brave police responding to tip-off feared for their lives' - that sort of thing".

* * * * *

Lydia didn't know how many hours she spent in the room. They had let her go to the bathroom and had brought a cheese sandwich and a cup of coffee. Then she'd been left alone. The light was left on. With no windows to gauge the passing of time, she didn't know whether it was night or day. Nor did she care. She just sat in her corner, twisting a strand of hair in her fingers. Round and round in her head, she heard: "Trust me" - her words to Ramon as they held each other. "I promise I won't let them hurt you" - her promise to herself.

She found herself praying for the first time since she'd left the convent school. She asked whoever might be listening to keep Ramon safe. She didn't ask for forgiveness for herself. She didn't deserve it. She had betrayed him. She held herself and rocked back and forth. And wept silently.

* * * * *

Elena, Lydia's mother, was on the patio reading her beloved book of Antonio Machado's early poems when she saw her husband arrive back in a taxi.

As he got out, it was clear that something was wrong. He didn't look well. Elena ran to the door. "Ave Maria! What happened to you, Alejandro", she shouted.

He waved her aside and went straight to the kitchen. He poured himself a glass of water, then went through to his study and sank into his old leather chair. Elena followed him in. He was acting so strangely, he was clearly not his usual self. "Alejandro", she said anxiously, "what's going on?"

Señor Alejandro Echevarria, the distinguished Professor of Mathematics, had spent the time taken to drive him home thinking of what he might say to his wife and later to his daughter about what had happened. This was one occasion when there was no formula to solve the equation. To his wife, he had resolved to tell her very little, bearing in mind what Salcedo had said. To his daughter – that was a separate question.

"'Well, Elena", he said, heaving a sigh, "you'll remember that two men came to ask me to go with them. Well, it seems that Lydia had got herself into some kind of trouble or other, but it got straightened out. I was a bit shaken up, but as the great playwright said, 'All's well that ends well'".

"Lydia, in some trouble? What trouble, Alejandro? My daughter does not get into 'trouble' as you call it"

"Well, she was this time. I suspect it was something to do with that boyfriend of hers. He's bad news but what can I do?"

"He's a very nice boy and he loves her and she loves him. Yes, he has some wild views but all young people do. You did in your time."

"No, Señora, no. I was too busy studying", he replied shaking his head vigorously. "I never went on demonstrations. I wasn't an agitator. But..." he paused. After a long pause, he went on, "I'm sorry, Elena, but that's all it's safe to say".

Elena was mystified. "Safe. What do you mean, safe?"

She didn't know what he was talking about, but her husband just looked at her. All he said was, "I have a splitting headache, Elena. Forgive me. I'm going to lie down".

She realised that was all she was likely to get till Lydia came home and she could ask her.

"I'll get you up for dinner, OK", she murmured. Then, as if it was an afterthought, "when will Lydia be coming home – you know, do I plan dinner for two or three?"

"I don't know".

Shaking her head, she went back to her well-thumbed copy of *Campos de Castilla*. After reading the opening lines of *The Wayfarer* several times she realised that she couldn't concentrate on anything till she found out what was going on.

* * * * *

Fulgencio took Lydia some coffee in the morning and told her she was free to go. She walked out blinking into the bright morning light, still wearing the jeans and blouse that she'd left home in all those hours ago. The jeans were split when she came off her bike and the sleeve of her blouse was torn, but she'd been able to wash her face and clean herself up. What she wanted more than anything was a shower. Then she would think.

She got a taxi home. As she walked in she expected to run into flak from her mother - where had she been all night - and her father - what was all that about, what had she done that the police wanted to know about?

Instead, her mother was standing in the kitchen, tears streaming down her face, holding a copy of the Diario. Seeing her, she cried out, "Oh Lydia, my poor darling Lydia". Dropping the paper, she threw her arms around her.

"Mami, what's the matter? I'm so sorry I was out last night. I can explain".

Her mother said nothing. She just picked up the paper and handed it to her daughter. The headline was as dictated by Raul. It was accompanied by a photograph of Ramon's body lying crumpled at the foot of the warehouse's stairs.

Lydia stared at it. She said nothing. She just stared. Then she let out an agonising scream, the scream of a gravely wounded animal. And she screamed and screamed - "No. No. No". Her mother tried to hold her, but she pushed her away and ran screaming to her room.

* * * * *

Both of her parents tried to get her to open her door but it remained locked. All that day and the next, they kept vigil, but she did not appear. Occasionally they could hear weeping but that was all.

Her father knocked on her door for the umpteenth time. "Lydia, mi amor, you have to eat something. Please open the door".

She unlocked the door then walked back to her bed and buried herself in the sheets. Her hair was a tangled mass. Her face was streaked with tears. The room smelled musty. There were tissues all over the bed and floor.

Hiding his shock at his daughter's appearance, Señor Echevarria said softly, "I've brought you some coffee, Lydia, and your favourites - little churros with extra cinnamon and sugar." He moved aside some of the tissues and set the tray on a side-table next to her bed. She drank the coffee thirstily. She ignored the churros. Her father, now that he had breached the first line of defence, was determined to stay as long as he could. He had promised himself that he would not ask her any questions. As her mother had said, she would talk when she wanted to. But he could not resist. It all came flooding out.

"What happened, Lydia? Your mother was asking but I couldn't tell her anything, because I don't know anything. What did those people want to know? What did they do to you? What can we do? People like Salcedo think they can do anything and get away with anything."

"Papa, I'm so sorry about what they did to you. Can you forgive me?"

"Well, that's the one good thing about the whole awful business. They had you locked up, but, thank God, they didn't seem to have hurt you - physically, that is. And, they never laid a hand on me".

"What?" she shouted. "I heard you. They were hitting you and you were very brave but couldn't prevent yourself from crying out. I'm so, so sorry, Papa".

"No, querida, that's the strange thing. They bound and gagged me, which wasn't very pleasant, but nothing else. You remember the two police. One damned fool thumped a chair with his hand to make it sound like I was being hit and the other yelled and screamed. It was very lifelike, I must say".

She lay there. She had not been saving her father. She had just been betraying Ramon. Shame and anger, at herself more than anyone else, washed over her.

Her father looked on as the anguish overwhelmed his daughter's face. "Lydia, what was it all about? Please tell me. You look as if you are in such pain. Your mother and I want to help. We love you."

She sighed, a sigh that came from the deepest depths of her being. "Papa, you must promise first that you will not tell anyone, not even Mama".

"Your mother and I have no secrets, Lydia".

"Then I cannot tell you. I'm sorry, Papa. Just believe the story in the paper – that the police got a tip-off and traced Ramon to the warehouse. And leave me alone for a while. I know that you and Mami want to do things for me. Please don't. Just leave me."

She turned onto her side with her back to her father and pulled the sheets up to her chin, her one hand seeking out a strand of hair and winding it round her finger. There was so much her father wanted to ask, so much he didn't understand. He wanted to take his daughter in his arms and hold her for ever. But he simply nodded.

As she lay there, he stood staring at her - desolate, powerless, forbidden from showing the love he felt in such measure. Eventually, he whispered, "We are here, we will always be here for you", and quietly closed the door. He was grateful that Elena did not see his tears as he blundered towards his study and the sanctuary of his beloved chair.

Chapter 13

Lydia and the Circulo Latino

Weeks passed. Lydia moved between her room and the kitchen like a zombie. Efforts to speak to her were ignored. She paid no regard to her appearance. She was losing weight. Her hair had long grown out of its elegant cut and fell across her face and down her neck. Her complexion took on a sallow, almost transparent aspect. Day and night were matters of indifference as she padded in her socks between her twin harbours.

There had been a muted reaction to the news of Ramon's death. Raul's contacts in the media ensured that the narrative of 'dangerous revolutionary' had taken hold before any counter-narrative could get any traction. Calls for an inquiry into the shooting were met with outraged support for 'our brave police' 'risking their lives in defence of law-abiding citizens'.

He was buried in the cemetery in his home town of Caguey. No-one knew where his parents had been buried - there was no family plot for the Aguirres. Bus-loads of students and trade unionists took over the little town for the day, marching to the cemetery and singing "We shall overcome". There were a few reporters but it had been decided not to waste any outside broadcast cameras, particularly as the biggest baseball game of the season was scheduled for that evening in Puerto Grande. President Barbosa would attend, though there was some doubt whether he would observe the tradition of throwing the first pitch. The truth was that he probably wouldn't be able to throw the ball far enough.

The day fizzled out. Promises to 'fight on' and calls for 'justice' were exchanged. Then they got back on the buses and went home, singing defiantly as they went.

Lydia did not go to the funeral. Ramon's friends and supporters were not surprised. She had said nothing nor done anything since his death. They had slowly begun to believe that he had just been a curiosity, someone from the other side of the tracks who had amused her. She had moved on. She was back with her society friends. They did not know how she spent that day – in bed, as ever, clasping her only photograph of Ramon to her breast, winding a strand of hair round her finger and weeping silently. At three in the afternoon, when his coffin was due to be put in the ground, she sighed and said goodbye.

As the weeks passed she began to make a plan. She would honour Ramon's memory in her own way. No-one must know. No-one would understand what she was going to do. But that didn't matter. She would be the one who really would get justice for Ramon. She may be destroyed in the process, but that hardly mattered. What mattered was what she owed to Ramon and to what he believed in.

*****

The party was quite something. Raul had spared nothing. The apartment in Roosevelt Tower was luxurious to begin with but now was decked out with magnificent displays of flowers. Handsome young men and women hovered with trays of champagne and hors d'oeuvres. All of Caribe's society had been invited to her house-warming. The more thuggish elements had accepted. The rest, the large majority, stayed away. "What was Lydia doing, consorting with Raul Salcedo?" had echoed round the cafes and drawing rooms.

Lydia looked beyond beautiful. Her smile was radiant as she greeted guests. She proudly showed them around the apartment. She strolled onto the balcony, her arm through Raul's. She could not thank him enough for his generosity in helping her to get the apartment, she repeated, and, yes, he really had paid the first six months' rent – how kind was that?

Her parents were not at the party. They had been invited, of course, like the rest of her family and friends. Most did not even acknowledge the invitation. Her parents once again had asked each other - how could she? Then they had written, declining the invitation. They thought it best to reply so as not to burn every bridge between them and their beloved daughter. But there were few bridges left in view of the events of the last few months.

She had done her homework on Raul. She knew that despite his reputation as a ladies' man, always surrounded by a coven of admirers, his preference in terms of sex lay with young men. He was exceedingly careful and Alberto was eternally vigilant on his behalf, but she had her own contacts and had soon discovered the truth. This made things easier.

There had been one occasion early on when she feared that he was going to 'seal the deal', as her College friends would have put it. Raul was entertaining some businessmen at a hotel and had told her to join him for dinner. It turned out that 'dinner' was to be champagne and canapes served in the penthouse suite. The moment she saw the set-up, she steeled herself for what else might be on the menu. Sure enough, after raising his glass to her, he put on a record of Edith Piaf and invited her to take off her clothes, item by item – first her shoes, then her skirt, then her stockings and suspender belt, then her blouse, then her bra and then finally her panties. She did what he asked. He remained seated in the ornate armchair throughout the show, glass in hand. As she stood there naked, he stared at her for what to her seemed like an eternity. She waited for the next act, for him to move towards her, to take off his clothes, to lead her to the big double bed in the other room. She had decided she would not resist but would not help. If he wanted her, he'd have to take her. But, he just sat there.

It slowly dawned on her. If sex is as much about power as, well, sex, she reflected, Raul had shown his power. Now he seemed more interested in himself as he ran his hand up and down his leg. He was still looking at her but his eyes were almost closed and he was far away in another place. That, she thought, was the sex bit. She didn't have to stay around for it. Slowly she picked her clothes up and went to the bathroom. By the time she came out, Raul was already opening the door. They left without a word and took the lift to the ground floor. Alberto was waiting in the car.

So, she realised, that was the deal. She could play the part of the courtesan without having to act it out. Raul could play the great lover, the conqueror, the man who had claimed the beautiful Lydia for himself. He would lap it up. To have one of Caribe's most well-known young women, beautiful and educated, on his arm, to flaunt in the faces of those who remembered his squalid past, would be a daily delight for him. She would play the hostess and mistress. But she would store away his secret. Secrets are power.

In her new life, she was reviled by those who knew her in the time when she seemed to care about the things that Ramon cared about. Those around Raul and El Presidente, by contrast, were entranced and mystified in equal measure. They loved to be a part of the circle that surrounded her. They were too careful to ask what she was doing with a brute like Raul, though they whispered it among themselves.

Raul rarely put in an appearance at the apartment. He called her on the phone most days. It was his way of controlling her and reassuring himself at the same time. She chatted politely and asked him what he was up to without appearing to show more than a passing interest. She graced his arm as required. Otherwise she led her own life, subject, of course, to the one condition – she belonged to Raul. There was to be no-one else. She was a beautiful caged bird.

She charmed her new society with her soirees and her tea parties for wives and girlfriends. She occupied herself in the cultural life of Caribe. One of the interests that she discussed with Raul was the literacy campaign which El Presidente had announced. He and Raul had little interest in literacy. They had a lot of interest in the money that they could cream off from the grants which charities in the USA were inclined to send to their less advantaged neighbours.

"Raul", she asked one day, "do you think you could persuade the Minister of Education to put some of the money my way?"

"What for, Lydia?"

"It would be nice to encourage people, especially young people, to study our beautiful language and literature. Perhaps also study its roots in Latin".

This was already too esoteric for Raul, but it seemed harmless enough. So, she got her money.

She rented offices and hired some staff and teachers. She began to organise classes, put on plays and hold readings. Many of Caribe's young artists - writers, poets, actors, musicians, painters - had refused to have anything to do with her. She was soiled goods. She got her money by sleeping with Salcedo. She represented everything that they hated and that Ramon fought against. He would be turning in his grave if he knew how he had wasted his love on this spoilt up-town floosie.

She heard all this. It wasn't important. Doing what she was doing was important. One idea that she was particularly keen to pursue was her Circulo Latino - a meeting place for those who wanted to explore the classics. In an interview with the Diario, she explained that "it would offer beginners an opportunity to learn Latin and, for those who already have some background knowledge, a chance to develop it further through study groups". Studying Latin she told the interviewer would, "offer a window into their own language as well as opening a door to the classics". She began to gather together a group of young people to help to run it. They'd heard what was said about her, but were prepared to get involved nonetheless. They were convinced she wanted to do something important for Caribe's cultural life.

Within a few days of the story in the Diario, a frail, middle-aged man showed up one late afternoon at the office. The staff wondered whether, perhaps, he'd come to the wrong place. He was wearing battered overalls, and sandals made from discarded tyres. He joked that he'd left his machete at home. Someone was in the process of asking kindly how they could help, when she emerged from her office. She introduced him enthusiastically.

"This is Professor Cesar Sanchez, everyone. He was once a Professor of Latin at the University, but fell out with someone. So now, sadly, he's had to find a job working in the fields."

He picked up the story.

"I was delighted when I read about your Circulo, Señorita. I would be so happy to give up a couple of evenings a week to spend some time with students again. I love teaching. Coming here would give me a second chance to introduce another generation to the glories of Virgil and Tacitus and Cicero and, Señorita and all of you, my favourite, Lucretius."

Misty-eyed, he went on, "You know, I once wrote an article arguing that *De Rerum Natura* was one of the great masterpieces of ancient literature. Now I'll be able to introduce others to it again".

The staff were bemused and looked at her questioningly. She smiled warmly. "You'll get used to the Professor. He's a bit of an enthusiast, aren't you", she said, turning to him. "But, first we must talk. Shall we go into my office, Professor Sanchez."

"Cesar", he protested. "You must call me, Cesar." Turning to everyone, he repeated, "Call me Cesar. I'm not a Professor any more. I'm just a cane cutter". And with that he followed her into her office.

Once she had closed the door, she embraced Cesar warmly. "Thank you for coming, Professor. Thank you for answering my call. That was a wonderful performance. You have won them over. They will believe in you."

"But I do think Lucretius was a great poet", he protested.

"Yes, I know. But that's not why you are here. I want you to be the teacher, of course. That's what I asked Melba to say when she made contact with you. But, the truth is that I want you to do something far, far more important. I want you to take on a special role for me. Yes, I want you to teach Latin and inspire our young staff. But I also want you to do something more; something that is dangerous. You have already lost so much that I hardly feel able to ask you. But there is no-one else I can trust. I know how much Ramon admired you and what you stand for".

"When you sent a message asking me to come, I didn't hesitate. I came because of Ramon. I knew the stories that I heard about you could not be true. Though we have never met, I knew that you were Ramon's girl. That was enough for me. Now what do you want me to do, apart, that is", his blue eyes twinkling, "from flirting with the young girls who will flock to my classes as I make them fall in love with Catullus?"

"Professor, I know you are the spiritual leader behind those who want to bring about change. I want to help. I want to help to avenge Ramon's death. I want to help to get rid of that monster Barbosa and all he stands for. I want to help to get rid of Raul Salcedo and his thugs. I want to help to rescue Caribe. And I want to work with you to do so" – all delivered with an almost frightening passion, as her fingers searched for a strand of hair to twist.

Cesar sat down slowly on one of the easy chairs by the side of her desk.

"Well. That's the morning spoken for. What would you like to do in the afternoon?"

She was about to protest when he went on, "Forgive me, Señorita. I know it's no subject for joking. I apologise. But you will accept, I imagine, that what you speak of, besides getting us shot, is something of a challenge, to put it mildly".

"Yes, I know, Professor. But I must try. I hope you will let me help. I can explain if you are willing to listen".

"I'm listening".

She began. "I have a privileged position. I have access to the powerful in Caribe. I have achieved this by taking Salcedo as my protector and consort. I am a disgrace in the minds of those I love and those who live in the circles that I used to live in. This is the price I decided to pay. No-one knows it with the exception, now, of you. I know that you will keep my secret. My aim is to give whatever information I can acquire from those I come into contact with to those who are working to overthrow Barbosa."

"You are going to be a sort of spy? And me, what do I do," Cesar asked in a hushed tone, as if people were listening. There was just the hint of excitement in his voice.

"What I want you to do, Professor, is to be my go-between. The Circulo will be our cover. You will be the Professor, I will be the socialite, dabbling in cultural things. We will meet from time to time. I will pass information to you. You will pass it to those who can do something with it. They must not know where it comes from. No-one must know of my role or my cover will be blown. At first, they will not trust you. But gradually, they will see that what you tell them is true and begin to act on it."

"Señorita, this is very dangerous", Cesar protested. "I am not afraid for myself, but you should know what you are getting into and what could happen to you. I have lost my job. I have been beaten. I have been to prison. But you? I dread to think what they would do to you."

"Raul simply would not believe anything bad about me. I am such a trophy for him - his Lydia, trapped in his amber - his defiant middle finger to those in Caribe who look down on him. He thinks I am a weak woman who needs his protection. Professor, he has a hold over me that I cannot even tell you. But what he does not know is that by working with you I am escaping his control."

"I confess that I don't understand half of what you say. But, if you want me to be a go-between, who, Señorita, is the other person who must not know of you but must trust me, if I can bring that off?"

"He's the leader of the sugar workers' union, Jose Gaudi. I'm not sure how much you know about him, Professor. I know what I know from Ramon who admired him though he told me once that he didn't entirely trust him. According to Ramon, his family had a long history of involvement in politics in Argentina. He was closely involved with Peron and his wife Eva when they were trying to improve living standards and strengthen the trade unions. But when Peron was overthrown in 1955, Jose Gaudi went into exile in Uruguay. A few years back, apparently, he came to Caribe for a labour conference and saw at first-hand the conditions of workers in the sugar plants. Ramon said that the leader of the sugar workers union at the time, someone named Caspar Rodrigo, took Gaudi aside and said, that with his experience in Argentina, he was just the person they needed in Caribe to build the union and stand up to the factory owners. With no family and no ties, Gaudi agreed.

"From what I understand, Professor," she went on, "Gaudi soon proved himself a formidable organiser. Beginning at a sugar mill in the interior, he gradually recruited workers into the union. With the stronger bargaining power this gave him, he extracted increasingly favourable terms for members. The backlash from the owners once they saw how successful he was becoming was, as you may remember, Professor, swift and violent. The progress that had been made for workers was reversed. Pay was cut. The right to holidays and health insurance was cut to the bone and strikes were broken up by the police and the Rurales. Barbosa hitched his wagon to the owners. He refused to deal with the unions and called Gaudi, by then the union's leader, a 'foreign commie' who 'we don't need in Caribe'.

"I've never met him, but from everything I hear from Raul and those around him, Gaudi is not someone to back down. His appearance must help. It seems he was a prominent rugby player in Cordoba when he was younger. From his photographs he looks like some Viking warrior with his barrel-chest and shock of red hair, on top of being over six feet tall. The way Ramon told it, his inheritance from the Scottish side of his grandfather's family (the Campbells) was not just his appearance. His politics are the polar opposite of Barbosa's. He's absolutely uncompromising. He's determined to see Barbosa brought down. But he has no illusions about the challenges he faces, the biggest being Raul Salcedo and his network of informers".

As Cesar listened intently, she continued, "I understand that Raul's spies originally were told that Gaudi shouldn't be arrested nor even harassed. They just wanted to keep an eye on him and let him lead them to whatever mischief was being planned. As the union became stronger and increasingly better organised, Raul told Barbosa and the factory owners that he would act when the time was right. But, now they've finally decided to act, their attempts so far to knock him and the union off course haven't gone to plan. Gaudi is elusive and the union is getting more and more powerful."

Cesar sat forward in his chair, sipping the coffee that Lydia had made for him. "An interesting character, your Gaudi, my dear," he offered after a pause. "I've heard about him, of course, but I steer clear of the union. It attracts too much attention". Looking at her intently, he went on, "For your plans to work, Gaudi and I will have to work together. We'll have to trust each other. Let's hope we can."

Chapter 14

Conway gets involved

Eleven people had been killed and dozens injured in the demonstration in the Plaza Garibaldi. The Diario denounced it: the trade union behind the demonstration and the strike was 'a plague infecting our island'; the union leader, Jose Gaudi, was a 'foreign agitator' and a 'lackey of the Communists'. The strike must be called off. Workers must get back to work. The young people parading in the streets were useful idiots, gullible pawns being led astray. 'They should be in classes - not in the streets shouting slogans they don't even understand'.

The strike was not called off. New pickets replaced those killed and injured in the police charge and subsequent fighting. Only a few workers on the night shift crossed the picket line. The rest stayed at home choosing to get by on the food distributed by the union rather than give in.

Conway had followed events carefully after his meeting with Cesar Sanchez at the shack in San Rafael. It was clear that something was happening in Caribe - some kind of seismic rumbling. There was a story here that London would be interested in - the local struggle between the classic authoritarian leader, for so long a feature of the area, and an emerging popular opposition, plus the growing influence of the politics of liberal democracy in the region and across the globe.

From what he could gather from his sources, President Barbosa had demanded to know why the strike and subsequent demonstration hadn't been stopped before it had started. Barbosa had told Ministers in a hastily convened meeting of his Cabinet that he'd just got off the telephone with the Chairman of the sugar factory's Board who was "getting increasingly pissed off". The US Ambassador had also put in his two cents worth of "What the hell's going on, Don Basilio?"

El Presidente had told the Police Chief and the Minister of Justice, "If you two motherfuckers don't get a grip on things, you'll find yourselves in jail with the goddamned agitators and students - not something you'll enjoy I can tell you".

Then El Presidente had called Raul. "What the hell's happening, Raul. I put you in charge and you're not delivering. I don't want dead bodies in the street. It puts the Americans off".

Raul had indulged Barbosa's petulance. He knew that the President had no-one else to turn to. "I'm on the case, Don Basilio. It's just a flare-up. We'll break up the strike in a day or so. We'll have the ringleaders where we want them - in jail or feeding the sharks".

El Presidente allowed himself a sigh and growled, "You'd better be right".

Conway made a habit of having a drink at the Hilton with Raquel, one of the journalists at the Diario who was sleeping with one of Raul's staff (purely work, she'd insisted). According to her, Raul recognised that the strike was effective because it was well led. Gaudi was a cut above the usual hot-heads he'd had to deal with. And it was well supported because they'd been smart in trading on the anniversary of the death of Ramon Aguirre. They'd made him into a kind of folk hero; a rallying point for those opposed to the President's increasingly oppressive rule. And their number was growing. Raquel's boyfriend had told her that Raul knew he had to do something. Life was too good to let anyone spoil it. But, she added, as he sat in his office in the gloom of the early evening, Raul had also wrestled with another problem.

While the police were supposed to be in charge of sorting out the trade union, it was Raul who was actually in charge. And, as Raquel told it, the sense around Raul was that odd things were happening. The strikers seemed to be a step ahead of the police. Tying the demonstration to Aguirre's death was something Raul hadn't anticipated - his informers hadn't warned him about it. Clearly, the union's organisation was both good and impressively secretive. And the shooting on June 26 seemed to be a calculated tactic - create a few martyrs and pile more pressure on El Presidente.

The story was acquiring legs. Conway began to try to line up interviews for the Globe with the various players. But no-one in government would return his calls and his visits to Ministries and Police headquarters were met with polite replies - "I'm sure the Minister/Chief will be very keen to get back to you. Thank you for calling/coming in". Officialdom in Caribe seemed to have the technique of saying Yes and then doing nothing down to a fine art. It was friendlier than saying No, but it had the same effect.

Local business leaders, particularly the sugar and tobacco bosses, preferred not to go on the record for fear of making an already difficult situation more difficult. Privately, they lambasted both the union leaders and the politicians, from El Presidente down, but, then, they always do, he thought. "If only countries could be run like businesses, we'd get things done" was the regular refrain.

Conway couldn't get anything from the union. The leaders were nowhere to be found after "the June 26 massacre" as it came to be known. They'd gone underground. He learned that Raul's men in addition to the police and Rurales were scouring Puerto Grande, arresting and beating people up who had the slightest connection to the union, and tipping others out of bed in the middle of the night to be taken in for questioning. There were leads but they led nowhere. Gaudi and his lieutenants were well hidden.

He'd hit the buffers. He couldn't report the story if he couldn't get the story. He was sitting on the sea-wall of the Malecon, gazing out at the sunset and its ever-changing reflection on the sea, when a small boy tugged his sleeve.

"Señor, Señor", he piped. Barefoot, he was dressed in shorts and a none-too-clean, once-white T-shirt.

Conway turned to look at him. He didn't think he'd seen him before - just another child begging for some coins - and waved him away.

"Señor, Señor", the boy repeated more urgently.

Reluctantly, Conway asked the boy what he wanted. The boy simply pointed to a boat that was making for the harbour. As he turned to look, Conway didn't see the boy slip a piece of paper into his pocket. There was nothing remarkable about the boat, but, by the time Conway had turned back, the boy had run off. What had the boy been doing? He pulled out a handkerchief to clean his sun-glasses, as if to focus better on the matter. There was a piece of paper pushed into the handkerchief. On it was,

8 CALLE DE LIMONES. 20.00 HOURS. SUETONIUS

Suetonius could only mean one thing - Cesar. Conway had picked Suetonius' book, *The Twelve Caesars,* off the shelf in Cesar's shack. Cesar had said that he would make contact. This was the contact.

Perhaps this was the breakthrough he was looking for. He went back to his hotel and went over his memory of that day. Cesar said he was being watched. He said he wasn't brave enough to do anything though he supported those opposing the government. He wanted to talk. He would make contact. But, why would Cesar want to talk? Why would he make contact if he was so anxious about falling foul of the police?

Clearly there was more to Cesar than Conway first thought. Using the little boy so expertly suggested a clandestine world which he was being invited into. Was it a trap, he wondered. He could get knocked about and then given the heave-ho out of Caribe. "Not such a bad idea" he joked to himself, remembering again how long it had been since he tasted a decent pint of beer. But he'd be sorry to miss out on it if there really was a story. Obviously, there was no-one he could ask. He had to trust his judgement and his judgement told him that he should keep the rendezvous but that he was entering a dangerous world. As Jeremy Brown had warned him and as he'd seen in the Plaza Garibaldi, the police didn't mess about. They broke heads and shot people with apparent impunity.

Conway had just read a spy book sent by a friend in England written by a new writer by the name of Le Carre. It had examples of what the book referred to as trade craft - how to escape attention and elude people who might have you under observation. "It might come in useful", he thought to himself and decided to try out some of this "trade craft" on what he told himself was his first underground assignment.

First, he checked his map to find the Calle de Limones. Then he went down to the front desk and asked where a particular restaurant was. "I've heard a lot about it", he said, drawing in the Concierge to confirm that it was worth a visit. Now everyone would know where he was going. "I think I'll give it a go this evening".

"The Murano is an excellent choice, Señor. It's on Las Monjitas street. Shall I make a reservation for you," the woman at the desk asked.

"No thanks. I'll call them myself later. I'm not sure when I'll have finished my work this evening".

"As you wish, Señor. Here's the telephone number. But I wouldn't leave it too late, because it is very popular".

"Thanks very much".

Back in his room, he dressed in a dark shirt and black trousers and pulled out a black baseball cap that he'd picked up at a game and never worn. Then, he removed everything from his pockets except his press credentials – just in case he had to explain himself. His cover story was that he was doing a piece on 'Puerto Grande After Dark' and the growth of the nightlife - clubs, bars, restaurants, cinemas and so on – as an indication of the strength or fragility of Caribe's economy.

He reckoned it would take around thirty minutes to get to the Calle. He left at 18.30. This would give him the chance to check it out. Using the stairs, he left by the back door leading to the car park. There was no-one around. Once outside, he set off, mingling with the crowds making their way home from work.

The policeman assigned to watch him noticed his outfit and smiled - "He's been reading too many books" - and moved off to follow him across town.

Conway stopped at a bar in the San Jacinto market - from where he could look down the length of the Calle de Limones -ordered a beer, deliciously cold after his walk, and began to read the international sports section in the New York Times. Disappointingly, there was only a short paragraph on football and no mention of the Baggies. The watcher sat on a bench in the Plaza from where he had a clear line of sight to Conway, and read the Diario. The minutes passed. Conway occasionally looked up and casually took in the Calle. Otherwise, there was nothing to interest the watcher, but his job was to watch Conway so that's what he would do.

To maintain his status as someone out for a walk and a beer, Conway strolled up to the bar after about half-an-hour to order another. The barman said he'd bring it over. After a few minutes, he brought the beer to the table and also put down a piece of paper which could have been the bill except that he'd already been paid, and went back to the bar. Conway looked at the paper quizzically. It wasn't a bill – he was sure he'd already paid. What was it? There was writing on it. He read it. It said,

LEAVE. YOU ARE BEING FOLLOWED. GO BACK TO HOTEL AND WAIT

His first instinct was to look around immediately. Then he realised that this was not a smart move and made it look as if he was easing the muscles in a stiff neck. No-one would have been fooled, but the watching policeman at that very moment was looking down at his paper checking his horoscope. Shouting thanks and goodbye to the barman, Conway got up and set off back to the hotel. "Well," he thought, "that was a bit of a disaster. But how did they know I was in the bar? Half of Puerto Grande must be following me!"

At the hotel, Marco, the concierge, asked him if he was going to try the Murano. Conway thought for a moment. It might improve the so-far wasted evening. "Yes, I think I will. Marco, could you get a table for me, please? Say for nine-o-clock". Then he went up to his room to freshen up.

There was some dry cleaning on his bed - a shirt. Strange, he thought. He hadn't handed in any clothes to be cleaned. He was just about to call reception and ask them to take it back when he saw the note pinned to it. It simply said,

LA PERLA. 22.30. SUETONIUS

Conway smiled. "Bloody clever", he thought. He looked up La Perla in his guide. It was a night club across the street from the Murano.

He didn't really enjoy his red snapper on a bed of rice and sweet peppers, washed down with a beer, too close to room temperature. His walk to the restaurant had been punctuated by standing in front of shop windows to check behind him and suddenly stopping to shake something from his shoe. He'd gleaned from his book (or from some other spy book –the new Len Deighton perhaps) that stopping to tie a shoelace was a good way of checking if you were being followed, but he wasn't wearing shoes with laces. If he was being tailed, and he assumed he was, he couldn't see anyone. And, the restaurant was full. The tail could be anyone he groaned to himself.

Just after 22.30, Conway paid the bill and left. Across the road, he plunged into La Perla. The first thing that hit him was the noise - *Jailhouse Rock* being played at eardrum damaging volume. The second was that it was almost pitch black. The third was the smoke from cigarettes and other substances. There were people moving about. He could hear laughter and sensed that there were people dancing.

Before his eyes could become more accustomed to the darkness, a hand took hold of his arm and he felt himself being guided through the crowd. A door was unlocked and then locked behind him He was led down a staircase and along a corridor lit by a single bulb in the ceiling half-way down. His guide was a young woman. She didn't say anything. At the end of the corridor was another door. She unlocked that then relocked it and led him up another staircase. The door at the top, once unlocked, opened onto what looked like a kitchen. Two men were standing inside, either side of the door. They locked it behind them and nodded to the woman. She led Conway from the kitchen through a sitting room to more stairs. After climbing up two more floors, they arrived at a corridor at the end of which was a large, sparsely furnished room – a sofa and three old wooden chairs and a table loaded with tubes of paint and a couple of large jam jars full of brushes. The floor was spattered with paint, mostly reds and greens. It looked like a painter's studio, which it was. Thick-looking curtains covered the windows. It reeked of turpentine and tobacco smoke.

The young girl spoke for the first time. "I will come to fetch you in an hour and take you back through the club. Then your tail will see you come out and report when you are safely back in the hotel". Then she left. Conway assumed that the police didn't know about the underground way in to get to the room.

There were two people in the room. One Conway recognised from the demonstration – Atilio the megaphone man and painter. "Must be his studio," he thought to himself, "and obviously, they must think he's harmless enough not to be locked up. Or maybe the house is watched to see what company he's keeping". The other person looked like a Viking. He was huge. His faded jeans and sweat-stained shirt suggested a man of action, not caring greatly for appearances. Without any introduction, the giant man advanced on him and shook his hand, greeting him in English with a strong accent, then dropped back into Spanish.

"Thank you for coming, companero. Sorry to have messed you about this evening but the police are a bit edgy and watching their own shadows".

"That's OK. What's going on? What am I supposed to be doing? You do realise, don't you, that I'm a journalist, not Dick Barton, special agent."

Gaudi frowned. "Who's Dick Barton?"

Conway explained that there was a BBC radio programme when he was a boy called 'Dick Barton, Special Agent'. He could see he'd lost them.

Gaudi looked temporarily nonplussed. "We don't want you to be a special agent. We want you to be what you are – a reporter, but reporting things that we tell you as well as whatever lies the government peddles."

"Oh! You want me to be impartial, is that it?" He didn't try to disguise the sarcasm in his voice.

"If you are impartial, you will recognise their lies and expose them", not backing down. "But, we have not invited you to talk about the government. We want you to know about us."

"OK. First things first. Who are you? Who are the 'we'?"

"You don't need to know names, Señor Conway. I'm the convenor of the sugar workers' union. Through the union we support the students and other opposition groups. Our aim is simple – to bring down this corrupt and evil government and replace it with a government of the people – the real people.

"Now", Gaudi went on, "here's what you need to know. A small group of us have had to go underground for a while because the police are leaning heavily on us and on the union. We keep one step ahead of them because of the information supplied by Cesar Sanchez whom I understand you've met. Cesar has been a member of the union from the beginning but his membership isn't in the records and he always says he's too frightened to join when anyone asks".

"Yes, that's what he told me," Conway interrupted.

"Cesar passes on information to me through a variety of contacts – the little boy on the Malecon, the watcher who warned the barman in the Plaza Garibaldi, Circe, the girl who brought you through the club. There are many others, Señor, handpicked by Cesar. Take Atilio here. He was one of Cesar's students. He was arrested, of course, after his performance at the demonstration and has been turned by Salcedo to spy on us, or so Salcedo thinks. They keep their distance from him so as not to alert us, which Atilio appreciates, eh, Atilio?"

Atilio smiled and nodded.

"Atilio has to report daily which he does by phone or occasionally at a bar. He gives them stuff that is just true enough to be plausible but doesn't help. Just last week, Atilio gave them the names of organisers for the union at two of the big mills. But you apologised, didn't you, that you could only find out their nicknames – meaningless, of course. Salcedo praised you for your efforts, didn't he? 'That's great Atilio, but can you try to get me a few more details, next time'". Gaudi smiled and the others laughed, especially Atilio.

"The little boy on the Malecon who tugged at your sleeve, Señor, was Tomas. He's Circe's brother. He came from San Felipe with his sister when she moved to Puerto Grande. Circe has her own reasons for hating Salcedo and wanting to help to get rid of him and his cronies", Gaudi added darkly.

"Nobody knows where Cesar get his information from. And, because we didn't know, at first, Señor Conway, we didn't trust him or what he told us. But we soon learned that it was always accurate. And with that information we've been able to stay one move ahead of the police, the Rurales and Salcedo – no easy job in a city which isn't good at keeping secrets.

"Most important, we get to know what the bosses are saying to the government. We know where the pressure's being applied. Our plans feed on this pressure and increase it. If the bosses are worried about supplies being delivered to the mills on time, we organise flying pickets and road blocks to disrupt the traffic, sometimes for days. Production suffers. El Presidente finds himself being shouted at in meetings. The bosses say he's losing his grip. If he doesn't turn things around, Señor, they've threatened they'll find someone else who can.

"So, Raul goes around arresting more and more workers and harassing their families. It does our work for us. It alienates people. It recruits them to the cause. And, when they're beaten and thrown into prison, they can't work, so – it's not rocket science, Señor – production falters. And, anyway, they only ever pick up the small fry. We're always able to melt away as if we've been forewarned, which in fact we have been, courtesy of Cesar".

Conway reflected while Gaudi was talking that he'd been reporting on the strikes and their effect on Caribe's economy for some time. Meeting Gaudi and learning about the underground resistance persuaded him that something more significant was going on than a stand-off between the union and the factory owners. Revolution was in the air. It would be repressed or the government would fall. Either way, this was a big story and he was in the thick of it. Here he was, sitting in a room getting the story from the horse's mouth. Clandestine meetings, secret messages, a frail ex-professor, an Argentinian Communist, and a barefoot boy – this was the stuff he used to read about in books about the French Resistance in the Second World War.

Circe burst in on Conway's thoughts.

"Señor, you must go now. Follow me". She led him back along the corridors and through the several doors until he found himself again in the darkness and noise of La Perla. "Go up the stairs and into the street, Señor. Turn right and follow the road. Your hotel is about fifteen minutes away. Please don't look round. Just go back and then go to your room. We will find a way to contact you when we need to". And with that she disappeared into the dark interior of the club.

Back at his hotel, Conway weighed up what had happened. There was indeed something going on in Puerto Grande and it had the makings of something big. And for reasons which he did not really understand, he had a ring-side seat. But, it was tricky terrain. If he just continued to file general interest stories, London would soon get bored. The reports would get spiked and he'd be on the wrong end of questions asking what the hell he was doing with himself. If he gave any detail, London would be delighted with what they could claim was a scoop but he would be putting people, and perhaps himself, in harm's way. He decided to sleep on it.

He was idly leafing through the Diario over his orange juice and eggs the next morning (his request for tea once again produced the treacly-thick coffee that everyone seemed to thrive on), when Conway saw a short item about an initiative being organised by the Circulo Latino. Citizens of Puerto Grande were invited to 3 Lectures on aspects of Roman history and literature. The Lectures were to be delivered by teachers from the University and held at the Circulo's premises on the Avenida Firmin over three Wednesday evenings in the following month.

He'd read about the Circulo some time ago. Ordinarily he would have made a beeline for it. But Jeremy Brown had told him that it was the brain-child, or toy, depending on who you spoke to, of Lydia Echevarria. Her refusal to engage with him when he tried to make contact after her party and her relationship with Raul Salcedo had persuaded him to give the Circulo a miss. He doubted London would be all that impressed with his taking up with "a bunch of losers studying dead languages", as Harry would no doubt put it. But, the entry into his life of Cesar, aka Suetonius, suggested that he should try again. The Circulo, he reasoned, just may be a way of reaching Cesar. And Cesar seemed to be the key to understanding what was going on.

Noting down the number, Conway went up to his room and telephoned the Circulo's office. He asked about attending the Lectures. The receptionist, Teresa, assured him that he would be very welcome. "No", she said. "There is nothing to pay. The Lectures are sponsored by a Foundation associated with the University of Chicago in the United States. And, if you would wish to, Señor Conway", she added, "Why don't you drop by this evening. As it happens, we are having a get-together over coffee at six-o-clock. Just some of the staff and students. It would be good to welcome a new face". Having little else to do, he'd readily agreed.

Conway planned to get there by around six-thirty. He had long adapted to the general norm of Caribe's life – that an appointed time was more a point from which to calculate when you might arrive than the actual arrival time itself. So, he was surprised when he got there to find about fifteen people already involved in animated discussion round a table on which there were beers, coffee and doughnuts. He had been ushered in by Teresa who'd waited for him to arrive. She looked every inch the committed student; glasses, dark hair pulled back and captured by a rubber band, and wearing a loose-fitting dress which gave no suggestion that there was a woman within. White socks and white pumps completed the ensemble. He had apologised to Teresa for being late and now he apologised to the group. They smiled and offered greetings. A chair was pulled up and, reading his mind, one of the students passed him a bottle of San Miguel. He introduced himself: he was Tony Conway, an English journalist, based in Caribe who, in a previous life, had been a classicist at University. He was intrigued, he said, by the interest in Latin and the classics and hoped that they didn't mind if he joined them.

The welcome could not have been warmer. They introduced themselves. Atilio, the artist whose apartment he'd been in the evening before, was one of them. Neither gave any sign of recognising the other. It seemed that the group was planning the arrangements for the forthcoming Lecture series. Conway offered to talk to friends in the British Embassy to drum up support, perhaps even a link between the British Council's office and the Circulo. This was enthusiastically welcomed.

Choosing his moment, Conway enquired, casually he hoped, "Is someone I helped after the June 26 Demonstration, who turned out to be an ex-Professor of Latin, involved in the Circulo in any way? I can't remember his full name but I think his first name is Cesar". He caught Atilio's eye. The slightest frown appeared on Atilio's brow. It seemed to say "Take care".

"Ah! Yes. That's Professor Sanchez", one of the students replied. "He comes in when he can. He's a cane cutter and lives outside the city. When he's here, he spends most of his time talking to Señorita Lydia about her plans for the Circulo. But, we all think the real reason is that he's got a big crush on her," she giggled. The others smiled. "Such a nice man. Always willing to help if he can", said another student.

Conway smiled with them. "That's a great story: someone working in the fields then travelling in to help to teach the classics to the next generation. Do you think he'd give me an interview?"

"He's very shy. And he's had some run-ins with the police in the past". It was Atilio speaking. "I doubt he'd want to draw attention to himself. He might be willing to talk about the Circulo, however. I'll ask Señorita Lydia and let you know. Do you have a card?"

Conway gave him one and also wrote the name of his hotel on the back.

The connection had been made.

The meeting at the Circulo went on for another hour before breaking up. A group of the students invited him for a beer at the Bodega La Estrella at the corner of Avenida Firmin and the Plaza Los Angeles. He wasn't sure how to play it. He assumed that he was still being watched and so was reluctant to expose the students to the police's attention. On the other hand, his watchers will have seen him going to the Circulo. So, going for a drink with some of the youngsters would be a natural thing to do. And, if the Circulo was Lydia's brainchild, Raul would know about it anyway. Presumably, this would also mean it was not something Raul worried about.

Conway decided that, for once, he could use his miserly expense account for a good cause. He ordered beers for everyone. They sat outside at the edge of the plaza watching people coming and going on their way home for dinner. The students wanted to know about London. The weather was the first topic. Then it was music, not Latin but "the King" - Elvis. Was he big in England? What did Conway think of him? They were shocked when he had to confess that he'd only vaguely heard of him, but couldn't remember much about him. The age gap between him and them was no more than a dozen years but it could have been a millennium.

Patricio was leading the charge on the music front. He looked the typical geek; baseball cap worn backwards, coke-bottle-bottom glasses, torn jeans and T shirt sporting a large photograph of 'The King'. Undaunted by Conway's inexplicable ignorance of Elvis, Patricio hit the ball out of the park when he asked,

"What's your view, Señor Conway, of this new group from Liverpool who are setting Germany on fire?" He'd recently been hitchhiking in Europe and was keen to show off how up-to-date he was.

"I haven't a clue", Conway replied. Patricio was clearly shocked by this further display of other-worldliness. In an effort to change the subject, Conway suggested, "Now, if you want to know about football ... ." They didn't.

More beers were ordered and several conversations broke out. Conway found himself sitting with a serious-looking, dark-skinned young man.

"I'm Carlos", he said.

"Hello, Carlos. I'm Tony. What drew you to the Circulo? Was it the Latin or the girls and the beers?" As soon as he had said it, he realised that Carlos did not appreciate the intended humour. "Forgive me. A silly attempt at breaking the ice. Seriously, please do tell me something about yourself."

Not entirely mollified, Carlos told him that he worked in a shop, his father was a taxi-driver, and that he wanted to be an actor and writer but there was no chance of ever being either.

"Why on earth not", Conway asked breezily, reflecting the egalitarianism of the Britain back home. "Surely, if you want to do something you just get on and do it, don't you?"

"Perhaps in your country, Señor, but not here. I am the wrong colour, I live in the wrong place, and I have the wrong background. What the Yanquis call three strikes against me. I come to the Circulo because it's good to be around people interested in reading and ideas and politics. They put on plays occasionally so I might be able to get a part. But my main interest here is in politics. I'm trying to get my head round Cicero. In translation, of course", he added self-consciously. "The teachers are great and it helps me to understand things. There's a new party called the Alianza which some of the workers have formed. I'm trying to help."

"Yes, I've heard of them. Tell me more".

"Well, there's not much to tell yet. They want to get rid of Barbosa and his crooks and get an honest government. It's as simple as that."

"Mmmm... . It's rarely as simple as that, though I do appreciate the clarity of vision."

"You are mocking me, Señor. I know you people think you are so superior with your traditions and history, but we natives can do things too."

The ferocity of Carlos' retort surprised Conway. "My dear chap," he began in best English mollifying mode, but Carlos had already got up and was on his way to join the others at the bar. He found himself alone- all a bit embarrassing.

"I see you just got a tongue-lashing from Carlos". It was Patricio, the music geek. "Don't worry. It happens to all of us. He's a bit of a loose cannon is our Carlos. Do you mind if we talk for a moment, Señor? I'm Patricio, as you may have heard - Puerto Grande's very own walking encyclopaedia when it comes to music. I shall call you Tony, if I may. Atilio asked me to talk to you. You should understand what that means".

Conway nodded, suddenly on high alert.

"We are having a conversation about music, Tony. I shall wave my arms about and mime with this beer bottle as my microphone. Assuming those watching you are awake, they will recognise that I am boring another poor soul with my passion for Elvis, the Beach Boys and all the other sensational products of the Yanqui music machine.

"Now, Atilio is keen that you do a story on the sugar workers' union and Señor Gaudi. He also wants you to meet Professor Sanchez. This is dangerous for us. But it has been decided that we should talk to you. We want you to raise awareness of what we are doing on a larger stage. Here in Puerto Grande, the Diario is owned, of course, by the bosses. The other papers are either too small or get shut down if they step out of line. So we get little attention. We need attention, Tony." At this point, Patricio stood up and, waving the beer bottle about, went into a wild routine. There was a combination of laughter, applause and friendly abuse from the other tables as he sat down. One of the students shouted, "Turn him off, Señor, if he gets too obnoxious". Conway waved an acknowledgement.

"Here's what we will do," Patricio continued, waving the beer bottle about in apparent ecstasy. "You will go to La Perla again tomorrow at 22.30. You will have asked Dolores over there to go with you". He pointed to the blonde at the bar. "It will look like a date. You will pick her up at her place. We will get the address to you. You will put it about at your hotel that you have found this fantastic club right next to the restaurant they recommended and have asked a young woman whom you met at the Circulo to go dancing with you. And she said yes. Circe will look after you and Dolores once you are inside. Dolores is one of us. Carlos, by the way, is not. Take care when you are around him". And with that Patricio leapt into the air and did a pretty awful imitation of Elvis that drew boos from the group.

Getting up from the table, Conway clapped and slapped Patricio on the back, then shouted goodnight to everyone, thanking them for their company. They shouted thanks for the beers. Then he set off for the Valencia. He hadn't gone far when he heard footsteps behind him. Turning he saw Carlos coming towards him.

"I wanted to apologise, Señor, for my rudeness. I know I'm hot-headed sometimes. Perhaps we could have another beer somewhere and talk. I'd like to let you know a bit about the Alianza so that you might write about us".

Primed by Patricio's warning, Conway held out his hand and shook Carlos'. "Don't give it another thought. No hard feelings. And, yes, it would be good to talk but not just now. I'm rather tired and need to get back to the hotel. Another time, perhaps". And with a wave he walked off.

Chapter 15

Conway files a story

They were sitting in a corner of the café in the Circulo, sipping soft drinks late in the afternoon of the next day. Conway was telling her about his talk with Patricio the evening before and she was smiling as he described the scene. It was the first time he'd seen Circe in daylight and he realised how impressive she was. It was not just her looks, though she was very attractive in a tall, languid model-type way. It was her personality – bright, sharp, practical, and very determined.

She turned the conversation to what had happened earlier in the day. She told Conway that she'd spent some time talking to Atilio and then running back and forth.

"Tell me about it," he urged her. He was keen to hear what she and the others had been up to. It was precisely the sort of background he needed for the story he was going to write, though obviously he couldn't name people and places.

* * * * *

Two men had called on Atilio in his studio at lunchtime. They came by the conventional route – through the front door on the Camino de Los Gatos.

The big fat one, Cristiano, did the talking. His side-kick, Javier, drew on his Marlboro and worked on looking tough.

"What've you got for us? The boss is getting pissed off with what you've come up with so far – a big load of nothing. You were at the Circulo last night with your pansy friends. What did you pick up? And what was the Englishman doing there?"

Atilio had to think on his feet. He made a play of looking for his cigarettes and then a lighter. Lighting a Chesterfield, he inhaled deeply and blew out a stream of smoke. Paying him a visit was not the standard approach. They must be under pressure from above. What could he give them to keep them happy?

"Well, boys, I'm glad you dropped by. Can I get you a beer?"

"No beer. Just talk".

"Well, I was going to contact you this afternoon at the usual time and report on the Englishman. It seems he's got this mad obsession with Señorita Echevarria - he thinks she's in love with him but won't leave Señor Salcedo. He thought he might be able to contact her if he came to the Circulo. We gave him the run-around. I think he's just lonely and love-sick but I thought that Señor Salcedo may be interested. I also picked up some news about a new newspaper that the Alianza is planning to start. One of the group at the Circulo told me about it but I can't now remember his name. I'll ask around."

"Is that it? An Englishman in love and a newspaper being planned. I have to tell you that Señor Salcedo's not going to be too impressed. You'd better do better than that if you want to stay out of jail".

"What use would I be in jail", Atilio shot back.

"What use are you out of jail? We'll want more, much more next time. We need you to get a handle on Gaudi and the union. Don't waste your time on the Englishman".

"Fine, I'll work on it. But it doesn't help if you come here unannounced. Friends may see you and then start questioning me and before you know it my cover will be blown. So, can we stick to the agreed procedure, please, gentlemen? It would be a pity to ruin everything when I'm getting close".

"Close to what, pendejo," was Javier's contribution.

Cristiano made for the door. "We'll see you soon. And don't disappoint us. We don't like being disappointed, do we Javier?"

They banged the door on their way out.

Atilio collapsed on the sofa. He realised that things were getting too hot. It was pretty obvious he wasn't going to be able to keep them at bay much longer. He needed some advice; he needed help. He was out of his depth. And, if they were going to pay him a visit whenever they felt like it, his place was no longer a safe house: it was a very unsafe house. He had to get word to Gaudi's people - they couldn't meet there that evening nor in the future. And, he needed to disappear for a while.

Atilio phoned Teresa at the Circulo.

"I think I left my sketch-book at the Circulo. I'm coming over to get it. I'm feeling inspired" and, mocking himself, "I don't want to miss the moment, do I?"

"Cometh the moment, cometh the man", Teresa mocked back. "I'll be here. Make sure you can get your ego through the door".

"Charming!"

There was nothing there to interest the listeners if they were listening.

"Is Circe here", he asked Teresa when he got to the Circulo.

"No. She's coming in later, I think".

"Can you call her, please, and ask her to come as soon as she can. It's a bit urgent".

Teresa nodded. "I'm not sure how to contact her. There's no phone where she lives. I'll try the Bar where she helps out sometimes."

Circe was there and said she'd be happy to come over. When she got there, Atilio took her aside. "There's a problem. We can't use my place any more. Can you get the message to Gaudi and ask him to let me and Conway know where to go. And tell the Englishman that the date with Dolores is off – she has to wash her hair".

"Very funny", Circe replied, then asked Atilio where he was going to be so she could let him know.

"I'll be doing some sketching on the Malecon. Tomas will be able to find me".

Circe hurried back to the Perro Negro Bar, warning Atilio to take care and to look out for Tomasito – "he's all I have".

After about half an hour, Atilio also left, his sketch-book and a satchel prominently under his arm. He walked down across town to the Malecon and settled on a bench where he started to sketch.

As she washed glasses and joked with customers, Circe began to work out what she had to do: get word to Gaudi, find out the new meeting place, then send Tomas to contact Atilio. She would leave it to Gaudi's people to contact the Englishman. The problem was that she didn't know how to reach Gaudi. She only knew that there was a chain of people at the end of which was someone who did know. The one person whom she knew who was in the chain was Patricio but where was he? She shouted to Ruben, the owner of the bar. "Is it OK if I make a phone call?"

"As long as it ain't a boy. Remember, Circe, I'm still first on the list when you decide to start dating".

"Don't worry. You're my man".

She phoned Teresa at the Circulo and asked if she knew where Patricio was. The good news was that Patricio didn't have classes that day and was making music, or what he called music, with his group in a back room. Teresa went back and interrupted them, shouting over the noise that he needed to go over to where Circe worked. "Back in a while", Patricio told the group. Then he hurried over to the Bar. He gulped down a limonsoda and picked up the tab.

Circe had written on the back,

NO MEETING AT A's. WHERE NEW PLACE? I'TELL A. U TELL ENGLISH.

Patricio downed his drink, shouted a "Thank you, Señorita" and left.

* * * * *

It was almost five-o-clock when a well-dressed, middle-aged woman came into the Bar and asked for "something refreshing – it's so hot out there". Ruben was about to serve her.

Circe brushed past. "I'll get it. You've been on your feet all day, old man."

"Hey, less of the old man, Señorita", pulling a face at the Señora.

Circe prepared a long drink of lemon juice, ice and just a touch of white rum and took it over. The two of them chatted for a while, sitting on the hard metal chairs as close as they could to the big fan in the corner. It was moving the hot air around without making much impression on the heat. Circe apologised - the air-conditioner was broken - but the woman shrugged, "no problem".

"I'm going to the Iglesia Santa Maria Magdalena this evening", she told Circe. "We're having a big service of thanksgiving and a reception to commemorate our twentieth wedding anniversary. Who would believe it? There'll be crowds of people there, some of whom I may even know", she joked.

"I've invited a young English journalist named Conway", she added. "I just met him. He seems like fun."

When the woman left, Circe called her little brother, Tomas. He was playing with some friends in a back room. He hadn't been to school that afternoon – some big meeting of the teachers he'd told her. She only half believed him, but he was a good boy and she enjoyed indulging him once in a while. She gave him a piece of paper that she'd folded up. On it was,

MASS AT 8. PRAY WITH US. IGLESIA SMM

She told Tomas to take the note to Atilio. "He's on the Malecon somewhere, sweetheart. Then come back here. You need to get to bed early tonight".

Tomas took off without a word. As he made for the Malecon to give Atilio the piece of paper, his mind was on ways of avoiding the threatened early night.

* * * * *

The crowds milling around outside the church provided cover. Gaudi and Cesar, both dressed as waiters and carrying trays, walked quickly through the church and down the steep steps to the crypt. Gaudi sported a chef's hat to cover the red hair. Candles had been lit, throwing shifting shadows onto the walls. The air was damp and there was a pervasive smell of mould. Atilio was already there. They greeted each other. Atilio had brought down chairs from the church upstairs. There was no sign of Conway. They knew that he was being watched and that he did not have their skills in evading attention - just in case, two of Gaudi's men were at the door to the crypt, ready to raise the alarm if necessary. Atilio had ensured that there was an alternative way out by prising ajar a door at the back of the crypt. It gave onto a staircase up to street level. At the top of the stairs, across a narrow passage way, dotted with potted plants and discarded stone statues, was the back door into what had once been the convent attached to the church. The nuns had moved on and it was now a large house, slightly dilapidated but still grand. It was owned by the well-dressed woman from the Perro Negro, one Señora Magda Gonzalez.

There was a knocking on the door at the back of the crypt. Atilio worked it open and shouted back to the others, "Conway's here". Conway stepped inside, sporting a flower in his lapel.

"I'm one of Señora Gonzales' guests", he told them. "Never met her before but she seems very nice. I got this invitation and then one of her staff took me back to her house, telling me to appear to be feeling unwell - the heat, you know. I was escorted to the back door and here I am. I'll have to leave in about an hour so I can emerge from the house looking suitably recovered."

There were smiles all round. Gaudi congratulated him. Cesar looked at him fondly and said,

"You are learning fast, Señor. Dona Magda is a good friend of ours. Her husband is a doctor. He treats Police Captain Gomes for his blood pressure. You would be surprised what patients are willing to tell their doctors, all in strict confidence, of course. And then Doctor Gonzales passes those confidences to his wife, in confidence, of course. And his wife passes those confidences to me, again all in confidence, of course".

Everyone was smiling. Conway marvelled at the underground network of supporters. Then it was down to business. Gaudi took the lead.

"Thank you for coming, Señor Conway. As I said last time we met, we want you to tell the world about us. Companero Sanchez will fill you in".

Cesar took over. "It is good to see you again, Señor Conway. I'm delighted that Suetonius has brought us together."

Conway smiled and nodded.

"Let me tell you what we are doing and what we plan. You will realise, Señor, that we have decided to trust you. I know that you will not betray that trust.

"Currently we have a well-organised programme of strikes and disruption, led by Señor Gaudi here. For the most part it's centred on Puerto Grande. Our next step is to extend it to other towns on the island. As you will appreciate, this takes considerable organisation particularly when the police and the Rurales are so active. Our aim is to paralyse the economy and pile increasing pressure on Barbosa. We expect him to respond with violence. We assume that he will bring in the army. This will be our cue to declare an armed insurrection. We will call on the army to come over to the people's side – some will, most will not, at least not at first. By then we will have obtained weapons and raised, if not an army, an armed group. We will then embark on the armed struggle. It will begin in one of the towns on the south coast, probably La Fortaleza. It will end when we enter Puerto Grande which we would expect to do by the Spring of next year."

Conway listened intently. He thanked them for their trust but reminded them that he was a journalist, not a partisan. He could see that there were the beginnings of a breakdown in public order and that the economy was struggling. He could report this, "but, if I'm going to report on the campaign as outlined by my friend Cesar here, I wouldn't last more than a week in Puerto Grande. I'd be picked up and asked (not so very politely) why I was lending support to the communist agitators and where I was getting all my inside information from. Of course, I'd refuse to tell them, at which point they'd put me on the next plane to God knows where, or, more likely, sling me off the Malecon for the sharks".

Cesar nodded. "I understand, but, there is a solution. What I propose, Señor Conway, is that you write a major piece describing the turmoil and the coming political storm and revolt against Barbosa. Then, you go underground. You would travel with Señor Gaudi's men into the countryside and report on the spread of the uprising and Barbosa's reaction. You would be in La Fortaleza for the launch of the armed struggle – what a coup that would be. Then you would send despatches from the front, telling our story, culminating in the entry into the capital".

Conway saw that Gaudi looked a little surprised and guessed that Cesar had not discussed this part of the plan with him. And on cue, Gaudi raised objections.

"Wait a minute, wait a minute. This won't work. Companero Conway will stand out and give us away; his reports will not be picked up by the world's press if he's stuck in some village in the hills without any sense of the wider picture; local people won't trust him; he isn't a trained fighter; he'll just be an encumbrance".

Before he could continue adding to the list, Cesar interrupted and waved the objections away.

"If there are problems, they will be solved. Señor Conway is a trusted and reliable journalist. He's also resourceful. And I'm sure the idea of being in at the beginning of a revolution will appeal to him".

What was being suggested was both daunting and exciting to Conway. He was not a war correspondent, but it couldn't be that hard, he thought, as long as you remember to duck. The one thing that caused him to pause was the coldness that he detected between Gaudi and Cesar. They addressed each other formally as Señor or Companero.

Clearly, Cesar knew that he needed Gaudi. He may have to hold his nose on occasions but that was a feature of the deal he had made with him. Conway assumed that Cesar had decided that the price would not be too high - that was probably why Cesar wanted him to be involved. Yes, he would tell the world. But his reports would also tell Cesar what he needed to know along the way, and, perhaps, keep Gaudi in check.

Conway sensed that the coldness between them was stronger in the case of Gaudi who clearly saw Cesar purely in instrumental terms. There was no warmth, far less love. Yes, currently, Cesar was central to the struggle. He could inspire people to join them. Cesar could get Gaudi to where he wanted to be. After that, Conway guessed that for Gaudi, it was a case of - "we'll see".

Conway saw that Cesar was a brilliant leader and organiser but, ultimately, he was the romantic, the lover of Caribe, the dreamer for a better future for her young people. Gaudi was different. His goal was power. With power, a new political order could be established. A foreign journalist could get in his way. Someone raised on the niceties of liberal democracies constantly looking over his shoulder and watching what he did might not always be appealing to Gaudi. There were things that sometimes needed to be done which might not pass muster in the salons of London or Paris or New York.

Conway realised that they were looking at him. He cleared his throat.

"Well, this is all a bit sudden. The people in London will like being brought up to date on the goings on here. But I don't know whether they would like me to go off like some latter day George Orwell or Hemingway and start reporting from the front. I can ask them, but they may say no."

He paused.

"So here's what I'm going to do. I'll file a big story as Cesar suggests and then put it about that I'm going to 'take the nation's temperature' by travelling around a bit. The aim will be to elude Salcedo and his watchers with your help and then link up with whomever you tell me to. After that I'll be filing copy from what I hope will be the front line. Let's hope I'm not filing from jail, describing my last night before they shoot me". He tried to make the last point come out flippantly but didn't quite succeed.

"Bravo, Señor Conway", Cesar cried. "Now that's out of the way, we must spend some time briefing you about what should go into what you call 'the big story'".

Cesar took about half an hour to set out the themes of the story he wanted Conway to write. Gaudi threw in the odd word from time to time, but it was clear who was in charge. Conway borrowed one of Atilio's pens and took notes on the back of hymn sheets which were lying about, abandoned, in the crypt.

Glancing at his watch, Cesar caught Atilio's eye. Atilio nodded.

"Now, we must disperse before the mass and celebration are over. Señor Gaudi and I will become waiters again", Cesar smiled, picking up the tray and napkin he had brought down. "You, Señor Conway, will return to Señora Gonzales' house. She will look after you. We will contact you in due course. And we must find somewhere safe for Atilio. He can't go back to his apartment."

Turning, Cesar smiled warmly. "Gracias y buena suerte. Thank you and good luck, Señor Conway. Te veo, amigo, I'll see you again, my friend", clasping him in an all-enveloping hug.

"We'll be in touch, Señor Conway", Gaudi said, putting on his chef's hat then offering him his hand to shake.

* * * * *

During the following days, Conway buried himself in work. The piece he was working on would make (or break) him. It had to be good. He set the scene by recalling for the reader the impressions he'd reported since he'd arrived in Caribe: attempts to grow the economy through tourism, the effects that the strikes and growing disorder were having on that project, the discontent of big business, particularly the Americans, with the disruptions in production and the consequent inability of the government to keep Caribe working, and the sense that relations between the government and the governed were increasingly fraught. Things were getting ugly.

He allowed himself to offer the prediction that if something were not done, and done relatively soon, the government of El Presidente would be under threat and could be toppled.

They liked it in London. They gave it a double-page spread inside the front page. It reflected the Globe's take on the world; that liberal democracies were under threat with dictators cropping up all over the place. The editorial declared: "We must support those fighting back". It went down well in the living rooms of North London. He was duly applauded and encouraged to press on. "Keep the stories coming" was the message from Harry.

Pleased with himself, Conway decided to give himself a treat. He'd spoken a couple of times to Dolores since their ill-fated 'date' which had had to be called off. He didn't normally go for blonds, but he found her bubbly personality and sense of humour, coupled with her good looks, very attractive. It was also not irrelevant that he hadn't been out with a girl since he arrived and was champing at the bit. So, he asked Dolores out.

He picked her up at her apartment. The transformation from the young woman in the Circulo to the person standing in front of him bowled him over. Her blonde hair was cut in a bob, Clara Bow-style. Her green eyes were outlined with just the right suggestion of mascara. Her pink lipstick was equally understated and all the more effective for being so. She was wearing a simple black dress with spaghetti straps and black shoes with two inch heels. Gold earrings and a gold cross at her throat completed the ensemble.

In the lift going down, he announced, "I've booked dinner at a nice place. I think you'll like it".

She leaned against the side of the lift and looked him up and down. Then she laughed loudly - at him or with him, he wasn't sure.

"Hey Tony, Tony! Loosen up. You're in the tropics, not in stuffy London. We don't go out to dinner at nice places. We go out to dance and drink and then drink and dance and then .... You OK with that?"

He nodded – lost for words. This was a far cry from the dating rituals of West Bromwich or Camden Town. "Fine. Yes. I'm OK with that. Very OK".

He let himself be guided from club to Bar to club. His footwork on the football field didn't prove much use when it came to dancing the sort of dance that Dolores enjoyed. But there were also the sorts of dances that he enjoyed – the sort where you get hot and sweaty and very close.

It was 2.30 in the morning and he was feeling the pace when Dolores suggested a walk along the Malecon. It was a beautiful, moonlit night and as they walked, he put his arm round her. She leaned into him and he found himself kissing her on the side of the head. She stopped and turned to him.

"What about a proper kiss, or is that the best you English can do?"

Accepting the challenge, he kissed her. Locked in an embrace, several cars full of late-night revellers sounded their horns and shouted the Spanish equivalent of 'Get a room' as they drove past.

Dolores drew back from him and said softly, "Well, Tony, shall we get a room? Do you think your hotel will mind if you offer shelter to someone who's missed the last bus home?"

"I'm sure they'd be very understanding".

Hand in hand they made their way back to the Valencia. The night porter barely noticed before slipping back into snooze mode. Once in his room, the pace quickened. Clothes were cast off as quickly as possible. Dolores stretched out on his bed, very attractive and very naked. Her skin was the colour of honey. She ran an appraising eye over him as he finally got his other sock off.

"Not bad, Señor. A bit pale for our Caribino tastes, but it will do". Then she pouted and asked, "Why are you still standing there".

He was about to say that he'd been trying to get his sock off but figured that it might do something to the mood. So, he went for the athletic approach and leapt onto the bed. Dolores screamed and then giggled. The sex was remarkable. She guessed that he had been starved for a while and that there was a danger that it could be over before she'd got started, so she took him in hand, so to speak, and the next half an hour was glorious.

Both thoroughly sated, they fell asleep, arms and legs locked together.

He woke at 7.30, his usual time, to find that Dolores was in the bathroom taking a shower. When she came out, it was his turn to beckon her to join him in bed.

"No, Señor, que no! You're all sweaty and need a shower", she protested, but jumped into bed anyway. The second time was equally fantastic. He had never been with a woman quite like this. Then, all business, she rolled onto her side and said, "I have to go, Englishman. I need to go to church."

"What? Why?"

She pointed to the cross round her neck. "I have to go to confession after all that sex".

He couldn't work out whether she was joking or not. "Are you serious?"

"Oh, Yes. Whenever I have sex, I go to this one church where the priest is very sweet. He hears my confession and insists that I go into very great detail. As I do, the knocking against the side of the confessional box gets more and more urgent. So I like to think I've done something to make him happy as well". She smiled her wide-mouthed smile. With a "See you around", she left.

Wow, was all he could manage.

* * * * *

Conway's piece in the Globe was picked up by the US press. The New York Times described it as "a fine piece of investigative journalism". The Wall Street Journal railed against its "anti-business" agenda in not attacking the strikes explicitly. While he was delighted with the attention, there were others who were not so happy. Jeremy Brown called him from the Embassy and urged him to "tone it down a bit, old chap." HMG didn't want to pick a fight with El Presidente while trade talks were going on.

The original copy of the piece had been intercepted as usual before it went out and passed to Raul. Conway knew that Raul would not try to strangle it at birth because he would just send another copy. Instead, he learned later that Raul had instructed Caribe's Charge d'Affaires in London to kill the story. When told that things didn't work like that, Raul ordered the Charge to publish a statement attacking the piece and demanding a retraction. When he saw the New York Times' story, Raul knew that his efforts at suppression had failed, even if the Wall Street Journal had come through for them.

Within minutes, Conway was summoned to see Raul. It may not have been possible to kill that particular story, but there wouldn't be any others.

Raul sat behind his big mahogany desk with the leather inlay. The air-conditioning was on full blast. The furniture was plush – a sofa and three armchairs arranged round a highly polished table. There were several photographs of Raul with El Presidente at various receptions and gatherings and one of Raul standing alone on the shore-line staring out to sea. It was noon when he was ushered into the office. He was wearing his number one outfit, the suit he bought in Piccadilly that he'd worn the day he arrived. Raul did not greet him, far less invite him to sit down.

Raul began by reminding him of the occasion of his 'disgraceful behaviour' at the home of Señorita Echevarria. "Did you take lessons in being an offensive fool or does it come naturally", he asked. The menace in his voice was that much greater because he spoke so softly.

Giving him no chance to reply, Raul went on, "The piece you just wrote for your newspaper. It is a disgrace. So, this is what you are going to do, Señorito. Within the next twelve hours you are going to write a letter to El Presidente apologising for the mistaken and insulting article that you submitted to your newspaper. You will explain that you fell in with some young agitators. You will admit that you abandoned the standards of proper journalism in favour of sensationalism which you hoped would get you advancement in London. We will publish this letter, expressing our regret but also our confidence that the goodwill between our two countries would remain as strong as ever. El Presidente will then invite the British Ambassador to the Palace and convey his displeasure. You will then have a further twelve hours to leave Puerto Grande or face arrest and its consequences. And, as time is running, I suggest that you start writing."

Although he did not expect a love-in with Raul, Conway was taken aback by the ferocity of Raul's reaction. He saw that it would be pointless to seek to respond, far less, argue. After a long pause, he simply said, "I hear what you say, Señor Salcedo" and turned on his heels. Not entirely sure that a knife wouldn't bury itself in his back, he opened the door, nodded to the guard and left.

Conway had twelve hours. He was never going to write any letter. He didn't think Salcedo really expected him to - Salcedo would favour the prison option. Conway didn't fancy going to jail nor what Salcedo had in mind for him once he was inside. So, he had to go underground. Cesar's plans for him contemplated this. They just had to be put into operation rather more urgently - and with great care. Raul's watchers would be all over him like a rash. He had to get word to Cesar. Cesar would know what to do to. But how to contact Cesar? He could try to get in touch with Atilio or one of the people he'd met through the Circulo, but that risked exposing them. It was not an option. Moreover, he accepted that he may have read a book about spying, but he was no spy himself. He had to admit to himself that he was out of his depth in that department.

The Bar on the corner of the Plaza was called the Bodega La Esperanza (The Hope Bar). Was this a sign Conway asked himself as he pushed aside the bead curtains and went inside? He ordered a beer. "Just the one", he thought - he needed a clear head. He settled himself and looked around. There was hardly anyone in the Bar but he assumed a watcher or two was nearby. He thought of going to the bathroom, climbing out of the window and going to ground but dismissed the idea. He didn't know if there was a window. He didn't know if he could climb through it, if there was. And he didn't know what he would do once he'd got out. So, it was a stupid idea, even if it worked in the films.

Nursing his beer, he floundered about in his head for ways of escape. Suddenly, he thought of Jeremy Brown. Embassies abroad existed among other things to look after Brits in distress. He was a Brit in distress and Jeremy was on HMG's service. The flaw was that Jeremy had not exactly been warm about his piece in the Globe - damage to trade talks and all that. Why would Jeremy damage the talks more by helping him? An answer occurred to him which he thought might work.

Conway telephoned Jeremy from the Bar and spoke to Rebecca, Brown's secretary.

"Hi. Becky, it's Tony Conway. Yes, it is hot today. Listen, can you please tell Jeremy that I've just been given a significant bollocking (pardon my French) by Raul Salcedo. I need to speak to Jeremy and the Ambassador to find a way of repairing any damage. I'm coming straight over to the Embassy. Meanwhile, could Jeremy, please contact Salcedo and say that you've heard from me and I'm extremely contrite. Jeremy should reassure Salcedo that everything will be straightened out."

He took a taxi to the Embassy and told the guard he was expected. Recognising him, the guard let him through. Conway realised that it was not at all a sure thing that Jeremy would go along with his plan. If he did, the next step was even trickier. Once he was safe in the Embassy, he needed a way to get out and go into hiding.

Conway needed Cesar's help: he needed to make contact. He settled on a plan. He decided to ask Jeremy to contact someone at the Circulo such as Teresa, and say that he was calling on behalf of the British Council. Jeremy was to say that the British Council wants very much to organise some Lectures on 'History across the Ages' and that someone had mentioned starting with the Roman chap, Suetonius. Jeremy needs to say that he understands there's a Professor Sanchez who visits the Circulo who might be able to give that Lecture. Given that there's some urgency in tying down the arrangements – budgets (she'll understand) - could she please get Professor Sanchez to contact Jeremy Brown at the British Embassy as a matter of urgency?

Conway and Brown sat in the same room as before. As he outlined his plan, Brown listened open-mouthed.

"Whatever possessed you to think I'd involve myself in such a hair-brained scheme? I don't understand a word of what you've been saying nor do I wish to. I did not call Salcedo as you suggested, nor will I. You must get yourself out of the mess you've created without my help". Dropping into full diplomat-speak, he went on "I will do nothing that imperils the warm relations that Her Majesty's Government enjoys with the government of Caribe."

Brown was somewhat taken aback by Conway's response. "Yeah, Yeah, I know. Queen and bloody Country and all that. Get real, Jeremy. They're all crooks."

Brown blinked and had just got out the words "I say...", when Conway went on,

"One of your jobs, Jeremy, is to protect us Brits and I'm a Brit who needs protection. Salcedo is going to throw me into jail and then do what he and his charming associates do to people in jail, if I don't write a letter saying that I got it all wrong. As you probably know from your sources, I didn't get it all, or, for that matter, any of it wrong. So, I need help. I plan to go underground. There's revolution in the air and I'm going to tell the world. You don't need to know the details. Indeed, it's best if you don't. But if you make the call I just spelled out, I'll be spirited away in one way or another. You will then report that I scarpered while you left me alone – further evidence if it were needed of the decline in standards of modern journalism. Salcedo will rail, but he knows which side his bread is buttered on. He won't let anything get in the way of the trade talks. You will persuade him it will all blow over - tomorrow's fish and chip paper and all that, though Salcedo may not get the image."

Jeremy sighed. "Here goes my career, such as it is. Sit over there and don't say or do anything. I presume something will happen. I don't want to know. I will tell my staff, if anyone asks, that you are just visiting and will be gone soon." Then Jeremy made the phone calls. First, to Salcedo,

"I'm sure things can be worked out. Look I'm so sorry, Señor Salcedo. A free press is one thing, a press that takes unwarranted liberties is another."

Raul thanked him and suggested they talk further once Señor Conway had written his second piece recanting the first.

Then Jeremy to Teresa, relaying the message as directed. Teresa thanked him. "I'll contact Señorita Echevarria straightaway".

Chapter 16

Lydia gets help

In fact, Lydia was ahead of them. Raul had called her an hour earlier in a foul mood.

"What do you think of your wonderful Englishman now? You've seen the piece he wrote. He probably showed it to you, come to think of it. Well, he's finished. He's as good as dead. I'm going to enjoy putting him in prison and letting Alberto loose on him".

"Raul, he's not 'my wonderful Englishman'. I haven't seen or spoken to him since that awful business at my party. I don't know what you're talking about. You're being ridiculous."

Raul slammed the phone down.

She immediately called Melba. "Could you please contact Cesar and ask him to come to the Circulo as soon as he can – it's urgent, Melba".

Melba grabbed her bag and flew out of the door.

Lydia put on some old blue slacks, a dark blue blouse and some white pumps. The aim was to look inconspicuous; she didn't want the watchers to report to Raul that she'd got dressed up and gone out. That would make him even more angry. Of course, the reality was that she'd look beautiful whatever she'd got on. She took the lift to the car park and climbed into the Buick.

Traffic was heavy. By the time she reached the Circulo, Cesar was already there. He was explaining to Teresa and the others that he'd taken half a day off - the first time in a long time – so that he could plan some Lectures with Señorita Lydia. They nodded and smiled. 'Poor, lonely love-sick old boy' was what they were thinking.

Lydia greeted Cesar warmly. "Professor, thank you so much for coming. We have such a lot to do."

"Please call me Cesar", he urged. The staff suffered for him.

"Come on, Professor", she said over her shoulder as she ushered him into her office.

Once inside, she closed the door and they embraced.

"They think you are in love with me and I'm a heartless brute for addressing you so formally", she said and smiled warmly.

"I am in love with you and you are a heartless brute. But there we are. Now, what can I do for you, Lydia my dear?"

"We'll talk about love another time. Right now there's an emergency. Raul is very angry about the piece that Tony Conway wrote. I know that you helped him a great deal. It was a great success in raising the profile of the struggle, but Raul is out for blood – Tony's blood. I have a soft spot for Tony. I've had to give up meeting him because of Raul's ridiculous possessiveness, but I still keep an eye on what he's doing, without him knowing, of course. He thinks I've gone bad, corrupted by Raul. It makes me sad, but it comes with the territory I've chosen. Now, back to the present. I know how important Tony is to your plans. I don't know where he is but he's in danger. You must protect him. It means that he'll have to go underground earlier than you planned."

Cesar nodded.

There was a knock at the door. Cesar immediately began to talk about a class he was planning on Lucretius as Lydia went to open it. It was Teresa. She relayed the phone conversation that she'd had with a person named Jeremy something at the British Embassy. At the mention of Suetonius, Cesar clapped his hands.

"Wonderful. Marvellous. A Lecture on Suetonius. I would love to do that Señorita Lydia. Yes, wonderful!"

"Teresa, I think you can tell the man from the Embassy that Professor Sanchez will be pleased to deliver a Lecture. You don't need to describe how he skipped for joy", she teased. "And please tell the man that we will be in touch very shortly."

When Teresa had left and the door was closed again Lydia raised an eyebrow.

"Ah, Yes," Cesar responded. "You don't need to know the details, but my enthusiasm was not entirely false. The message means that we know where Señor Conway is. He's with the British diplomat in the British Embassy. We have to get him out of there quickly and hide him. We have to come up with a plan."

She nodded, understanding that some coded message must have been passed to Cesar. She marvelled at his calm decisiveness. She saw what Ramon had seen in him. Like Ramon, she loved him too - a brilliant man capable of so many things.

He was soon out of the office, blowing a kiss to her which caused her to wag her finger at him to general amusement. As she stood at her door, he called Teresa over.

"Is your young man Patricio around, please? I'd like him to go on an errand for me, if he'd be so kind."

Teresa said that she was sure that he would but that he wasn't her 'young man'. "Not everyone round here is love-sick, Professor," she teased.

"At your service, Professor". Patricio had appeared from a back room followed by the noise which he called making music.

"Ah, my dear Patricio." Cesar put his arm on Patricio's shoulder and guided him to a quiet corner. "Patricio, please get a message to our friend.

The English is in the British Embassy. Our friend must get him out and get him underground. And he must not embarrass the Embassy. Now, repeat what I told you."

Patricio did so. Cesar suddenly laughed aloud and said for all to hear, "And what did *she* say?"

Patricio laughed too. "Wait for the next instalment, Professor", he shouted as he left.

Teresa was intrigued. "What was that all about, Professor", she asked.

"Oh nothing", Cesar replied. "He's still your man!" Teresa began to deny it but he had wandered out of the door smiling and waving.

Chapter 17

Conway at the Embassy

Conway needed to get out of the Embassy and hide somewhere for a while. He had to believe that Cesar would get the message and be able to pull it off.

His confidence was not misplaced. Gaudi was in a safe house in a side street just off the Plaza Garibaldi. More exactly, it was a garage with three ways in and out. There was a cot bed, a table and chair. Three telephones sat side by side on the table. Guards stood inside at each door. Another three lounged at a table in a bar on the Calle Florida with a view of two entrances to the garage. The third entrance was covered by two men apparently working on a car with the hood up.

Gaudi went into action the moment he received Cesar's message. He put the word out that he needed someone who knew the layout of the British Embassy. Within half an hour Nino had phoned him. Nino was the most senior of his lieutenants. He had fought his way out of the Barrio La Joya, home to Luis and his family. Determined to better himself, he'd joined the union at seventeen. When he met him, Gaudi had spotted his intelligence, his ambition and his ruthlessness and brought him into his inner circle. Still only a young man of twenty-seven, he was Gaudi's 'go-to' man. Tall, slim, carefully turned-out, with skin the colour of café-au-lait and with the darkest eyes, he was undoubtedly handsome. He had a ready smile which did not wholly disguise the toughness underneath.

Nino told Gaudi, "I've found someone who used to work at the Embassy as a gardener".

Gaudi was impressed. "Excellent. Can he be trusted?"

"Yes. He works at the sugar factory now. He's one of us".

"Good. Here's what you have to do. I want to find a way out for Conway which looks like he's escaped. So it has to be over a wall or something like that. Then I want him picked up and taken to Rio Culebra. There'll be someone at the church who'll look after things from there. I'll leave the arrangements to you. Talk to your man and find out the best way out. Then let me know. I'll get the message to Conway."

After a few minutes, Nino telephoned back. "There's a wall in the corner of the garden which is covered with purple bougainvillea. The English will have to pull it aside. Tell him to wear gloves - the thorns on the bougainvillea are really mean. The wall isn't high. The English should be able to climb over it. There will need to be a car waiting for him. My man suggests just after midnight. You'll need to check about security patrols."

"Thank you, Nino. Good work. I'll find out about security then give you the precise time. Call me in half an hour".

Gaudi's contact in police headquarters told him that the police drove round the perimeter of the Embassy every hour on the hour - it took no more than five minutes.

When Nino phoned back, Gaudi told him to have the car waiting after midnight as soon as the police patrol had passed the wall and gone around the corner. He then wrote a message setting out what had to be done. One of the guards took the motorbike from the garage and drove to the Embassy with an envelope marked 'Special Delivery - for Jeremy Brown's eyes only' - Gaudi had checked the name that Teresa had given him. After some argument, the envelope was accepted by the Embassy guard and taken inside.

The guard handed it to Brown when he came down. He took it back to his office and opened it cautiously. Inside was another envelope marked 'For Conway's eyes only'. Brown was in two minds. He hated the idea of things being done behind his back particularly if they could blow up in his face and embarrass him and the Embassy. But, he also recognised the benefit of not knowing what was going on so that he could claim later that he was duped. The latter reasoning won the day.

Conway was still sitting in Brown's office reading whatever he could find to pass the time - at this point it was 'The Glories of the English Riviera' with several flattering photographs of Torquay - the Imperial Hotel, the Harbour, Torre Abbey, Babbacombe beach. Brown held out the envelope.

"For you", Brown said. "I don't want to know. I trust it relates to your leaving here."

Conway read and re-read it. "Thanks. Yes, it does. Is there a place I could hole up in the garden till I leave? I want to get out of your hair as soon as possible."

"There's a gardener's shed somewhere at the back of the garden which I'm sure you can make yourself at home in till, as you say, you leave. I don't want to know how," he added loudly.

"Great. Thanks so much Jeremy. You've been an absolute star. I won't breathe a word, but one day I'm sure you'll get your reward"

"At this point, I don't want a reward. I just want to keep my pension".

* * * * *

It was eight in the morning. Conway had slept like a baby for four hours with the blanket as a pillow after his escape from the Embassy as the getaway car headed south. While he was just setting off on the next stage of what he'd called his "adventure, Jeremy Brown was telephoning Raul's office.

"I'm afraid to have to tell you, Señor Salcedo, that Señor Conway absconded from the Embassy during the night. The Ambassador will, of course, apologise in person to El Presidente and make the strongest possible representations to Conway's employers. I do hope that you and the President will accept my profound apologies. I am sure that this minor affair need not interfere with the smooth progress of our current trade negotiations".

"Thank you for calling me", Raul responded. "I accept your apology, Señor Brown. And, I appreciate the offer, but here is no need to trouble the President".

Raul reasoned that it was best for the President to know as little as possible. Raul fumed inside but knew that there was nothing to be gained from picking a fight with Brown. He needed the trade negotiations to succeed, but the real target was "that damned Conway" and those whom he was supporting. They must be hunted down.

As a final coda, during the night, a car had drawn up outside the Hotel Valencia. Two men carrying bags had shown passes which looked genuine to the woman on duty at Reception and had gone up to Conway's room. They collected up his belongings. They would be taken to Rio Culebra. Gaudi knew that Conway could not do his job without his personal effects around him. It was a thoughtful thing to do, but the thoughtfulness was about Gaudi's needs not Conway's.

Chapter 18

The Road to La Fortaleza

After six hours of driving Conway was delivered by Gaudi's men to the people waiting at the church in Rio Culebra. Dawn was just breaking. The church stood in the middle of a dusty road lined with flamboyant trees with their magnificent red flowers. There were a few houses, what looked like a shop, and a Bar. That was it. He really was in the middle of nowhere.

His new guides and protectors introduced themselves. They were both women, sisters, Ines and Sylvia Fonseca. They looked like teenagers, not the rugged mountain fighters that he had imagined. Before he was able to indulge his prejudices any further, the two had kissed goodbye to the driver and his colleague and had pressed a rucksack on him. They were all business, as if to say this isn't a Sunday School outing.

"There's some water and food and a pair of boots in the bag." This was Ines. "You may want to put the boots on now. We will be walking for a couple of hours before we reach camp. We may bump into one of the Rurales' patrols. So, no talking, and If we come across one, do exactly what you are told. Now, let's go."

Conway changed into the boots and hurried after them, strapping on the rucksack as he went. This was to be his new life for the next several months, he thought. He felt exhilarated. The march took him away from the little town into hilly country, dotted with little fields of sugar cane and groves of banana trees. They skirted the dwellings, keeping out of sight. Not all of the locals were sympathetic, Ines explained. They feared what any change, or worse, upheaval would do to their fragile hold on survival. They preferred the devil they knew.

Camp turned out to be a large shack in a clearing bordered on all sides by lush vegetation. Tall ceiba and avocado trees provided shade and also cover from any spotter plane that the army might use when things became more serious. There was a main living room with a kitchen attached and five other rooms used as bedrooms. The bathroom was outside at the back, as was the shower. Conway's room was clean and tidy which was not hard when there was only a single bed, a table and chair and a small wardrobe which stood in the corner, ready for his clothes once he had more than the ones he stood up in. He cheered up when Ines told him that his belongings from the hotel were on their way, including his books and notes and typewriter. They already had a good supply of paper, she added.

His despatches - this was the word that Ines used and which he adopted - should be given to her or one of her colleagues.

"They'll be taken to a safe house and then sent to your Globe by a secure means that you don't need to know about. Salcedo's men, the Rurales and soon the army will be combing the island to find you and to intercept the despatches, but they won't succeed. When the time comes, we'll move you to La Fortaleza where we'll launch the armed struggle. Then, as the struggle intensifies, you will move with us so you can report from where the action is. We're making arrangements to establish more camps and ways of getting the despatches delivered".

All of this was delivered with clipped military precision. Clearly, Ines was someone to be reckoned with.

* * * * *

As predicted, in the face of the growing concern at the breakdown of order and the apparent inability of the police and Rurales (not to mention Raul) to do anything about it, the President had called on the army to 'root out' the 'agitators and traitors'. He ordered them to 'do whatever is necessary'. Civil rights (such as they were) were suspended. Martial law was declared across large parts of the island.

The President's response played directly into the hands of the insurgents. Gaudi issued a call to arms. The Diario and radio stations refused to report it but posters, leaflets and graffiti all carried the message – 'El Presidente's days are numbered - the people are taking up arms against his corrupt regime'. Young people were urged to take to the streets in shows of solidarity. A pirate radio station began broadcasting, calling on members of the police, the Rurales and the armed forces to abandon El Presidente and come and join the revolt. The implication was clear. Barbosa should realise that the uprising was everywhere. There was no need to tell people how to join the insurgents – they already knew.

Conway reported these developments. His despatches, once published in the Globe, were picked up across the world, sometimes as minor items on the back pages, sometimes, especially in the United States and parts of Europe, with growing interest and concern. And with that interest came growing pressure on President Barbosa.

As promised, Conway was in La Fortaleza when the armed struggle was declared. He'd been driven there overnight in an old truck loaded with fertilizer, installed in a sack with air holes, amongst the other sacks. At the checkpoints set up by the Rurales and the army, the driver, an old farmer named Jaime, with his wife Cecilia, exchanged greetings with the guards.

"You're all doing a fine job, young men, making sure law-abiding people like us can carry on our business", Cecilia shouted through the window as Jaime nodded agreement. "You want some beans and rice and a tot of rum?"

They were waved through with grateful thanks.

After four hours, they rolled into La Fortaleza and drove into a warehouse by the docks. Conway was extricated from his sack and gulped down the fresh air, tasting the sea on it. Jaime and Cecilia said goodbye and drove off without another word. New people took him in hand. There were no introductions. He was told that he would be taken to a safe house once it was dark. He was to remain where he was until then. They gave him a bottle of beer and a sandwich of soft goat cheese and drove off.

Conway sat in a corner, hoping that his typewriter and papers, as well as his other stuff, would also reach La Fortaleza. A figure appeared through the gloom. Before he had any chance to react, the figure came hurrying over to him and embraced him. It was Atilio. He'd made his way across the island to join the others, handed on from contact to contact. Conway was delighted to see a familiar face. He hadn't seen Atilio since he'd had to take refuge in the Embassy. It was good to see him well and active and, with time to kill, Conway peppered him with questions. Atilio had remained under cover in Puerto Grande until it had become too dangerous, so naturally Conway wanted to know what he had been doing and how the struggle was perceived in the city. They talked for hours, while he took notes on the back of order forms lying about in the warehouse. An insider's story would go down well with the Globe, lending authenticity to the despatches he was filing.

Once taken to his new digs, as he thought of them, he put together two despatches. The first described the first-hand experiences of a rebel (giving Atilio the name Geronimo in a moment of romanticism) who described life in the capital under martial law and the escape to La Fortaleza to take up arms. The second despatch was marked as 'From La Fortaleza' and described how he had been brought there (no details) and how he would be reporting the campaign as the rebels advanced against the government. He gave both despatches to Ines who had arrived a few hours earlier. Then, after another beer and another sandwich, he settled down under his mosquito net to spend his first night as a war correspondent.

The next day he got his scoop. Gaudi had arrived in La Fortaleza with truck-loads of supporters, armed to the teeth with a variety of weapons, including small arms stolen from army garrisons. The police and Rurales had melted away in the face of the show of force. The closest army garrison was twenty miles away in San Cristobel. The rebels' sudden appearance in the sleepy coastal town had taken them by surprise. Urgent messages were passing between the army, the local police, now ensconced six miles inland in the police barracks in Vallejo, and the government in Puerto Grande.

Gaudi wasted no time. Momentum was everything. He addressed the small crowd which had gathered. His staff had made sure that the local radio stations and newspapers would run the report that they helpfully provided. "The armed struggle against the evils of the President and his corrupt gang has begun", Gaudi declared, promising "a rapid victory" and then a government which would "end poverty and bring education for our young people and jobs for our workers".

For his part, Conway allowed himself to reflect, "Let's see!"

For the next five months, from the end of the summer, through the hurricane season, the winter and the spring, he kept the world informed of the struggle.

Chapter 19

'Events' at the Circulo

Lydia watched as the revolt gathered pace with a growing sense of satisfaction, even pride, tinged with concern for the safety of Cesar and his network. She was not concerned for herself. She had chosen this path. She had made her promise to Ramon, after the two promises, first to him then to herself, that she had failed to keep. She would get justice for him and for those he stood for.

She decided it was crucial that the Circulo carried on despite the government's crackdown. It was the only way that she could feed information to Cesar. He had stayed in the city rather than join Gaudi in La Fortaleza. The struggle needed people, money, arms and information. These were Cesar's responsibilities. She was a vital source of information. But, he was out in San Rafael and, because he was watched, he needed to carry on working in the fields. His visits to the Circulo, therefore, as cover for their meetings were crucial even if increasingly dangerous.

Lydia decided to speak to Raul. She had invited him for coffee, so that, as she put it, he could escape for a while from the pressure he was under from all the things that were going on. Unusually, Raul had accepted. He was tired and needed a break. He left Alberto downstairs in the lobby and went up to the apartment. They sat facing each other in the living room in comfortable armchairs. She had on her uniform of blouse and jeans with a ribbon holding her hair back. Raul, as ever, was dressed formally - dark suit, white shirt and blue tie. His shoes were immaculately polished. Melba, always on the alert when Raul was around, had brought them coffee and some mallorquinas and then retired to the kitchen leaving the door ajar. The bright morning light was diffused through the blinds - picking up motes of dust as they danced in the air. It was quiet without being peaceful.

Before long, Lydia had moved the conversation to the Circulo.

"I know you think the Circulo is just a folly – that the sort of things we do are a waste of time – but I want to help you", she urged on him.

"What can you do? How is sitting around talking about books and putting on lectures about people who've been dead for thousands of years going to help me put that bastard Gaudi in a coffin," he muttered between clenched teeth. "And sometimes, you know", half wearily, half angrily, "I wonder whether in fact I can really trust you – whether you secretly support what Gaudi and his gang are doing – that you still carry a torch for that hot-head. You had his photograph hidden away, for God's sake".

It had been a while since Raul had questioned her loyalty. It was usually when he felt particularly threatened and wanted to lash out. She knew the signs and knew how to deal with them.

"Don't be so silly, Raul. You really can be ridiculous sometimes. Here I am sitting in an apartment with you, asking about how I can help you and you still want to bring up the past. It's the past, my dear Raul. You know that hot-head as you call him was just an infatuation – the appeal of opposites. I've grown out of it. I'm Raul's woman, happy to grace his arm, charm his friends, even if some of them are somewhat unsavoury, and spend his money." She said the last with a laugh in her voice. "Now, let's get back to what I was talking about, or do you still want to pout and distrust me?"

Few would have dared to be so direct. Raul was, as all agreed, unpredictable. It wasn't wise to cross him. But, at the same time he exuded a strange sense of dependency. Gradually, subtly, Lydia had begun to shift the balance of power and control in her direction. Raul needed her. He could speak to her without fear of being shouted at as he was by El Presidente, the Americans, and all the others who were on his back. She was on his side, or at least not against him – when most were. He knew that she had not forgotten what had happened in that room all those months ago. He knew that her conversion to 'Raul's woman' did not make sense. But, then, he did not understand women. And, more important, he wanted to believe that she was his woman. He wanted to believe that she had moved on from the hot-head; that she, at least, was there for him. Believing filled the emptiness where his soul was supposed to be.

She let the silence hang. She could almost feel the tension, the tug-of-war between Raul's doubts and his almost child-like wish to be free of the distrust and betrayal and pain which increasingly constituted his world.

"So, alright. Talk to me. Tell me what you have in mind. I've told Alberto to wait. And before you talk, get me some more coffee."

"Of course, my dear," Lydia replied warmly. She had won. He wanted to stay, to be safe with her. She understood that the order to bring him coffee was his attempt to regain control. She played along with it.

She put the fresh coffee on a side table and granted him one of her million dollar smiles. Then, sitting down and crossing her elegant legs, she began, twisting a strand of hair as she spoke.

"Well. Here's what I've been thinking. What I want, as I've said, is to help; to help you, and to help our little island which is going through a rough patch. I want all those business people and Americans you spend so much time with to believe in us. So, how about if we use the Circulo to put on 'events' for them every couple of weeks? There would be drinks and dinner and some music and dancing and, perhaps, a show of paintings or photographs. Of course, most of those we invite would just come for the free drinks and dinner, but we could invite some of the Circulo's regulars, especially the girls, to liven things up".

"We'd be saying that life goes on in Puerto Grande. Your businessmen and Americans will see us having fun. We'll show them we're not put off by a few misguided young men with straggly beards trying to stir up trouble. Yes, we've got martial law for a while till you get on top of things, but we've also got exhibitions and music and dinners and a civilised life".

Almost as an afterthought she added, "Of course, I'll need some money, Raul, to do these things but it will be money well spent I think."

She paused. Would Raul embrace her idea? Or would he dismiss it as the sort of thing a society woman would think of as the rebels inched their way forward – tea and cakes and conversation to persuade the businessmen that the strikes and disruption, not to mention the bullets, were no more than minor inconveniences, soon to be dealt with like a case of measles?

Raul stared at her for a while. She knew what he was thinking – would she actually like him if he agreed. He wanted her to like him. That was her victory – the great reversal of roles that she had painstakingly engineered since coming to Roosevelt Tower. He still thought she was his to command. But, any acute observer would have seen the opposite.

Finally he spoke. "OK. Go ahead, my dear. I don't think it'll make a damned bit of difference, but it might keep a few of my tormentors onside and it will give you another opportunity to spend my money".

She had won again. She jumped to her feet, all enthusiasm and smiles. She planted a big kiss on his cheek. "Thank you, Raul. I'm really grateful. Now, go back to your office," she continued, shooing him out of the apartment. "I have work to do. The first meeting is next Wednesday. There's no time to lose.

"What? Don't look at me like that", she laughed. "I knew you'd say yes, so I've already started to plan. And, yes, you are free on Wednesday – I made sure of it".

Raul frowned and then permitted himself his smile. Let her have her little victory.

Chapter 19

A second front

Once on her own, Lydia went back to her thoughts. How could she help 'the cause' as she thought of it? There was the intelligence which she continued to glean from mixing with Raul and those she saw as courtiers around Barbosa - the pinch points in the economy, problems of supplies, difficulties in shipping - all of which were passed on to the union leaders and suitably exploited. Strikes were called, supplies, particularly of fuel, went missing, truck-drivers were intimidated if they didn't cooperate with the union.

But Lydia wanted more. With the call to arms in La Fortaleza, there had to be more she could do. There had to be a second front; an attack from inside the capital to assist the one from outside. Her solution was simple – hostages. She would put together a team to kidnap wives and children of the Americans and of the local business leaders and hold them as hostages. Nothing, she thought, would undermine trust in the government and in Raul in particular more quickly than if wives and children could not be protected. The hostages were not to be harmed. They were to be treated as she was treated. She smiled to herself at the added satisfaction of paying Raul back, if only vicariously, for what he had done to her.

The 'events' she planned to hold at the Circulo would be the key to the plan's success. She would take advantage of meeting whoever might come, and of the conversations she would have with them, to identify suitable targets. She would learn about routines; nannies, schools, favourite shopping destinations, security arrangements at home, and all the other things that would allow for a successful kidnap. She would then pass the information to Cesar. Ransoms could be demanded which would help the cause financially. But far more important, the victims, or rather their husbands and fathers, would lose even more confidence than they currently had in the ability of the government to govern. And, of course, there would be a huge backlash from the police which would alienate the general population even more.

The 'events' worked better than Lydia had dared to hope. After a slow start, more and more people had been drawn to the chance to eat and drink and talk (not many danced) and forget the world for a few hours. The men drank and smoked and played pool in one of the back rooms. The woman gossiped and complained about how hard it was to get good staff and what a pain it was that the locals didn't speak American.

Lydia had taken Cesar aside on one of his visits – he was supposed to be giving a Seminar on "The contribution of Lucretius to the theory of the atom". She told him that she had postponed the Seminar because it clashed with one of her forthcoming 'events'. As she drew him into her office and closed the door, he asked "What 'events', chica?"

She sat him down in one of the armchairs and fetched him a cup of coffee. "You look tired, viejo. Take care of yourself. We need you".

"I *am* tired. Cutting sugar is young man's work. I'll try to take care of myself, though I'd try harder if I was more than just needed. I'd like to be hugged or even loved occasionally."

She had never seen this side of him before. He was always the joking, smiling teacher, or the serious revolutionary. What she saw now was a lonely man, his family dead, cut off from the teaching he loved, and dedicated selflessly to a cause which brought only struggle and danger. She threw her arms around him, tears welling in her eyes.

"We have each other, my beautiful, lovely Cesar. It doesn't matter that no-one else knows what we do. We don't do things for ourselves. We believe in something. We fight for it. And, we'll win."

She held his scarred, calloused hands in hers and looked into those blue eyes which currently had lost their sparkle.

"Smile for me, viejo. That will make it right for both of us".

"Less of the 'viejo' señorita", he snorted and gave her a smile. They embraced, holding on to each other, taking refuge in each other.

Breaking off eventually, Cesar sat down and said, "Now, tell me about these 'events'. What do you want me to do?"

Lydia explained her plan. Cesar was impressed at how simple it was yet how devastating it could be. He also saw what needed to be done.

"I'll have to put a team together and train them how to do a kidnap and I'll have to find a safe house where the hostages can be kept. It's not going to be easy with the police and the Rurales all over us. But, my dear Señorita Lydia, we'll do it". Dangerous as it was, he seemed invigorated by having a new challenge to meet.

They agreed that the Circulo would be the base for recruiting the team. Cesar was watched wherever he went. The Circulo was about the only place where he could organise what needed to be done. His attendance was seen by his watchers as benign. They just reported that he'd been, stayed for a couple of hours and then gone home. It was seen as a sad pilgrimage to a world which otherwise no longer had a place for him.

Over the months, the initial hostility both towards her, following her taking up with Raul and moving to Roosevelt Tower, and towards the Circulo had faded. The Circulo had become an established part of Puerto Grande's cultural life. Young people were increasingly coming and going, for lectures, meetings, music and the general companionship that it offered. There was still an emphasis on Latin and languages but there was much more besides. New members were regularly signing up, so no-one paid any attention to a group of four who had recently joined. They included a couple of young men who seemed obsessed with fast cars. They weren't the usual sort - one asked whether the forthcoming lecture on Julius Caesar was in honour of the guy who invented the fancy Mexican salad (he'd been a chef for a while) - but they were made welcome nonetheless. Circe would hang out with them from time to time. They seemed to spend most of their time in a back room poring over street maps. To enquirers they explained they were organising a road race which they hoped the city would agree to if the Circulo sponsored it. People nodded and left them to it.

In fact, the group was the kidnap team. During one of his visits to see Lydia, Cesar made a show of introducing himself. The team were sitting in the café area drinking Coca Cola, chatting with some of the girls. Cesar ambled over. He said that he'd heard about the proposed road race and had had an idea. Did they think the cars could be made to look like chariots like in that movie Ben Hur? It *was* the Circulo Latino after all. The group smiled indulgently. "Well, it's an idea," one of them said, "as long as I get to be Charlton Heston. I've got the body for it". The others guffawed and threw stuff at him.

"Hey, why don't you come on back, Señor, and we'll show you the plans," another of them said.

"I'd love to and please call me Cesar. Everyone does. Except Señorita Lydia", he added, contriving a hint of sadness in his voice.

Once in the back room, alone with them, Cesar embraced each in turn. He thanked them warmly for joining the struggle. Their job would be dangerous but very important. They all came highly recommended by his contacts. They shuffled uncomfortably and said that they were honoured to do their part.

Conscious that they could be interrupted at any moment, Cesar said,

"Let's get down to business. These are the targets of the first two kidnaps, the date, where they should be snatched, and the location of the safe house. The precise details are for you to work out. No-one is to be harmed," he emphasised. "Wear masks at all times. In the safe house, the hostages should be put in the room I've marked on the plan of the house you've got. As you can see, it has no windows. There's a bathroom next to the room; its windows are boarded up". Turning to Pablo and Jaime, two of the drivers, he told them, "You should melt back into your usual world until I contact you again. You others will stay with the hostages and remain on guard until you get fresh instructions. All understood?"

They all nodded. There was silence for a moment. Things had suddenly become serious. Then they stood and each shook Cesar's hand. As if on cue they began to laugh and clap Cesar on the back as they wandered out of the room. "Yeah, Yeah, old man," one of them was saying, as Cesar continued to insist that making the cars look like chariots would make the race more authentic.

* * * * *

After five 'events' over a period of two months, Lydia had decided on her first two targets. She chose well. Mary Baxter was the wife of an American banker who travelled a lot, as she had put it. She clearly suspected that Mr Baxter did not devote his energies exclusively to Mrs Baxter. Mary was in her mid-forties and staring into the abyss of middle-aged loneliness. Her visits to the events at the Circulo were clearly a high point in a drab life. Indeed she had asked if she could join one of the study groups, having been introduced to a sculptor named Octavio Flores.

"Honey, he's an artist and you know what that means", she told her friend Alice breathlessly and with hope in her heart.

Another attraction of the 'events' was the booze. Mary found that a couple of rum and tonics took the edge off things. Conversation became easier and she could forget she was married to a cheating bastard. Thankfully, he was always busy or travelling when the 'events' were on, which meant that Mary could be on her own in the crowd for a while.

One evening, Lydia joined Mary and a couple of others at a table, bringing over a tray of drinks 'courtesy of the Circulo'. They were all bosom buddies in no time. Giving her apparently undivided attention to Mary,

Lydia had no trouble in learning of Mary's love of a particular restaurant '"with the cutest waiters"'.

"I'm a real regular now," she gushed. "I go every Thursday without fail. I have to leave at two on the dot, unfortunately – I could spend all afternoon watching those waiters, honey – but I have to get back home to let the cleaner in. You can't give them a key, can you? You just can't trust 'em."

Betty Lloyd was also a perfect target. Joyce Lloyd came to the Circulo to "indulge mahself in some culture" she confided in her broad North Carolina accent. In fact, culture never got a look in. When Lydia sat with her, all Joyce did was to talk non-stop about "mah baby Betty". Betty was ten years old and Joyce and Greg's only child. "They told me after the surgery – no more kids for you." So Betty was her life, Greg being another who was regularly absent Stateside, at his law firm's main office in Raleigh. Without prompting, Lydia learned the minutest details of Betty's life. Her visit to her friend's house on Thursdays was just one such detail.

"I let her walk, honey, 'cause it's just a hundred yards or so and it's down a quiet little street with no cars. It does her good to have a bit of independence, as long as it's safe, of course. It's still safe, you know, but, ah don't know what we'll do if those madmen in the hills start coming our way. But Greg says they won't and he knows about those sorts of things."

It was just after two-o-clock. After lunch at her restaurant, Mary Baxter was walking back to her car down the quiet side-street where it was easier to find a place to park. She was wondering whether that third rum and tonic had been wise. A young man stopped in front of her, a hat pulled low over his face and spoke to her in rapid Spanish. Flustered, she stopped and began to try to explain that she didn't understand. Her confusion was compounded by the fact that another young man and what appeared to be his girl-friend had taken her by each arm and lifted her off her feet as a car drew alongside. They both had scarves over their faces. The car door was thrown open and she was bundled onto the back seat. Mary tried to shout out but the breath was knocked out of her when the young woman sat on her. It was Circe. She blindfolded Mary. Jaime gunned the engine and the car sped off while the two young men went on their way without acknowledging each other.

It was all over the evening news. A note had been received by Radio Central, the biggest radio station in Puerto Grande. It was from a group calling itself "The Avengers". It read "We have the Yanqui oppressor Baxter's woman. She will be returned unharmed when you pay $10,000." It was signed "Soldiers for a free Caribe".

Outrage turned to turmoil when Betty Lloyd disappeared later that same day on her way back from school. She always walked to her friend Patty's house on Thursdays – the school was close by and Patty's mother would then give her a ride home. But that Thursday she did not show up. Two men had approached Betty. A car drew up with Pablo at the wheel and she was bundled into it and sat on, this time by David, before she realised what was happening. She was blindfolded. Mario, the other man, disappeared down a side-street.

Greg and Joyce Lloyd were beside themselves. Where was she? The note delivered to Radio Central told them. It was the same as the Baxter note except that it referred to "the Yanqui oppressor Lloyd's daughter".

* * * * *

Three days later, Lydia organised a de-briefing session with Circe at the Circulo.

"Did everything go to plan, Circe? Do we have to make any changes", she asked

Circe sat sipping a cold drink of lemonade. In her quiet, serious voice, she told Lydia,

"We took the Baxter woman to the safe house outside the city. The other car soon brought the little girl Betty. The boys said everything had gone without a hitch. They climbed back into the cars, pulled the scarves off their faces, and made a bit of a show," she smiled, "throwing up gravel to make a flashy exit. Then they went back to the Barrio Catania where they both live. Pablo told me they replaced the licence plates (just in case). Then he went for a beer and Jaime went to bed".

"David and me, with our scarves on our faces, put Mary and then Betty into the room the Professor told us about and took their blindfolds off. They screamed and shouted and the little girl cried a lot. We took Mary's handbag and frisked her, then we took Betty's school bag. We didn't say a word – we just pointed to two chairs and told them to sit. Then we gave Mary the sheet of paper which the Professor had given us. She was sobering up fast by that time and was terrified. She looked at the paper and then read it out to the little girl".

"What did it say, Circe. I never saw it?"

"It was in English, so I didn't really know, but clever-clogs David speaks English and told me that it said something like, 'You are hostages. You will not be harmed provided others do as we ask. There is no point in shouting or trying to escape'. It said that there were bottles of water, and that we'd take them food. If they needed the bathroom, they had to knock three times on the door and one of us would fetch them.

"Then David and me went into the kitchen. I remember David smiling and saying, 'We did it, Circe'. I told him to calm down - it had only just started. He had to stay alert. Then I took the first watch. I went through to the room where I could see the road and the land around us and hunkered down. David, bless him, made coffee and brought me a cup. Then he went off to the bedroom and lay down and we waited."

As she listened, Lydia's admiration for Circe's calm leadership grew. "Thank you, Circe", she said. "Thank you so much. You were brilliant."

Chapter 21

Raul manages the fallout

In the aftermath of the kidnappings, the police and army rounded up the usual suspects. Beating them up and throwing them into jail didn't produce any information. No-one knew anything.

Raul was at his wits end. The business community made it clear to him in phone call after phone call and angry meeting after angry meeting that 'it had to stop'. *He* had to do something, or *they* would. The threat was not spelled out in detail and was all the more ominous for that.

El Presidente saw himself attacked on two fronts – Gaudi's men massing in the hills on the south of the island and now these kidnappings. This was on top of managing his new bride, Carmen Martinez, and the fall-out from her unlikely marriage to someone deemed unsuitable by those who saw it as their role to make such judgments. The Cardinal Archbishop had refused to let the Cathedral be used for a third time. They'd had to settle for a country church in Varadero and pass it off as 'El Presidente showing solidarity with his people'. Carmen was not amused. And then there was all this 'commotion' as she saw it, interfering with the gilded life she had imagined would be hers. Managing her would have been a full time job at the best of times. And this was not the best of times. What a mess!

Raul could see that El Presidente was beside himself. Barbosa's fuse was ordinarily pretty short. Now he looked ready to explode, banging his tiny fists on his desk and yelling at anyone who made the mistake of coming within range. Raul watched as his President berated army commanders and spent hours on the phone with the American Ambassador and business leaders seeking to reassure them. Yes, the kidnaps were a shocking development but they just showed how desperate the rebels were. He knew that Barbosa didn't even convince himself.

Two days after the kidnaps, Mary and Betty were found wandering on the highway near the airport at seven-o-clock in the morning. A taxi driver took them to the central police station, where they were taken to a conference room and offered a cold drink. Raul listened to the recording when he got to the station. It didn't make for happy listening.

"I'd like some coffee". This was the Baxter woman. "And Betty here would like a Coke, I guess - is that right, dear? We, Betty here and me, we were driven to the entrance of the airport and just left by the side of the road. Can you believe it? It was awful and nobody came to rescue us from that hell-hole. What is it with you people? Are you the police or what?" Mary was apoplectic.

"Did they hurt you, Señora Baxter?" This was Sergeant Lopez.

"No. No-body hurt us, if you don't count being snatched off the street, sat on in a car, and stuck in some Godforsaken shack."

"Did you have anything to eat?"

"Yes, they fed us, if you count rice and beans and a bread roll twice a day as feeding us. And Betty here hates beans, don't you, honey?"

Betty nodded, tears welling in her eyes.

"Did you know any of the people who kidnapped you?"

"No, I didn't, and you didn't neither, did you, dear."

Betty shook her head this time.

"Would you be able to recognise them, do you think?"

"They all wore scarves over their faces. How in God's name are we gonna recognise them. And," she added as an afterthought, "here, they gave me a note". It was in Spanish and English. She began to read it out to one of the police officers:

"It says, 'As a gesture of goodwill, we are releasing the two hostages. The corrupt government must surrender or we will take many more hostages.

From now on we will not return them'. It's signed 'Soldiers for a free Caribe'. Now what in the living hell is that all about?"

Raul had been notified at once. He let the President's office know and then went directly to the police station. Once he'd listened to the tape, he didn't hold out hope of finding out much more, but, nonetheless, went through to the room they'd been put in and sat down to question them himself. As he feared, it was soon obvious that they couldn't tell him anything useful. The kidnap had been well-organised and carried out. And the note told him that this was only the beginning. There would be more kidnaps.

Raul saw he had two choices, both of which were bad. He could call on the business community to take special precautions in the face of the threat of more kidnaps. Or he could suppress the kidnappers' note, ignore the threat it contained, claim that the kidnaps were a one-off which had failed, make clear that no ransom had been paid, and encourage everyone to carry on as normal while the President dealt with the local disturbances in the south of the island.

He explored the two options with El Presidente over the phone from the police station. Barbosa raged at him - the world was falling apart and he was to blame. If he hadn't caught the kidnappers by the end of the day, he'd be the one in jail. Raul let Barbosa get it all off his chest. It was just desperation and not a little fear. He knew that Barbosa had no-one else to turn to because he didn't trust anyone else. They were both alone, dependent on each other while they watched their world collapse around them.

Raul brought El Presidente back to the options. They both saw the first option as suicidal. It was tantamount to saying that they couldn't protect their own citizens and the business community. Business and their American supporters would bring the government down without waiting for Gaudi's revolution. They had to go with the second option – keep their nerve and carry on as if they were on top of things.

As a strategy, it might have worked had not a copy of the note which had been given to Mary Baxter been sent to Radio Central and broadcast at midday. It was picked up by the Diario which ran a special edition, condemning the kidnappers but, ominously, calling on El Presidente to "cut out this cancer threatening our island". Raul immediately worked the radio stations and gave the Diario an exclusive interview. The "so-called note" was a fiction, he said. "There was no such note. It was dreamed up by an over-enthusiastic young reporter. Yes, the kidnap was an outrage, carried out by a disaffected group of criminals. It has clearly failed. What's important", he emphasised, "is to get on with building prosperity in Caribe under the leadership of El Presidente".

The interviews took some of the sting out of the threat in the note but the mood in the capital, particularly in the Convento district and amongst the Americans in Roosevelt Tower, was one of tense unease.

Chapter 22

One more time

    Once they had been questioned, Mary and Betty had been taken home exhausted. Police guards were posted outside, more to stop journalists getting to them than to protect them. The first thing Mary did was to book a flight to New York. She would stay with her sister. She called her husband and told him that she'd had it with living in the goddamned third world. He could stay if he wanted but she was out of there.

Betty's mother, Joyce, was beside herself with relief. But for her too, the kidnap had been a step too far. Greg had flown down from Raleigh to be with her when he heard what had happened. He agreed with Joyce that she and Betty would be safer in Raleigh - they could move back into their old house which his sister was minding for them. He would have to survive in Puerto Grande on his own.

Lydia had planned another 'event' at the Circulo to take place five days after the release of Mary and Betty. She wasn't sure whether it should go ahead. The mood in the business community, especially among the Americans, was febrile. But amazingly more people than usual showed up. They all wanted to talk about what was going on and what they should do. The Circulo gave them a place to do so. She found the irony delicious. The Circulo was seen as a haven of safety even as it was the place where she plotted the downfall of everything these people stood for.

She had decided that another kidnap was required to edge people a little bit closer to panic. Again, Lydia chose carefully. It was to be a young newly-wed local girl, Soledad, the daughter of a moneyed land-owner, who had married one of Caribe's best known politicians, Leonardo Fuentes, twenty years her senior. She knew Solly from school - spoiled and addicted to shopping. So she got Solly a ticket to the forthcoming fashion show at Saks Fifth Avenue on the Avenida.

"You'll love it. I'm far too old to go but it's just right for a new bride", Lydia gushed.

Soleded needed no persuading. "I'd love to go, darling".

The ticket prompted those visiting the show to use a side door in an alley so as to avoid the crowds milling around the front doors, hoping to see someone they thought they recognised. Pablo was parked down the alley with the engine ticking over. The kidnap team was Circe, Mario and David. A cab dropped Solly off at the corner of the Avenida and the alley. Dressed in her favourite yellow linen dress, cut daringly low, and wearing a broad-brimmed straw hat, she looked fabulous. Not sure what to do, she showed a doorman on the front door her ticket.

"Where do I go," she asked.

He pointed her down the alley.

"Go through the yellow door, Señora, just a few yards down on the right".

As Solly neared the door, David, walking quickly, bumped into her. As she stumbled, Circe and Mario came alongside, their faces wrapped in scarves. Solly was lifted off her feet. The car pulled up and the back door flew open. She was inside the car with Circe on top of her and Mario beside her before she could get a scream out of her lungs. Pablo sped away. As the car hurried through the traffic, Circe put the blindfold on Solly.

"Lie still and keep quiet".

They were so pleased to have pulled off another successful grab. What they didn't know was that Soledad's father had hired a bodyguard for his daughter.

He was an ex-policeman named Lorenzo, known to everyone as 'Gordito' given the forty pounds of excess baggage he carried around his waistline.

He was not the world's greatest bodyguard – most of the good ones had been called up to form the basis of a Special Forces Group.

He'd got out of the taxi with Soledad and waited for her to go in through the front entrance. There was just time, he figured, for a quick cigarette before she found her way in through the crowd and he had to go in with her. It was while he was finding his cigarettes and then trying to get his lighter to fire up in the breeze that Soledad was snatched. When he heard the roar of the car engine in the narrow alley, he looked up and saw the car speeding off. Then he saw David walking towards him on his way to the Avenida, pulling off the scarf which covered his face.

Lorenzo drew his .38 revolver. David was about thirty feet away when he saw the gun. He turned and raced away down the alley. Lorenzo got three shots off. None hit David, but one ricocheted off a bicycle leaning against the wall and hit one of the guests who had decided to leave early and was at that moment coming out of the door. She collapsed. The bullet had torn through her thigh and she began to bleed heavily. Lorenzo, who was not too quick-thinking at the best of times, wrestled with what to do – should he chase after the guy running away or should he look after the woman whom he'd just shot and was now lying on the ground screaming? He opted for the latter. He didn't want to have someone die because of him. He'd never work again.

Lorenzo, the police, the emergency services, staff from Saks and from the fashion show were all trying to do something. In the end, the medics got control. They put a tourniquet on the woman's leg to stem the bleeding and took her off to the Santa Trinidad Hospital. The police took over. Eventually, Lorenzo was able to get through to them the fact that he had been guarding Dona Soledad (or "supposed to be guarding" as one police officer put it), that she'd been kidnapped, that he'd shot at one of the kidnappers who'd escaped, and that, unfortunately, one of the shots had hit that poor woman. The police called for a roadblock but Lorenzo's description – a young male with a scarf on his face – wasn't exactly gold dust in helping them to find him.

Meanwhile, Pablo delivered Solly and his fellow kidnappers to the safe house and drove off.

Circe guided Soledad into the room where the others had been kept and took her blindfold off. She frisked her and took her handbag - it was a Gucci bag. Circe had heard of them but had never seen one before -it looked just like any other bag. Soledad started to shout and threaten - her father would do this, her husband would do the other. Circe ignored her - she was just another spoiled brat. When she'd run out of steam, Circe gave her the piece of paper that she'd given to Mary Baxter - the one about being a hostage - and left her. Mario was making coffee so she just concentrated on watching the road and waiting.

* * * * *

Lydia sat down that evening and put the television on to watch the news from Canal Uno, the public broadcasting channel. The kidnap and shooting topped the news. She smiled as Soledad's father and Leonardo Fuentes, speaking to the television cameras, demanded action. The President and Raul were both named as having "allowed this total breakdown in law and order" to overtake the capital. And what with rebels advancing through the island, it was clearly the time, they said, to look for new leadership. There. Someone had said it. "Yes", she said out loud. "Yes, that's exactly right. It *is* clearly the time!"

The President, when he saw the news, was both furious and terrified. If he didn't get a grip, he was finished. Yet, he couldn't get a grip, nor could his army, nor anyone else. "What's happening, Raul," he asked plaintively. He poured himself a glass of rum, knocked it off and slumped down. "I need to think", he mumbled.

Next day, there were demonstrations in Puerto Grande. Lydia could see them from her apartment. They had been orchestrated by the unions and attracted wide support and not just from workers. Students and mothers with their children also took to the streets, the women carrying hastily put together placards - "Keep Our Women and Children Safe". The Union banners called for the removal of El Presidente and the formation of a "People's Government". The Police looked on. The Rurales were itching for a fight but their orders were not to inflame things even more.

Soledad Fuentes was spotted sitting on a bench in the Plaza Garibaldi. She was still wearing a blindfold and her hands were tied to the arms of the bench. There was a gag in her mouth –fashioned from the ultra-expensive silk stockings she had chosen to wear for the fashion show. Their current role was to prevent her from screaming and shouting which they did admirably. It was the owner of one of the cafes who saw her as he was opening up. He ran inside and called the police. Then he went over to Soledad. When he took her blindfold off and removed the gag, Soledad stared at him in terror then slowly looked around.

"Where am I?" and "Untie me" were the first things she said.

"In the Plaza Garibaldi, Señora. And, hold still while I get a knife to cut these knots. I've called the police," he added. "They should be here soon".

There was no thank you from Soledad. She sat on the bench as if in a trance. When the police arrived she reached for her handbag which her kidnappers had tied to her waist.

"I was told to give you this", reaching into the bag and handing them a note. It read: 'We are returning Señora Fuentes. This is our final act of clemency. The next hostage will not be so lucky. Fuentes and her oppressor family are living on borrowed time. They must go."

As before, it was signed, "Soldiers for a free Caribe".

When the police reported her release to Raul, he told them to destroy the note. Then he contacted her family and El Presidente.

Once safely returned to her husband, the family put out a statement:

'While we are overjoyed that Soledad is safe and well, we condemn the government of President Barbosa in the strongest terms. Our capital city is a jungle. No-one is safe. We demand that the President and his henchmen resign forthwith"

The Diario ran the statement on the front page next to the copy of the note from the kidnappers which, as with the other kidnaps, had also been sent to them. By publishing the note, the Diario was clearly hedging its bets as to whom to side with. If support for El Presidente was ebbing away, the Diario had to make sure it picked the next winner.

* * * * *

Lydia stood at the window looking down on a group of demonstrators as they advanced on the Convento. She hoped no-one would get hurt. She had been a little unnerved by the shooting at the fashion show. Any further kidnaps would be more dangerous if people started using bodyguards. She was very protective of the group she thought of as "the boys and girls". In particular, she'd watched Circe's growing involvement and leadership with admiration. She didn't want them to get hurt if it could be avoided. She decided that there would be no more kidnaps. They had served their purpose.

Now she needed to let Cesar know of her decision. But he had not been to the Circulo for a while. She didn't know where he was. She also made another decision. She would scale back activities at the Circulo. No more kidnaps meant no more 'events'. She would simply put a notice in the Diario saying: "Señorita Lydia Echevarria regrets to announce that the much-loved 'Events' at the Circulo Latino will be suspended until the current period of unrest is over". Her young people, as she saw them, would be encouraged to direct their energies elsewhere. Lectures and classes would be suspended.

Melba came in from the kitchen and joined her at the window.

Pointing to the demonstrators in the street below, Lydia asked her, "What do you think, chica?"

"I think you have done very well, Señorita. I am so proud of you."

Lydia stared at her in disbelief. "What can you mean, Melba," was all she could manage.

"Do you think I am blind, Lydia? This is Melba you're talking to - the Melba who looks after you." She had never called her Lydia before, but it seemed natural. A sort of intimacy had suddenly settled on them.

"I have known all along. You are my Lydia. You would never have anything to do with that pig Raul except to destroy him. So, I am proud. But, don't worry. I'm Melba, the maid. I know nothing. I see nothing. I just love my mistress."

Lydia looked at Melba for what seemed an age. Then she took her in her arms and held her. Nothing was said. Nothing needed to be said. She sobbed quietly. Melba brushed away her tears as if she were the mother that Lydia could no longer turn to. Eventually Melba stepped back. Reaching out, she straightened Lydia's hair and fussed with her clothes for a minute. Then she pointed to her stockings and said, "Look, I still have the ones with the zig-zag seams". They both smiled. Melba went back to the kitchen. Lydia felt less alone.

Chapter 23

The despatch

Conway moved as the rebels moved. He was with the unit led by Gaudi who had proved himself as formidable an organiser in the skirmishes with the army and the Rurales as he was in the factories. The key was his clear vision and ability to command. People followed him.

As they made their way across the country they met only sporadic opposition. It was obvious that the army, besides being poorly trained and ill-equipped, had no stomach for a fight. Many of the officers were lazy and corrupt. If they weren't siphoning off fuel to sell on the black market, they were arranging drug deals or diverting soldiers' pay into their off-shore accounts. It was no surprise that Gaudi's ranks were swollen as much by deserters from the army and the police as they were by recruits to the cause. The Rurales stayed solidly loyal to the government because they had nowhere else to go. They had preyed on people in the countryside for years. There would be no amnesty for them if things went badly. They'd be hanging from lamp-posts or so they feared.

So the Rurales put up the greatest resistance as Gaudi advanced. In one fierce fire-fight, one of their units was dug in along a river bank holding a bridge over the Rio Bravo which a group of the rebels led by Nino, by then Gaudi's number two, had to cross if they were to get control of a section of the Carretera Central, the main highway across the island. The engagement lasted most of the day. An attempt to cross the river higher up and come round behind the Rurales failed. The river was too fast-flowing to ford and, in any case, the Rurales had posted a platoon to fight off such an attempt. Atilio, brave as ever, was leading. He was cut down when the Rurales opened fire from their concealed position.

The attempt was abandoned soon after. The bridge was finally breached when the Rurales ran out of ammunition and retreated. Atilio's body had been carried back and there was a short ceremony before he was laid to rest by the bridge in a hastily dug grave, a crude cross marking the spot. Nino promised his men, "when we have triumphed over these criminals we will come back for Companero Atilio and give him the burial he deserves". Conway found that strangely comforting.

Conway was deeply saddened by the death of the man who had become his friend. In his next despatch he wrote of the slow but unstoppable progress being made by the rebel forces. And he wrote also of the price that was being paid. He eulogised Atilio, using his real name rather than the nom de guerre of Geronimo that he'd given him. Atilio was a young artist, he wrote, committed to celebrating beauty who had turned his back on his calling to answer a different and more pressing call – the liberation, as he saw it, of his country. It was a bit over the top. He kept reminding himself that he wasn't Rupert Brooke. But he couldn't hide his feelings. Here was a young man giving his life for a cause. The nobility of the venture must not, he wrote, be allowed to go unremarked.

Word came back to Conway not long after (he didn't have a clue how the communications worked) that, yes, Harry did think it was way over the top, but the punters loved it. Geronimo/Atilio had been part of the story - he'd appeared in quite a few despatches once he'd left Puerto Grande and joined the rebels. They grieved over his death. Conway had given them their first martyr, even if his death was one of dozens that the rebels had suffered.

Once they had fought their way through to the highway, there was nothing between the rebels and entry into Puerto Grande, sixty miles away, except the increasingly rag-tag army and a die-hard group of Rurales. The rebels had nothing to fear from the air force. Gaudi had heard about Paddy Mayne from one of his rugby-playing friends back in Argentina. Apart from playing rugby for Ireland, Mayne had led the British SAS after the capture of the founder David Stirling. What had fascinated Gaudi about the SAS in North Africa was their particular operational skill in going behind enemy lines and destroying enemy airplanes while they were still on the ground. Gaudi used this technique to devastating effect in one of the most daring attacks of the campaign. The rebels in two co-ordinated night attacks had destroyed eight of the ten airplanes that were air-worthy in assaults on the Air Force's two principal bases, one outside the capital and the other in the centre of the island at Monterrey. It was a stunning reverse for the government's forces.

With the capital just a few days' march away, Gaudi and Nino had set up camp in a hamlet called San Pedro just off the highway. They were made welcome by the locals who had previously only known the hard life of share-croppers but were now being promised a better life. Gaudi invited Conway to sit in on the war council. They wanted him to report what they were planning so that the world's press, or at least those that were interested, could be there at the finish line to bear witness.

The plan was to strike a devastating blow on the demoralised army and mop up the Rurales. They would then demand the resignation of the government. What should happen to El Presidente and his henchmen was still to be decided. The rebel forces would muster at San Rafael a small town on the outskirts of Puerto Grande. From there they would enter the capital on May Day in honour of the workers who had supported the struggle.

Conway recognised the reference to San Rafael and knew that they were talking about Cesar. He figured that the plan must be to pick up Cesar and let him lead them into Puerto Grande. Conway took Gaudi aside and asked him whether it was alright now, at last, to name Cesar in the next despatch. It would be a chance to bring the great man out of the shadows and let the world know who personified the cause. Gaudi demurred. He and Nino wanted it to be a surprise.

"Let the people see just a simple man like them. Someone they don't know but who has fought for them quietly and with lethal effect for years. If you want, Comrade Conway, you can describe him in your despatch as 'a humble cane cutter who was a teacher till he was banished by the oppressive government'. But, No. No name."

Conway accepted the decision though he wasn't entirely persuaded that a name would make much difference, particularly if Gaudi was saying that no-one knew about him anyway. He wrote the despatch. It made the front page of the Globe and was picked up particularly in the United States. Some Senators were becoming alarmed at the threat to the business interests that they existed to protect.

After a couple of days the rebels moved out. The slight delay was to give the army a chance to review its options and decide whether in fact they wanted to fight. In the event they decided that they didn't. The army commander sent a personal message to Gaudi:

"The army will not resist your entry into the city," it read, "if you guarantee that my officers and men will be treated respectfully. Those who wish to remain in the army should be allowed to do so. Those who wish to leave should be able to do so without recrimination".

In his reply, Gaudi accepted the terms of what he called "your surrender", but insisted that, to show their commitment to the new order, the commander should assign a unit to join one of the rebels' units in 'dealing with' the Rurales. There was no love lost between the army and the Rurales, whom they regarded as ill-disciplined thugs, so the commander readily agreed.

The next day, the last stronghold of the Rurales was overrun. Those who were not killed in the fighting were taken off to be held in an abandoned army camp till someone decided what to do with them. The wounded were left to be looked after by the others without anything besides rudimentary medical supplies.

Gaudi was ready now for the march into Puerto Grande. It was Sunday April 28th. There were over five hundred of them in the central group. Another hundred or so were following behind, looking after supplies and guarding against any pocket of resistance. Another two units, of about fifty men each, were on either flank, making sure that the progress of the central group was smooth, unopposed and welcomed. Gaudi and Nino decided that the march should be in three stages, about twenty miles a day. The final stop would be on the outskirts of the city so as to enter on May 1st. The slow procession through the countryside and the small towns and villages would give them time to show themselves to their countrymen. It would generate increasing enthusiasm among the locals in the country and growing anticipation in those in the city.

At every step, the rebel soldiers were greeted as conquering heroes and showered with presents of rum and sweetmeats and baskets of fruit, and not a few kisses. The excitement grew. That Sunday night they set up camp outside El Pico alongside the Highway, putting up tents, taking over rooms in the little village gladly made available by enthusiastic locals, or, in the case of many, just sitting around parked trucks, drinking beer and singing far into the night. Gaudi, who had exercised iron discipline throughout the campaign, turned a blind eye to the beers - they deserved a drink.

Early in the evening, as the camp was being set up, Conway was at his typewriter, sitting at a table under a lemon tree, when he saw a jeep move out from the throng of men and women and set off along the Highway towards the capital. Nino was sitting alongside the driver.

Conway called to Ines Fonseca who was standing outside a shed smoking. "Where are they off to?"

"They're going to collect the Professor, so he can join the march into Puerto Grande".

"Oh! Really? I thought they were going to pick him up in San Rafael where he lives and drive in from there".

"Maybe there's a change of plans. I don't know. Ask Companero Gaudi". Grinding her cigarette into the ground, Ines went back inside.

Conway tried to get to see Gaudi, pushing his way through the crowds milling around, dodging the back-slapping and holding up his bottle of San Miguel whenever another was pressed on him. The atmosphere was one of happy contentment. They had survived and had won. They were full of expectation for a future without El Presidente. When Conway finally made it through the pack, he was told that Gaudi was in a meeting. He went back to join a group who were sitting eating beans and rice that they'd heated in billy cans.

He had this feeling. Something wasn't quite right but he didn't know what it was.

The noise outside woke him. He struggled to disentangle himself from his mosquito net and looked at his watch. It was two in the morning on the Monday. There was a great commotion outside the house Conway was billeted in. Lamps were being lit and people were shouting. He dragged on his shirt and trousers, pulled on his boots and hurried outside.

"What is it?" he asked the first person he came across.

"I don't know, Señor, but it looks as if something has happened. Perhaps the army has changed its mind," he added, only half in jest.

"There's been an accident" someone else shouted as he ran, "a terrible accident".

Conway shouted to a young woman coming out of another house. "Someone says there's been an accident. What's happened?"

She came over. It was Teresa whom he had last seen at the Circulo all those months ago. She was sobbing and wringing her hands. Tears were streaming down her face.

"Oh Señor Conway, Tony. It's awful. It's too awful".

"What's awful? What's happened", alarm entering his voice.

"It's the Professor, Tony. There's been a terrible accident", she wailed and broke into more sobbing.

"Which Professor? Do you mean Professor Sanchez – Cesar? That can't be right. Nino went to fetch him a few hours ago".

"Yes", she said through her sobs. "Yes, our beautiful, wonderful Professor Cesar."

"What's happened to him", Conway shouted, barely controlling his voice.

"He's been killed, Tony." Then she repeated over and over, "How can it be"?

Conway was dumbstruck. Yesterday Cesar was going to lead the rebel army into the capital, today he was dead. Teresa was right. How could it be?

Slowly, Conway began to put together a picture of what had happened. Gaudi had sent a message to Cesar that there was a change of plan. Nino would come to get him and bring him to the camp. Gaudi needed to brief him on certain developments in his dealings with the President's office and, in particular, with Raul Salcedo. Cesar could still do his triumphal entry, indeed he could travel with the rebels for the last day, showing himself to the people and the cameras before entering Puerto Grande.

Gaudi had then sent an order to Pablo, the driver, telling him to pick up Cesar at nine-o-clock that Sunday evening in San Rafael and drive him to the cross-roads in the middle of Vieques, a dusty one-horse town about twenty miles outside the capital. There would be a jeep waiting with Nino and a driver. Cesar was to transfer to the jeep so that Nino could bring him back. Pablo was to go back to town.

Conway got the next part of the story from Nino as they sat opposite each other across a table under the lemon tree an hour before dawn. No-one was interested in sleep and, anyway, Conway wanted to hunt down the story. Moths banged into the hurricane lamp hung from a branch and bats wheeled and dived. He was grateful for once that Nino was a chain-smoker and that he smoked the foul-smelling local Royals. The smoke kept even the most persistent mosquitos at bay.

Nino described how, "I was the one who raised the alarm. I'd driven back into the camp like a bat out of hell with the car horn blaring".

Rebels lying around drinking and telling jokes had suddenly sobered up and run to his car. Pushing them away, Nino said he headed for Gaudi's hut. He shouted, "Look after Ephraim", his driver, who was slumped on the back seat where Nino had laid him. There was blood everywhere but it wasn't Nino's - he was unhurt.

According to Nino,

"We got to Vieques first and were parked, waiting. As Pablo drove towards the cross-roads, there was gunfire from both sides of the road. Pablo's car was hit; it veered off the road, hit a post and burst into flames. A stray bullet also hit Ephraim in the head - God what a disaster! He died instantly. I opened the car door on my side and rolled clear, shooting into the cane fields with my carbine, aiming at where I thought the gunfire had come from because I couldn't see anyone. No-one returned fire. When I could get close to the burning car - the heat was tremendous - it was clear that Pablo and Cesar were dead, killed by the gunfire or by the inferno."

Conway asked him about the group which had staged the ambush.

"There was no sign of anyone. They seemed to have melted back into the tall stands of sugar cane which stretched away into the distance on either side of the road. Obviously, they'd eluded the units on the flanks which Companero Gardi had posted there precisely to stop such attacks. I ordered a 'search and destroy' mission the moment I got back to camp, but so far there's nothing. It looks like the ambushers have vanished."

"I drove back with Ephraim's body. He was a boy – just 17. As I said - a single bullet through his temple. Dios Mio! Once I'd reported to Companero Gardi, I sent a party to recover the bodies. It get worse, Señor Conway. When they got back the men reported that the heat from the fire was so intense that, apart from a copper bracelet with his initials on which Cesar wore for his rheumatism, all that was left were bones and ashes. The men collected them up, though they were not sure what related to Cesar and what to Pablo, and put them in a box. I ordered them to put the box in one of the huts in the camp till we could decide what to do. We were in shock. What a catastrophe!"

Conway knew that he had to file his despatch. But what was the story? Professor Cesar Sanchez who was the father and spiritual leader of the revolution and, he had assumed, the President-in-waiting, had been killed. What should he make of what was going on? Was there something he was missing? The low key response in the camp – just put the remains in the hut – shocked him. And the circumstances of Cesar's death were mysterious, at best. Where did the ambushers come from? How was it that they got clean away? How did Nino's driver also get shot, and by a single bullet to the head, while Nino came through it all unscathed?

Conway reflected that there was only the closely-knit inner circle around Cesar who knew who he was and what he had done. The fact that he operated clandestinely meant that otherwise he was relatively unknown. He had let Gaudi be the figurehead. To protect Cesar, Conway himself had never mentioned him in his despatches. And, when he had finally suggested doing so in his despatch about the rebels' imminent entry into Puerto Grande, Gaudi had specifically told him not to. At the time it had puzzled him. Now he was more than puzzled. To all intents and purposes, Cesar had disappeared before he had appeared.

Conway had made a commitment to himself when he started out on the campaign to stick to the facts in his despatches. He had pledged that he would be the neutral observer. But there was a jigsaw here and some pieces seemed to be missing. Should he try to complete the jigsaw? The plan for Cesar to climb aboard a tank in San Rafael had been agreed weeks earlier. It would be wonderfully symbolic – the humble cane-cutter making a revolution for his fellow workers. But the plan had suddenly been changed. Instead, Cesar was to be driven to a little town in the dark and then swopped over to Nino's car and driven back to camp. Why couldn't Pablo have driven him all the way, if Cesar really was needed in the camp? It didn't make sense. Gaudi's staff had explained that he needed to discuss certain important matters with Cesar in advance of their entry into the capital. But this seemed odd. They had been communicating clandestinely for months without difficulty. Why the sudden need for Cesar to leave San Rafael after all this time for a face-to-face meeting?

He sat on his bed early on the Monday morning as preparations to strike camp for the second day's march went on around him. There was a pervading sense of sadness among the very few in the camp who knew of Cesar and his role. Most of the rebels, if they'd heard of the shooting, just thought of it as another casualty. Gaudi and Nino had done nothing to disabuse them. There was no calling people together, no ceremony, no speech about the loss of the father of the revolution on the eve of its success. There was only talk about how to manage the choreography of Gaudi and Nino leading them into Puerto Grande on the Wednesday - May Day.

Conway faced a dilemma. If his despatch said what he thought was happening he would be teetering on the fine line between describing and speculating, a line he'd always tried to keep the right side of. And, his speculation was dark. Moreover, it would bring him into conflict with Gaudi, because his speculation was that Cesar's death was just too convenient. It cleared the way for Gaudi. It buried Cesar's role along with his charred bones. There were still the few who knew the truth, but, he reasoned, if Gaudi was ruthless enough to get rid of Cesar, they wouldn't pose much of a problem. And, it dawned on him how exposed he himself was - he was one of that few who knew about Cesar.

And what if he were wrong? Gaudi was a brave and successful leader who had fought a victorious campaign, initially against significant odds. His commitment to the welfare of those around him and to those in the towns and villages they marched through had been clear and made him immensely popular. Gaudi may indeed have changed his mind and decided that Cesar should lead them for their final day rather than just from San Rafael. He may have wanted to spend the last couple of nights of the campaign with his partner, making plans but also celebrating what they had achieved, as they moved through the countryside. Gaudi may have wanted Nino to pick Cesar up just in case Pablo was being followed by some die-hard Rurales, because he was confident that Nino could deal with any such situation. Indeed, that may have been what happened. Nino, for once, had been surprised, with tragic consequences.

Conway sat in the clammy heat staring at the keys of his typewriter hoping that they would decide and write the story for him. He got up and poured himself some iced water from the flask Teresa had brought him. This is where you find out what you believe in, who you are, he mused. It was the time to grow up, though he didn't fancy the idea that growing up risked going the way of Cesar and Pablo. Nor did it reassure him that here he was, in the middle of nowhere, surrounded by jubilant rebels high on victory and led by a seasoned, tough campaigner. Few would notice if *he* had an accident also.

He made his decision. He reported on the rebels' victorious progress towards Puerto Grande – V Day Minus 2, he called it. This gave him the opportunity to flag up that his next despatch would describe the triumphal entry on V Day. Then he changed the mood. He told his readers that victory, as ever, was tinged with tragedy. The man whom he had seen as the father of the revolution, the spiritual leader, had been killed. He reported the account as conveyed by Nino, well-known to the despatches as Gaudi's Number Two. Then he made the leap.

"I've been reporting on the revolutionary movement in Caribe since I arrived a year ago. I've followed the rebels' campaign from its beginning in La Fortaleza over five months ago," Conway wrote. "During that time, especially in the months leading up to the uprising, I've seen the interactions between Mr Gaudi, the Union Leader and subsequently the military commander, and Professor Sanchez. They became increasingly fraught. They clearly had different visions of the future after the overthrow of President Barbosa. Now Cesar Sanchez is dead. Is it only me who wonders whether his death is just too convenient? Is it just me who asks whether the circumstances of his death are at the very least mysterious? So far, I haven't been able to put my questions to Mr Gaudi. I shall keep trying."

The rebels were beginning to move off when Ines came hurrying over. Conway had just finished packing his old and battered rucksack (almost for the last time, he thought) and was heading towards the road. He spotted Ines coming towards him.

"Hola, Ines. What is it?"

"Hola, Señor Conway, Tony. I'm sorry but our communications team couldn't send your despatch. There seems to be something wrong with the system. I'm sorry".

Ines handed him back the typewritten sheets, then went on:

"Just as we always do, for security reasons, you understand, to make sure the despatch doesn't inadvertently give something away which may endanger the campaign, I showed it to Companero Nino. He was very angry, Tony, at what you say about Professor Sanchez's death. He shouted at me: 'There was nothing mysterious. Conway knows what happened. I told him myself'. So he wants you to remove that allegation - he called it an 'accusation'. He hasn't told Companero Gaudi yet. Perhaps, when you've revised the despatch the system will be up and running and we'll have another go at sending it."

So there it was. Change the story or it wouldn't go out and Gaudi would be told. Curiously, being confronted with what he thought was proof of his suspicions made Conway calm rather than anxious. Yes, Nino's account might be true, so, yes, Nino would be entitled to be displeased. But Conway didn't think so.

The challenge energised him. It was his turn to be angry. He was going to say his piece and let those in Caribe and the wider world make up their minds. But that meant sending the despatch and staying safe. He had to work out a plan.

Conway stood by the side of the road watching Ines head off in her combat fatigues and boots – a kind of revolutionary chic he thought to himself. A tank had been brought up, one of those that the rebels had commandeered from the army. Gaudi, Nino, and a couple of others were clambering onto it. A photographer was taking pictures. He waved and shouted, "Hey, Tony, you want a photo for your story?" But, Gaudi waved the photographer away and ordered the tank driver to "get going". The photographer just about scrambled aboard.

Three of Gaudi's staff didn't join the others. They stood to the side on a dusty little square, waving the fumes and dust away.

"They're watching me", Conway thought to himself. "Well, let's see. Nothing venture and all that".

Drawing close to them he said to the oldest-looking man. "I assume you're heading towards the capital". Pointing to the jeep behind them, he added with a smile, "Are you driving or walking? I must say driving is my preferred option".

None of them smiled back.

"We're driving but we're not going to the capital, Señor", the oldest one replied. "We have to go somewhere else first. You can join us if you want. You'll be able to get a ride to Puerto Grande from there."

Was there a hint of menace in his voice or was he becoming paranoid? Conway wasn't sure.

"Thanks. I'll catch them up and walk."

"Suit yourself". The three men turned away and headed over to the jeep parked under a jacaranda tree covered with magnificent indigo flowers.

Conway set off, glancing over his shoulder till he was sure they had driven off. "I don't get paid enough for this", he complained to another of the jacaranda trees.

The march soon became a trudge as Conway made his way down the highway, chewing the dust kicked up by those in front. His encounters with Ines and then Gaudi's men had affected him deeply. For so long he'd imagined the moment when the rebels would enter the city - happy and hopeful for a better future. It had kept him going through the deaths, the gunfire, the drenching storms, the mosquitos and tarantulas, the loneliness. But now the vision had lost its lustre. Yes, they would be getting rid of the hated President and his henchmen and, yes, they believed in the cause, but which cause was actually triumphing? He felt sick at heart. Was he exaggerating, getting things out of perspective? Was he just tired and foot-weary, seeing demons where there weren't any? He didn't think so. His instinct told him otherwise.

He was a different Tony Conway from the one who'd climbed over the Embassy wall. It was all a bit of a jape then. Now, the seriousness closed in on him. His early dealings with Raul had made him inclined to sympathise with the rebels. The last several months had reinforced that view. He'd seen the violence meted out to people by the army and especially the Rurales, he'd witnessed the corruption as schools went without basic supplies while local officials lived the high life, he'd seen the bodies, he'd shared the victories, he'd mourned Atilio. He had learned what staging a rebellion, becoming part of a revolution, involved. But then there had been Cesar's death. Everything for him had changed. He'd been brought crashing down as the politics of revolution replaced the dreaming and the fighting. He didn't like what he thought (no, what he knew) he'd seen. He needed to say so.

These were the thoughts that occupied him as he walked along at the back of the column of young men and women, drunk on their happiness, their success, and not a little rum. There was a sadness in him, a knowing quality which was in such contrast to the mood around him. In their combat fatigues, carrying their rifles, the men wore their unkempt beards as if they were an entry ticket to Valhalla, while the women argued about wanting to look their best (some even mentioning lipstick and tying a ribbon in their hair) while wanting to look like the rough and seasoned veterans most of them were.

Without thinking, Conway broke away from the main column as it made its way to the village of San Salvador where they would camp and spend the Monday night. In just a couple of days they'd be entering the capital. There'd be no more camps, no more sleeping on the ground, no more water bottles and billy cans. They would march to the Plaza Central, soon to be the Plaza de Independencia, and then the party would start. The future could look after itself for a day or two

Conway decided to make for the capital straightaway without waiting another two days. He wanted to file the despatch that Ines had handed back to him and then be an eye-witness to the end of the campaign. He veered off the Carretera to follow a country road which would loop round and cross the highway higher up. He was settling into a steady pace when an old green weather-beaten pick-up truck passed him and drew up ahead. For a moment he thought it was the three men from earlier on, but then he remembered that they had a jeep. As he caught up with it, the driver leaned across and shouted through the open side-window. It was an old man, a cigar jammed between his lips and a battered straw hat on his head,

"You goin' to the city, Señor", he asked. "I can give you a ride if you want. Ain't it all so exciting? All these young kids wanting to change the world. I'm gonna get me a ring-side seat for when they get there".

Conway thanked him as he climbed up into the passenger seat, moving an old rifle gently onto the back seat. "Yes, I am going into Puerto Grande and yes, it is exciting."

"I s'pose it'll all end in tears like it always do but it makes a change from fishing." Then, "You ain't from round here", looking sideways at him as he started away.

"No, I'm from England. I'm a journalist. I've been following the campaign".

"That so?" Then he turned the car radio up, as if giving a ride to an English reporter was the most natural thing in the world, and began to sing loudly and out of tune. "Hope you don't mind me singing, Señor," he shouted. "Driving's the only time I can sing. If I do it at home, the missus throws things at me".

I can see why, Conway thought, but smiled as if in appreciation.

At the edge of the city, he asked the driver, whose name he learned was Tito, to drop him off.

"You sure, Señor? I can take you right in if you like. I like the company. I ain't had an audience for my singing in years".

"Well, all good things have to end, Tito. Thanks again. Can I give you any money for the petrol?"

"No, thanks, Señor. Was a pleasure". And he drove off.

Once Conway had got his bearings, his feet took him unerringly to the Circulo. When he got there, a sign pasted on the glass doors told him it was closed until further notice. He turned away disappointed, unsure what to do next and feeling lost. Then, though it was still early afternoon, he noticed a light on in a room to the side. He went back and knocked. At the fourth knock, he noticed the bell – he'd forgotten there was a bell. He rang it and very shortly a figure appeared and peered out to see who was there. It was Circe. For reasons he didn't quite understand, his heart sang. Circe was special.

She opened the door, pulled him in, shut the door behind him and, without saying a word, hugged him tightly to her. She took him through to the room she had been in, their footsteps echoing in the empty space which was once alive with the chatter of young people.

"I'm back here working on my journal. I keep the light on just in case one of the old gang comes by. Sadly, no-one does. It's just Patricio and me. Do you want to say hi to him, he's playing his music somewhere?"

She went to the door and called him. Patricio appeared looking more than usually dishevelled. The moment he saw Conway, his eyes lit up.

"Señor Conway, Tony, how wonderful to see you. How are you? You've been away a long time. We've followed what you've been writing, haven't we, Circe? It's been brilliant."

"But you haven't seen the last despatch – suddenly not so brilliant".

They both looked at him. "Why? What's happened Tony", Patricio asked.

Not knowing how to say it except by saying it, tears welled in his eyes as he told them, "It's Cesar. He was killed last night".

"What? It can't be", Circe shouted. Patricio slumped as if he'd just been punched in the stomach. He stayed bent over for a while, his hands on his knees. Then, he put his arm round Circe and sat them both down on the old stuffed sofa. Neither said a word. They just sat and held each other, crying and rocking quietly. Eventually, Circe broke the silence. "What happened, Tony?"

Conway sat across from them in one of the hardback chairs. He put his rucksack down and put his face in his hands. "Give me a minute, while I wash my face and go to the bathroom. Then we can talk".

"I'll make some coffee", Patricio volunteered, to give himself something to do, Conway suspected.

"Not for me, thanks. A Coke would be great if there is one".

"I'll check".

Patricio was back in a few minutes. He put two mugs of coffee on the table. "No Coke, sorry. Just a glass of water."

"Thanks. That's fine."

Conway began. He told them what had happened from the moment he'd seen Nino leave the camp to the moment Nino'd arrived back and described what had happened. Conway told them of his suspicions which, to him at least, had become certainties. They fired questions at him, their anguish and anger competing with each other.

Reaching into his rucksack he produced the despatch that Ines had returned to him.

"This is the despatch I've written. It tells the story as I've just told it to you. I must send it. It's important that another account, a truer account, is heard before Gaudi is able to write his version of history. I need your help to get it to the Globe. And then I need to disappear once it's sent. So do you, I fear. You know too much about Cesar and his role. You are a threat, you and all the others."

Circe looked at him tearfully.

"We will help you, Tony. Of course we will. And we will take care. We are used to it. As for the others, there are very few others, I'm afraid. We are the only ones in the network who are left in the city, except for Señora Gonzales – you remember her, the woman who lives opposite the Iglesia Santa Maria Magdalena. Señor Gaudi knows that she was part of Cesar's network, but he will not touch her. She is too prominent and her husband, the doctor, is too well-loved. And people just wouldn't believe him anyway if he accuses her. We will take you there. She will hide you.

"It will be like old times," she added through her tears. "We should go now, before everything starts to go wild as they all reach the city."

Conway was once again amazed at Circe's self-control and ability to take command. He was content to put himself in her care as they left the

Circulo and made their way through back streets to Señora Gonzales' house. When Circe knocked, Consuela, her maid, opened the door.

"Señora Gonzales is not at home, chica, but you're all welcome to come in and wait for her."

Consuela took them through to a pretty sitting room, light and airy. The walls were covered with books and paintings, some of them portraits of the Señora when she was younger. She had been a considerable beauty. The furniture was equally light – rattan chairs with embroidered cushions and lamps with silk lampshades on low tables. She brought them lemonade with ice. Conway didn't realise how thirsty he was – apart from the glass of water at the Circulo, he'd had nothing since he'd left the camp that morning. He gulped down two glasses and then, realising his lapse in manners, held his hand up as if to say 'forgive me'. Circe smiled indulgently.

It was half an hour, during which they barely spoke, before Magda Gonzalez appeared. She was wearing a grey tailored linen suit which showed off her still-slim figure. In her high heels she seemed tall and almost regal. She entered as if onto a stage and took them all in with a sweep of her arm.

"Well, look who's here. How wonderful to see you all. It's Tony isn't it? Welcome – again - to my humble home. Hola Circe. Hola Patricio. Now, what's going on? Tell Magda".

Before Conway could open his mouth, Circe took over. She told the story that Conway had told them. When she got to the death of Cesar, Señora Gonzalez shrieked and held her head. Consuela came running.

"What is it, Miss?"

"Oh! Someone has died. It's too sad".

Consuela crossed herself. "Can I bring you anything?"

"Some brandy for all of us, please. And coffee, except for Señor Conway - peppermint tea for you, eh, Tony?"

He nodded his thanks.

Slowly regaining her composure, Señora Gonzalez looked at Conway and said, "I fear you are right in your suspicions. They were too different, Cesar and Gaudi. I saw it when they were together. Towards the end, I don't think Cesar entirely trusted Gaudi or Nino. But they had gone too far and they were winning. I think poor Cesar just hoped things would come right. But", she added with tears again in her eyes, "they didn't, did they?"

She stood up, straightened her suit and clapped her hands together, becoming the practical doctor's wife.

"So what do we need to do? Circe mentioned a 'despatch'. Is that what you called it? Let's find out how we can send that off to your people in London. Then we need to put you up here for a while, Tony. I'll get Consuela to prepare a bed in one of my husband's consulting rooms - off limits to all except doctor and patient, you understand. And we'll get your clothes washed and you can take a shower. You can use some of my husband's clothes till yours are ready. They may not be to your taste, they certainly aren't to mine but he doesn't listen, but they'll do for the moment. And you two young things", pointing to Circe and Patricio, "you'd better make yourself scarce. You've had quite a lot of experience recently of surviving underground. Use it. Disappear but keep in touch. Now, the 'despatch'".

Conway was impressed. No wonder she had been close to Cesar. This, he thought, was a woman who was used to getting things done. He pulled the despatch out of his rucksack again. Magda took it from him and pursed her lips.

"We need to know where to send it and how to send it. My husband has a whole host of stuff in his office which may help. I don't understand the first thing about it."

Patricio spoke for the first time. "I may be able to help, Señora, if you show me where to go".

They all followed Magda as she went down a long corridor lined with what looked like wedding photographs. At the end on the right there was a large room which was both office and consulting room for when Dr Gonzalez saw patients away from his clinic. Patricio inspected the equipment on the doctor's desk. Patricio asked Magda whether her husband had one of those facsimile machines that he had read about in the technical journals that he devoured - they were expensive but could be useful in sending medical records and the like across the country or abroad. Magda looked at him quizzically and shook her head. "I haven't a clue".

In the end, Patricio decided that the only way he could think of to send the despatch from the office was by telegram. So, sitting in the doctor's chair, he phoned the telegraph office. Luckily, despite all the impending commotion, there was someone on duty.

"What's your name, please"

"You can call me Mia. It's short for Amelia".

"OK, Mia. It's going to be a very long telegram."

"That's OK. It's a bit quiet here today what with everything happening. It'll give me something to do".

Thanking her profusely, Patricio began dictating. The name and address of the person the despatch was to go to was on the front sheet. All the other names had been changed to letters of the alphabet as a precaution.

"It's the first draft of a chapter of a new novel, Mia. It's a bit of a secret."

"How exciting".

It took Patricio over half an hour to dictate it all. When he'd finished, he thanked Mia again and added "Not a word now". She laughed and said "Of course, Señor. You can always trust Western Union".

Magda broke the mood. "What now, Tony."

"I need to call London. Is that OK, Magda? I need to explain the coded alphabet names and who they refer to".

"Go right ahead".

The evening shift was putting the first edition to bed when Conway got through to the desk and filled them in. He gave them Magda's number in case they needed to call back. Bill Humphrey, the duty editor, was surprised to hear from him and wanted to chat, but he cut him off,

"It's urgent, Bill, so could you get on with it straightaway, please."

"Yes, Sir", came barking through the static.

They all regrouped in the main living room. Consuela had made dinner - mushroom risotto - which she served in the dining room. They were all so hungry that almost nothing was said above the expressions of satisfaction with the food. Then it was Magda again.

"Children, go", she commanded Circe and Patricio. "But keep in touch. You can reach me through Father Benedict, or Consuela who goes to the shops each day at ten in the morning. And take care". With that she shooed them out through the back gate into the little alley opposite the church.

Then, "Let me show you where you are going to sleep, Tony, till we decide what to do with you". Picking up his rucksack she marched ahead. On the second floor there were two rooms marked 'Patients –do not disturb'. She opened the door to the second room. There was a bed, an easy chair and a writing desk with a chair. A tiny bathroom was attached. After over five months sleeping rough, it looked like the Ritz to Conway.

Thanking Magda warmly, he watched as she closed the door. He'd take a shower in a moment, he thought. As he lay on the bed, he remembered that he hadn't slept the previous night. "I'll just rest a minute" he mumbled. He was asleep within seconds.

Chapter 24

Flight

Raul was no longer interested in protecting Barbosa from the news of what was happening. He knew it was all over and needed to get Barbosa to realise it as well. Then they could do what was necessary.

The news reaching El Presidente had been increasingly bad for weeks. The pressure from all sides, business, commerce, banks, the Americans, even the Diario, not to mention the very disgruntled Dona Carmen, was non-stop. The reports from the army were of defeat and retreat. The air force, such as it was, had been destroyed in devastating fashion. The Rurales were fighting but they were a mob who couldn't be expected to do anything other than try to save their own skins.

Raul was at the receiving end of Barbosa's worst tantrums.

"You shout at people, Raul, you set the police on demonstrators, you've fired dozens of my army officers, and what the hell has it achieved? A big fat NADA", Barbosa shrieked. "That bastard Gaudi is winning. I, El Presidente, am losing and losing badly and losing fast. Do something, for God's sake".

Barbosa had given orders for contingency plans to be drawn up. In other words, how he was going to get out before Gaudi's people laid hands on him. If they got him, they would do to him what he would have done to them. They'd shoot him or string him up: probably the first, then the second, like Mussolini.

Raul went to see Barbosa the morning the radio reported that the army was preparing to do a deal with the rebels. El Presidente had issued an order that no deal should be contemplated under any circumstances. He, El Presidente, would prevail. He would drive the rebels back into the sea. None of officers still in the army had even bothered to read the order.

Barbosa could fight if he liked. They had no desire to die for him and his cronies.

Raul found Barbosa apoplectic at this refusal to obey their President. But, as he asked the President when he arrived at the Palace, "What are you going to do about it?

"Presidente," he went on cuttingly, "you're beginning to sound like the Queen in that film 'Alice in Wonderland' which we saw at the British Embassy. You know – shouting 'Off with their heads'".

That had brought El Presidente up sharp. "Oh! You think you can turn on me as well, do you?"

Raul bit his tongue though he wanted to say, "No, I'm just telling you what in your heart you've known for weeks."

He watched as Barbosa sat there fuming impotently. El Presidente had taken to muttering to himself, issuing orders to aides and officials who either were not there or, if they were, simply ignored him. Increasingly he had only two settings – anger, self-pity, shouting, weeping, and flying into rages or, when the switch flipped, collapsing in tears.

Raul was the principal target of Barbosa's fury – what he wouldn't do to him once they had defeated Gaudi. But Raul no longer paid Barbosa any attention. Raul was a survivor. They called him a chancer. It was true. To him survival was taking whatever chances were there to be taken. The war was lost. It was time to move on. He was all business.

Choosing his moment when there was a lull in El Presidente's lamentations, Raul put his hand on Barbosa's shoulder and quietly conveyed the news,

"I've arranged with a pilot I know to fly us out to Miami if necessary. And, in my view, Don Basilio, it is necessary."

Barbosa stared into space wanting to say something but there was nothing to say. He didn't like being called Don Basilio. He was El Presidente. Was Raul trying to tell him something? If so, what?

Raul continued, relentlessly,

"Presidente, the army has capitulated, like it or not. The rebels will be at the outskirts of the capital in a day or so. Knowing Gaudi, he'll want to do something grand like making his entry on May Day which is on Wednesday. So I've arranged the flight for this evening. I suggest you talk to Dona Carmen and tell her to pack her best things. Then choose who comes with you. With luggage, there's only room for four on the plane so that means one other besides you, me and your wife. Dona Carmen will want to bring her mother, but you may have other ideas."

Barbosa's head was spinning. "But where shall we go? Where can we live? And, what's May Day?"

"Don't worry about May Day. You have enough to buy a place and live well, as long as Gaudi doesn't come after you for the money".

"Is that possible", Barbosa asked, suddenly child-like and fearful.

"It's possible but unlikely. The money's well hidden. Now I suggest you concentrate on the here and now. Go and talk to Dona Carmen and get yourself organised. I've made all the necessary arrangements - papers are being destroyed as we speak. Police Captain Gomes has organised two cars. There will be a jeep in front of us and one behind for security, both under Alberto's command. We leave here at six-o-clock. Please check your watch - it is now eleven thirty in the morning".

Raul turned and left. El Presidente mechanically checked his watch. Then he looked about him. He was going to lose all this. He gulped back his tears. No, he thought. I'm El Presidente. I will not leave my island. But the surge of passion passed as swiftly as it came on. The image of him standing in front of a wall with a blindfold on was enough to propel him out of the room and go in search

* * * * *

Gaudi and Nino had spent quite some time during the last weeks of the campaign preparing to take power. One of the questions they returned to often was what to do about Barbosa, Salcedo and the rest of those close to him. They both assumed that when they were within reach of the capital and things got too hot for him, Barbosa would make a run for it. How should they react? They disagreed vehemently.

"I'm in favour of letting him go", Gaudi said. "It'll confirm our narrative - that he's a corrupt coward who's plundered and looted Caribe and then run away".

"Respectfully, I don't agree, Companero", Nino replied. Unlike Gaudi who had come to Caribe only recently, Nino Acevedo was a Caribino. He had seen his life as an aspiring doctor blighted by the prejudice that ensured that a dark-skinned man from the interior would never get near Medical School. It was his barely contained bitterness that drove him to join Gaudi's struggle, and his obvious abilities that had led him to become Gaudi's trusted second-in-command.

"Barbosa should be caught and put on trial so that everyone would be in no illusion as to the crimes he is guilty of", the vehemence in Nino's voice surprising Gaudi.

In a rare example of compromise, Gaudi gave way. Barbosa would be captured.

Nino immediately set about creating what he called his 'snatch squad'. A hand-picked unit of thirty men with six jeeps would launch the operation on the Monday when the rebels' column was two days out from Puerto Grande. The planning was left to a young sergeant, Emilio, whom his colleagues called Zapata, on account of his name and his bushy moustache. The capitulation of the army made it easier for Emilio to organise his unit and rehearse the planned operation. There was no fear of sudden ambush except from a few Rurales who could easily be dealt with, not least because they were running out of ammunition.

Emilio sent four men on foot and in civilian clothes into Puerto Grande on the preceding Saturday. Their job was to reconnoitre the Palace and confirm Barbosa's whereabouts and the strength of the force protecting him. They reported back on the Sunday in mid-afternoon. Barbosa was in the Palace with his wife and Salcedo, plus a number of others, including police. The only guard they could detect was a unit of police under the command of Captain Gomes. The army seemed to have vanished. Most important, they reported that a police officer whom one of the unit had known in a previous life had told them that plans were being made for El Presidente to leave. The policeman didn't know any details beyond the fact that the escape was planned for the Monday evening.

Emilio spelled it out to Nino as he briefed him on the Sunday night. "In other words, tomorrow evening, Companero".

"You'll just have to bring the plans forward, Emilio".

Emilio nodded. The unit was told to be ready to move at dawn. The time of the snatch was brought forward to fourteen hundred hours on the Monday afternoon, just two and a half hours, though they didn't know it, after Raul had spoken to Barbosa. The jeeps set off in the early light, travelling in convoy into Puerto Grande through back roads. Occasionally, people in bars or standing around talking, stopped and stared. Some pointed excitedly. But for the most part, their progress was unremarked.

The Palace was a grand building in the birthday cake style of architecture, full of turrets and balconies. It could well have been designed by Walt Disney. Once through the gates, there was a sweeping drive ending in a forecourt on which stood two sentry boxes painted in the national colours of red and blue. The gates were unmanned and there was no-one in the sentry boxes. The army really had surrendered, Emilio thought. His column sailed through and drew up in the forecourt. The plan was to split into two: one group under Emilio was to force an entry through the front;

the other under Victor was to take the back. But, as soon as Victor's group rounded the side of the Palace and tried to make their way to the grand rear entrance, they were met by heavy fire from automatic weapons. A unit of Special Forces created within the police to guard the Palace had positioned itself so as to control the rear and the tree-lined avenue that led from there to the main road beyond. Victor's group had to fall back.

At the front, Emilio's group quickly forced their way into the Palace. The plans of the Palace that he'd got hold of were out of date. Instead of a small reception area from where they could launch their attack, they found themselves in a large open space with a sweeping staircase up to the next floor. At the top of the staircase, there was a landing from where police now opened fire. The group scrambled back and took cover outside, dragging two wounded colleagues with them. Emilio realised it was not going to be as simple an exercise as he had hoped. Rather than knocking over a demoralised bunch of ill-trained police, these were people who clearly knew what they were doing and were going to fight. Emilio called up Victor on his walkie-talkie and they huddled down against a wall at the side of the Palace to plan what to do.

Inside the Palace, when they heard the gunfire, Barbosa and Carmen stood rooted to the ground, shaking and not knowing where to turn. Their luggage was all upstairs as was Carmen's mother who Carmen had insisted should be the fourth passenger on the plane.

"What are you doing, Raul? What's happening," Barbosa squeaked, tugging at his sleeve, like a lost child.

"I'm trying to find out what's happening: who's doing the shooting".

"What are we going to do," Barbosa yelped, the presidential authority drained from his voice.

"Be quiet, Señor, and let me find out", Raul shot back. He made call after call then finally shouted "OK" into the walkie-talkie and signalled to the other two to follow him.

"We can't wait till this evening. We're leaving now", he barked.

Following Raul's lead, they hurried down a back staircase and made their way to the grand back doors. There were two jeeps outside full of police, armed to the teeth. A single car raced over to them. Alberto was driving and shouted, "Get in". They scrambled in. Carmen's anguished cry of, "My things! What about my things? And where's Mami?" died in her mouth when she saw the guns. One of the jeeps hurtled off towards the avenue and then the main road. The car followed. The other jeep manoeuvred itself to cover the back and both sides of the Palace, with a machine gun mounted on the back, while the Special Forces took up positions. Their orders were to hold the rebels off for half an hour and then surrender. El Presidente should be airborne by then.

In the car, Raul explained to the terrified Barbosa and Carmen that he had been able to re-arrange the flight. The pilot was waiting at the air-force base on the edge of the city. It had cost another $25,000 but he was sure that El Presidente would not begrudge it. Barbosa nodded weakly. The jeep and Alberto drove fast, with Alberto checking his mirror every few seconds. They ate up the distance and reached the base in just over fifteen minutes. The jeep stopped at the entrance while Alberto drew the car alongside the small plane and shouted for them to get going.

Barbosa seemed paralysed at the foot of the steps. Raul had to drag him up and into the plane. Then he went back for Carmen. Her hair was blown around by the wind from the propellers as she climbed the steps and instinctively she made to stop and get it back into shape. He pushed her inside unceremoniously and then shouted to the pilot to "Move it" as he closed the door. The luggage was left bandoned in the car. The pilot had left a mop and bucket in the tiny galley. Grabbing the bucket he lurched towards his seat and none-too-soon positioned it between Barbosa's feet as he threw up. As he did so, he heard gun fire. The jeep at the entrance was engaging rebels in three jeeps which were about to force their way through. The plane took off as bullets flew everywhere. Alberto meanwhile raced across the base and crashed through the gate marking a side entrance, leaving the police in the jeep to fend for themselves. Once on the road, he made for Puerto Grande and the Boss' friends who would hide him. He told himself that if the Boss couldn't take him on the plane, at least he'd try to protect him. He hoped it was true.

Chapter 25

The news breaks

It was early on the Tuesday morning, when the telephone rang. Melba answered. "I'll see if she is in", she said.

"She's in, Melba. Don't mess me around. Just fetch her". It was Raul.

Melba hurried to find Lydia. She was listening to Armando Manzanero's *Voy a apagar la luz* which always made her cry. She was crying when Melba burst in. Hearing the music, Melba reached out and held Lydia's hand for a moment. She knew it was Lydia's way of talking to Ramon, telling him, as the song says, that 'I'm going to turn out the lights so that I can think of you ...'. Then Melba said softly, "Señor Raul is on the phone and he won't go away. He sounds angry, but then what's new these days"

Lydia sighed. She lifted the needle up and handed the record to Melba to put away. Then she went through to take the call.

"Raul, how are you? I haven't heard from you in a while but I imagine you've been busy."

"Yes, Lydia, very busy. But I didn't call to discuss my workload. I rang to say goodbye".

"Goodbye?" she repeated, her voice betraying her shock.

"Yes. It's all over, I'm afraid. And I offer you my congratulations".

"What can you mean, Raul?"

"What I mean is that you and your little Professor won. El Presidente lost, so I lost."

She wasn't sure how to proceed. If Raul really was calling to say goodbye, she could acknowledge what he was saying without admitting anything.

But, it may be a trap. Raul liked traps, especially if they meant he could hurt someone. So, she continued,

"I can't begin to think what you are talking about, Raul. I'm sorry to hear that you think the government is about to fall. You'll remember I did try to help a little. And I'm mystified by your reference to my little Professor. Who can that be?"

"Bravo, Lydia. True to the part you've been playing so well for so long. I don't know how you did it but I'm sure you did do it, you and your damned Professor. Because of you, I have to start again, though this time," he added ruefully, "at least I'll have some cash in the Bank."

"I'm sorry Raul. You're not making any sense. I'm sorry you are down. You've been very kind to me and I do appreciate it. Perhaps you'd like to come over and have a drink and you can explain what's got into you".

"No more drinks, I'm afraid, my dear Lydia. And no more need to act as if you cared. Anyway, it's a bit far to come for a drink. We're in Miami, you see".

"Miami?" she repeated incredulously.

"Yes, Miami. You know, the Miami in Florida. But, forgive me. Don't let me forget. I left the best news till last. Gaudi is in charge. Your Professor? He's dead. He got himself killed. Sad, isn't it, that he'll miss all the fun."

She had dropped the telephone. She grabbed the back of a chair to support herself. Was this another example of Raul's apparently limitless desire to hurt? Or was it true? No, it could not be true. Cesar was so looking forward to the procession into the capital and then setting about the task of putting a smile back on the face of his little island. She stood there, her face drained of blood. Melba broke the silence. She had replaced the telephone and was looking at her mistress.

"What is it?"

"Raul says that Cesar has been killed".

"Ay Dios mio", Melba exclaimed as she crossed herself, then covered her face in her hands.

"Raul says he's in Miami. He says that Barbosa is finished and Gaudi is in charge. I don't know whether any of it is true or not. If it's true, we shall have won only to have lost. This Señor Gaudi is not the Professor."

Lydia made no mention of herself but Melba knew what she would be thinking – that if the Professor was indeed dead, she had now lost two men whom she had loved, who had given her a reason for living.

They both sat lost in their thoughts. At last Melba asked, "How can we find out? It's no good getting sad if it turns out not to be true".

"You are right, querida. But there's no-one I can contact. Perhaps there'll be something on the radio. Can you turn it on, please"?

Melba drew the shades to keep out the harsh morning sun and put the radio on. She went off to make some mint tea. When she came back, they both sat there listening in the muted light. Martial music was being played. Then a solemn voice intoned:

"Once again, we bring you the news that President Barbosa, his wife and his Chief of Staff, Señor Raul Salcedo, have fled the island and are seeking refuge in Miami in the United States. They escaped on an airplane after the President's guards had exchanged fire with a contingent of the rebel force. We will update you on this dramatic breaking story as soon as we have more information.

"In other news, the rebel army is within sight of the capital. The leader, Señor Jose Gaudi, is expected to enter in triumph within a day. This morning he issued the following statement:

"'Friends, Comrades, Citizens of Caribe, our struggle is over, our victory complete. The coward Barbosa has fled. Caribe can breathe again.

Tomorrow, May Day, the day when we honour workers, we will enter our Capital City. It will be a day of rejoicing. The struggle has been hard and long. Many have given their lives for the cause. We were sad to hear of the death of the elderly Professor reported by the foreign writer, Señor Conway. His death was one of many. We grieve them all. We are grateful to Señor Conway for telling you and the world the story of our march to freedom. We can forgive his confusion over the role of the Professor – he has let his romantic imagination get ahead of the facts. We held occasional conversations with the Professor but that was all. Now, it's a time for singing and dancing, for throwing off the shackles of oppression and for greeting a new dawn and a bright future for Caribe. I will celebrate with you in the Plaza Central tomorrow".

Lydia sat in numb desolation. This is what she had achieved – that this man Gaudi rather than her beloved Professor should triumph. Cesar was dead. Cesar was dead. It echoed in her heart. First Ramon then Cesar. She hadn't protected either.

Melba looked at her mistress. She looked as if her life had stopped. She was just sitting there, as beautiful as ever but with a look of abject despair in her eyes. Melba loved her. But what could she do? As Melba went over to her, the radio was reporting what was described as the story written by the English journalist who had been with the rebels from the start. It had appeared in London and been picked up in a number of capitals and in Puerto Grande. Señor Conway was describing the Professor as the leader of the revolution and suggesting, no more than suggesting, that he had been killed by Señor Gaudi's forces, that he'd been eliminated so that Señor Gaudi could claim power.

"Clearly, it was this story", the reporter went on, "that had caused Señor Gaudi to point out the Englishman's confusion". The reporter then made the decision of his career. "Clearly, Señor Conway was confused, as Señor Gaudi has explained. Now is not the time to allow dangerous rumours to fly around. Now is the time to greet and salute Señor Gaudi and his rebels and call them what they are, the saviours of Caribe". The reporter had chosen his job prospects over any abstract notion of 'the truth'. He would not be the last.

"So, it's a 'dangerous rumour' that Cesar was the leader of the revolution," Lydia murmured. "Poor Cesar. Poor Caribe". She took Melba's hand and held it for a moment and then let it drop. "What will happen? I can't think any more. We'll just have to sit here, Melba, and watch and wait. There's nothing more we can do".

Lydia looked spent, floored, desolate. Melba nodded and took the tea cups back to the kitchen. There was comfort in doing something. She uttered a silent prayer that God, whoever He was and wherever He was, should show mercy. Melba suggested to God that her mistress had suffered enough. Was God listening?

Melba's prayers were interrupted. Startled, she heard her mistress shouting "No, it can't be" and ran back to her. Lydia had dropped the phone again and, this time was crying so bitterly that her whole body shook.

"What is it"?

"I rang Mama's home number. I just wanted to speak to her. I wanted to hear her voice after so long. I wanted to tell her and Papa how much I loved them. I wanted to tell them the truth. But there was someone else in the house – a man I'd never heard of. He told me that they had moved to Mexico two months ago. He said they told him that they couldn't live in Caribe any longer. And, no, he said, he only had a poste restante address for them, nothing else, no phone number, nothing. Oh, Melba, I can't go on."

It was time for Melba to be the mother Lydia needed and which the childless Melba wanted to be. "We will get through, Lydia mia", Melba whispered as she took her in her arms and stroked her hair. "We will get through. We must be strong for each other. Come on. Let's put you in bed for a while. Things always look different after you've slept a while."

Melba guided Lydia to her bedroom and left her to undress while she made her a drink. She boiled some water and made a cup of camomile tea. Then she crushed two sleeping tablets into the tea and took it through. Lydia hadn't moved. Quietly, Melba helped her to lie down. Then she gave her the tea and pulled over her an old, much loved quilt that her mother had made. Tip-toeing out, Melba closed the door behind her and had another word with God.

Chapter 26

Lydia stays

While Lydia was sleeping, tossing and turning as dreams became nightmares, Circe was making plans.

Circe knew that Magda Gonzalez was right. "You have to get out of Puerto Grande as quickly as possible, chica. It is too dangerous here for you."

But, besides herself, there was someone else to think of – the one who had looked after her and inspired her.

"I must see her before I leave," Circe thought to herself. "That's the one thing I have to do. I just have to contact her. I'm the only one, besides Cesar, who knows what she has done. And now that Cesar's dead, what should I do about the secret I've been guarding? Does she want me to say nothing, or does she want me to tell the people of Caribe what she did for the revolution? She'll tell me what's best, I know".

But, first, Circe had spoken to Patricio. He'd taken her hand and said,

"It's going to be a bit scary for a while, Circe. I'll be meeting Teresa when the rebels reach the outskirts. We're going to hide out in the city for a while to see which way the wind's blowing. Do you want to join us? "

"That's very kind, chico, but no thanks. I'm going to pick up Tomas from his friend's house - there's no school because of everything going on in the city - and head for the countryside. I can't go back to San Felipe, it's too dangerous if people come looking for me, but, I have friends in Dos Pinos about ten kilometres on - far enough to be safe, I think. They'll look after us while I get Tomas settled and work out what to do. I tell you, Patricio, I'm scared about the future. It won't be the future that our beloved Professor Sanchez talked about."

"What do you think you'll do, Circe?"

"I'm going to carry on with my painting", smiling and trying to change the mood. "Atilio spent hours teaching me the mysteries of oil painting. You know, he said once that I have 'real talent'. Yes, you know, 'talent', like you and your music," laughing.

"God, I hope you're not that bad," he joked back, both trying not to part on a sad note, not knowing if or when they would see each other again. The time at the Circulo had been so intense. And now... .

"Now to get in touch with her", Circe said to herself as she waved goodbye. At the Bar where she helped out, Ruben, the owner, saw her come in and greeted her warmly.

"Circe, can you work all day tomorrow", he asked as they exchanged pecks on the cheek. "Please. I'll need all the help I can get with all those thirsty soldiers coming into the city. And I need to look after you – it won't be safe and you're my girl".

"Yeah, yeah, your girl, like all the others", Circe mocked him. "I don't know about working. Can I let you know later?" It wasn't a good idea to let on that she was leaving the city, not even to Ruben. "But, hey, Ruben, can you do me a favour? Can I use your phone again, please? And, no, it's not a boy".

"Go ahead", he said laughing.

Circe dialled Lydia's home number. The phone rang for a long time till eventually Melba answered.

"Hello, Señorita Echevarria's residence".

"Melba, it's me, Circe from the Circulo. Is Lydia there please? It's urgent".

"Hola, Circe. I'm afraid Lydia is sleeping. You've heard the news about the Professor. She is devastated."

"Yes, Melba, I have. It's too, too awful. That's why I need to speak to her. I know it's the worst time, but help me please. It may not be safe for me to come to you, so could you please ask her to meet me at the Circulo in an hour's time. There won't be any lights on, but I will be inside. Tell her to ring the bell twice".

"I'll try to make sure she'll be there but I can't promise. I've given her some sleeping pills."

"Do what you can, please, Melba. It really is important."

It was three hours before the bell rang twice at the Circulo. Circe had almost given up. After collecting Tomas from his friend's house, Circe had packed a rucksack with clothes and toiletries for her and her little brother. He had his school back-pack which she'd packed with some food for the journey. They had been playing cards for what seemed an eternity. Poor Tomas was getting tired and crabby and wanted to go home. He didn't know yet what was going to happen: that he would not be going home; that they were leaving once his sister had had a chance to talk to the Señorita. Circe planned to take the bus which left the city to the west, avoiding the rebels who were coming in from the south. When they reached Laguna they would catch the bus to Dos Pinos, though it was getting so late that they might miss the last bus and have to spend the night somewhere in Laguna.

When she heard the bell, Circe ran to open the door and let her in. Lydia looked bedraggled. Her eyes were puffy and her face paler than pale with no trace of make-up. She had a scarf over her head and was wearing old jeans and her black flat pumps, with a light blue sweater which would ordinarily have complimented her dark eyes but on this occasion merely offered a contrast between light and dark. They fell into each other's arms and held on. Tomas hugged her too, though he could only reach her waist. For a moment neither knew what to say. The death of Cesar had changed everything. Their world would not be as they had dared to hope. There would not be a smile on Caribe's face, they feared, with Gaudi in charge.

Circe broke the silence. "I'm going away, Lydia. It's too dangerous here for me if they start coming for those of us in the network. But what about you? No-one knows about you and Cesar except me, and I won't tell. They think you were part of Salcedo's crowd, so you may be in danger too. Do you want me to tell anyone what you really did for the cause. They can't hurt you then. I could tell the Englishman Conway before I leave."

"No, Circe. You must get away and look out for yourself and this beautiful little brother of yours," bending down to kiss Tomas. Lydia reached for her handbag and pulled out an envelope full of notes. "Here's some money. It will help and I don't need it. I will look after myself. They will come for me, I'm sure".

Circe looked at her. There was a quality of resignation in her, a kind of tragic beauty about her.

"Lydia, thank you, thank you so much. The money will help. But you. If you think they will come for you, you must leave. Come with me till we can put a plan together. You will be safe with us."

"I know, chica, but I will stay. I made my choices a long time ago and now I must see them through".

Circe was conscious of the time and the need to leave, but felt that she must not abandon her without making one last try. "What's this talk of choices? What choices, Lydia? The situation has changed. We have Gaudi instead of our Professor. You owe Gaudi nothing. Come with us."

"You are right, Circe. I owe Gaudi nothing. But there are others I do owe something, indeed everything to. So, I will meet that obligation. I will pay my debt".

Circe did not understand – how could she? Ever the sensible, practical young woman, she was unable to understand the mood, the sort of meditation that her friend had lapsed into. She just saw a problem in front of her – her adored friend's safety – and wanted to solve it. Resignedly,

Circe managed "OK" and sighed deeply, then said, "Come on sleepy head" to Tomas who had been watching them through drooping eyelids. "I will get word to you, Lydia, one way or another, and let you know where we are. The invitation is always there. I love you very much, sister. May you stay safe."

And with that, she turned, picked up the bags, took Tomas' hand and left, fighting back the tears.

"I love you too, Circe. You are the best", Lydia shouted after her. Then she too left, closing the Circulo's front door behind her for what she reflected sadly would be the last time. Slowly, she made her way through the velvet soft light of early evening to the apartment in Roosevelt Tower.

Chapter 27

Tea with Magda

Conway sat sipping tea with Magda Gonzalez that Tuesday morning as they discussed what he should do. He was torn. He wanted to stay not just to report on what would be happening tomorrow outside in the streets on V Day, on the flight of Barbosa, and the fate of those left behind. He also wanted to dig further into the death of Cesar. But, he knew that when Ines had given his report to Nino, he became a marked man. And now that the report had been published, his accusation, as Nino saw it, would mean that he could say goodbye to any contact with Gaudi and those around him. There would be no interviews. No final coda to the campaign. He could observe from a distance and file a last despatch but even this carried a risk. There could easily be another 'accident', this time involving 'the foreign writer'.

These were the thoughts he shared with Magda. She nodded.

"You may not be in any danger, Tony. It could be that Gaudi and those around him will be too drunk with success to bother with you. But I doubt it". Lapsing into English, she went on, "You have rained on their parade big time, as the Americans would say." Back in Spanish, she went on, "They will not forget nor forgive. There would be an 'accident'. So, my dear Tony, this is what we will do".

"I will telephone the man at the British Embassy whom you dealt with". Conway was about to interrupt and say that this particular man was the last person whom he could turn to, but Magda went on, "I will ask him to send a car for you, explaining that you may be in danger. You should be able to get to the Embassy without anything happening. Gaudi won't want to start his reign with an international incident. Once in the Embassy, your man - what's his name?"

"Jeremy Brown".

"Yes. Well, Mr Brown will make contact with Gaudi's people, extend congratulations on behalf of his government and offer to get you out of their hair by putting you on a flight to Miami. You will agree not to write anything or give an interview repeating your 'accusations'. Then off you'll go to the airport. Of course once you are back in London you can do and say what you like. Jeremy Brown may not be best pleased, but he'll have moved on soon, you're not coming back, and Gaudi needs the trade deal that Barbosa was negotiating."

Conway was seriously impressed. "Have you ever thought of running for President yourself? But seriously, it's a great idea, but what makes you think Brown will play ball?"

"Oh, he'll play ball. My husband looks after a number of the Embassy staff. I'll just remind our Jeremy that it may be pay-back time for all that my husband has done for him - call-outs in the middle of the night after eating the wrong things, or being bitten by one of our less friendly spiders, not to mention the occasional bout of the clap - all free of charge, of course".

He was completely bowled over. "My Heavens, Magda, you are a genius".

She inclined her head though she did not dissent. "So let's get to it", she said, all action again.

Conway sat sipping tea as she phoned the British Embassy and asked to be put through to Mr Brown. "It's Dr. Gonzalez's wife", she advised the person on the other end. "And could you please let him know that it's urgent. Yes, I'll hold on", she added. Then, after a couple of minutes, he heard her say, "Mr Brown, how kind of you to take my call. You'll remember my husband, of course. Yes". Then, "I'm well thank you", followed by, "Interesting times we are living through, don't you think."

Without waiting for an answer, Magda went on, "I have the young English journalist, Tony Conway with me. He's having a cup of tea - very English. He's in a spot of what I think you call 'bother'. As you will know, he's written something about Mr Gaudi which I understand that Mr Gaudi has taken against. It may expose Mr Conway to danger. So, he needs help. This is what I've planned". She then set out the plan that she'd described moments ago.

After a couple of 'Yeses' and an 'Of course', Magda smiled broadly and said, "Thank you so much, Jeremy. I may call you Jeremy, may I? Wonderful!"

She put the phone back in its cradle. "Well that's all fixed. Your friend Brown wasn't entirely 'over the moon' do you say, but he got the point. The car will be here in forty minutes, so shall we have another cup of tea?"

Conway could only sit back in admiration. His "thank you, Magda" was heartfelt and she recognised it. She got up and gave him a kiss on the top of his head.

"You've done us and Caribe a great service, Tony. It is I who should thank you. Now we have a new fight on our hands, and we'll have to fight it without your help, I'm afraid. We will miss you".

They sat lost in their thoughts – Conway hoping that he'd get through the next few hours unscathed, Magda dwelling on the future and how to keep Cesar's dream alive. He went up to the room in which he'd spent what looked like his last night in Caribe, packed his things and came down again. Consuela cleared away the teapot and cups.

"Ah! Here's the car", Magda exclaimed.

Conway got up and joined Magda at the window.

"Blimey, Jeremy's driving and he's got the little Union Jack flying on the car. He's not taking any chances. I'll go out, Magda. You stay here.

"I can't thank you enough", he added, offering a peck on the cheek. Magda pulled him close and hugged him. "Please ask Jeremy to excuse me if I don't come out", she said. "It's better if you leave as if you were one of my husband's patients". Then it was "Goodbye, my friend," and she turned away as he made his way to the front door.

The moment Conway put his bag on the back seat and climbed into the Embassy's black Morris Oxford, Brown pulled away. He was wearing his usual lightweight fawn suit, brown suede slip-ons, a blue shirt and the inevitable College tie, his brow glistening with sweat and his mouth firmly set. He appeared to be concentrating on the busy traffic and didn't acknowledge him. There was no effort at conversation. Indeed, the atmosphere was not so much cool as arctic

"Thanks for going along with Señora Gonzalez's plan, Jeremy" - his attempt to make a crack in the ice if not break it.

Brown was having nothing of it. "Well it was that or you causing another bloody international incident. Look, Conway, you've got your job to do as have I. You are causing me grief right now so the best thing is for you to keep quiet while I get us to the airport".

"The airport! I thought we were going back to the Embassy. I need to make some phone calls and touch base with one or two people".

"You can phone from Miami or London. There won't be any touching base, I'm afraid. Gaudi's man Nino wants you out or you'll find yourself falling off the Malecon - his words not mine."

"What about tickets and stuff?"

"There's an envelope on the back seat. It has a one way ticket to London via Miami and a temporary passport, just in case you need it. There are a hundred dollars in twenties and, Conway, an invoice. Her Majesty's taxpayers are not footing the bill nor am I. I'd appreciate it, therefore, if you or your employers would reimburse me here. And just to be clear, I don't give a toss what you think about Gaudi or his friends. What you don't understand apparently, is that I and the Embassy have to work with whatever the wind blows in. If one of our compatriots decides to shit all over their show, it makes our job that much more tricky, if you get my drift. At the very least you could have warned us what you were going to say. Then we could have crafted something that put some distance between us while making it clear how important we regard the freedom of the press. But, no you wanted your moment in the sun and I'm the one getting burned while you go home to sodding wherever it is".

"Belsize Park, actually", he offered, almost instinctively.

"I don't fucking care where it is", Brown hissed. "Look. Do me a favour. Just get on the plane. And when you get to London, write a few pieces on the Arsenal or whatever, and let Caribe get on with what it's going to get on with".

"I couldn't write about the Arsenal. I support West Brom." He couldn't resist being flippant. This was a different Brown from the buttoned-up version he'd previously dealt with. Brown was obviously angry, but why? Yes, he'd embarrassed him and the Embassy by going over the wall but that was months ago. Since then he alone had been the narrator of the revolutionary campaign - a British journalist, Brown could proudly boast. There'd been his scoop about the launch of the armed struggle, followed by a string of pieces which had been widely published and seen his name put forward for an award. And then he'd produced the piece about the mysterious and suspicious death of Cesar. He didn't regret it. He thought it ought to have been said. He was proud he had said it. He could see that he had put Brown and the Embassy in a difficult spot but he didn't think it was entirely fair to throw him under the bus so as to keep in with Gaudi - someone who might not be the nicest person to keep in with anyway. He suddenly thought of those Lectures on Cicero at University about the challenge of steering a course between principles and politics in a time of revolution. He wished he'd paid more attention.

Brown could see there was no point in replying to Conway. They were on different wave lengths, wrestling with different challenges.

They sat in silence until Brown pulled up outside the Departure Lounge.

Conway opened his door then reached over to retrieve the bag and the envelope that Brown had put on the back seat.

"Bye, Jeremy. Thanks for the lift".

Brown drove off.

* * * * *

Conway spent the hours on the plane to London writing his last despatch. He explained that he was filing it from London. Sadly, he said, he would not be in Puerto Grande for the revolution's V Day. The new rulers had taken umbrage at his suggestion that it was Professor Sanchez who had been the father of the revolution but that he had been 'conveniently' killed, clearing the way for the Argentinian Union leader. He ended by thanking the staff of the British Embassy for their support in facilitating his departure. In a final flourish, as a memorial to the Professor, he promised that he would continue to investigate the circumstances of his death.

At the Globe, Harry met him at the door and shook him by the hand. Dropping into street vernacular, he shouted "You did good, my boy", provoking laughter and applause from those who had come down to say 'Welcome back'. Harry, once in his office, said how pleased he was. "I didn't know whether sending you there would pay off - either in terms of something happening or in terms of you being able to be a proper reporter. But we hit the jackpot. It all kicked off and you produced a stream of great stories. Well done, son. Now, let's see. Take a couple of days off and then I want you on the Profumo business. There's still stuff to dig up".

Conway stared at him in disbelief. "Harry, I'm knackered. I've been living in tents and God knows what for months, being shot at occasionally, and then having to get out pretty sharpish. How about a bit of a rest?"

Harry broke into a laugh, hugging his ample stomach. "Just joking, son. By all means have some time off. We've talked about it and here's the plan. You can have a month off on full pay, courtesy of the Head Boy. I was against it, I might say, but he's a softy. Then we'll give you a four months sabbatical. You write the book. We serialise the book. We make some money. You make some money. And you become famous, or should I say, more famous?"

So, that was the arrangement. All that was left was for Conway to head for the George on Haverstock Hill. He had dreamed of sitting in the corner of his local pub with a pint and a bag of plain crisps for months. Now he was doing just that. He sat there in his old jeans and a loose sweater (yes, he had put on a bit of weight). He bought all the newspapers and slowly began the process of re-entering the world that had been his only world until Caribe.

Chapter 28

Justice

It was a bright warm May Day morning when the rebels entered Puerto Grande. Gaudi, Nino and as many others as could cling on drove into the Plaza Central on the old tank, the caterpillar tracks wreaking havoc on the metalled roads. Estimates put the number of people in the Plaza to welcome Gaudi at close to a hundred thousand. There were flags and placards and banners everywhere. The mood was one of contagious excitement and optimism.

The optimism for the future was the counterbalance to anger at the past. Barbosa had not been popular from the outset and the combination of his corruption and random cruelty had ensured that it was not long before he was despised by all but the few who caught the crumbs from his table. The crackdown which had followed the launch of the rebels' campaign had made things worse, if that were possible. It had brought into the open the henchmen who did his dirty work for him, principal among whom was Raul Salcedo. According to the radio, he had escaped with Barbosa. Those who had not escaped could expect that the fury which the crowd had hoped to direct at him would be redirected even more bitterly at them. There was, in other words, a dark side to the mood of excitement. It meant that the desire for revenge, for the rendering of an account, was also in the air. Gaudi knew that he must play to both emotions if he was to consolidate his power and rid himself of those who might oppose him.

The next two days were declared to be public holidays. Work would begin after the weekend. Till then the citizens of Puerto Grande and all over the island had a party. And it was some party. Bars overflowed, bands played. Day became night became day. Hugs and kisses and more were exchanged. Love was in the air, in the park, on the beach, and in the bedroom.

Gaudi, Nino and the senior team set up headquarters in a nondescript office block downtown in the Calle Formosa near the Malecon. The plans they had made for communicating with the people were quickly put into operation. The Diario was taken over and renamed La Lucha (*The Struggle*). The existing staff were thrown out none-too-ceremoniously and Ines Fonseca was installed as the new editor. A similar change of management took place at Radio Central and at various local radio stations. Stories which had been prepared in the final weeks of the campaign, celebrating victory and rejoicing in Gaudi' leadership, began to be broadcast. The first was a statement by Gaudi himself:

"Fellow citizens, we will hold elections within the next six months. This will give you a chance to judge us and what we have done in your name. Until then, I, Jose Gaudi, will serve as Interim President and my second in command during the campaign, Nino Acevedo, will serve as First Minister. We are your friends and colleagues. We do not want nor need titles. They are a hangover from the past, the time of oppression. Just call us Companeros – that's what we are."

In the early weeks, changes came thick and fast. To consolidate his power, Gaudi integrated into the existing army those of his forces who wished to continue to serve, under the command of senior rebel leaders. Those who wished to return to civilian life were awarded a generous grant so they could re-integrate into civilian life. An education programme was announced with a target of one hundred percent literacy within three years. A public health programme was launched. Teachers, doctors and nurses were required to spend a year in the countryside after qualifying before being able to work in the larger towns and in Puerto Grande. To pay for these measures, banks were taken over and the state took majority shareholdings in the sugar, tobacco and agricultural industries. An Economic Council, chaired by Gaudi was to manage the economy. To 'ensure stability', as he called it, Gaudi announced that the Alianza would be outlawed and other 'political groupings' would need to be authorised by the state.

The reaction was swift and predictable. Amidst international condemnation, led by the United States, there was a mass exodus of those who could leave - Americans and wealthier Caribinos. The airport was clogged for weeks as flights left for Mexico City and Miami. Those who had seen the writing on the wall had made sure to transfer their assets out of the island. The less perceptive (or more trusting) saw their assets confiscated as the price of obtaining a permit to leave. Unsurprisingly, tourism which had been withering on the vine in the past years anyway, completely collapsed. Hotels stood empty and staff were laid off.

Those who could not afford to leave hoped for the best, peering into the future in the hope of seeing the new dawn. Others settled in for another bout of political musical chairs in which the names might change but the reality wouldn't.

* * * * *

As they had marched on the capital, Gaudi and Nino had talked most evenings late into the night about what they would do once they'd reached Puerto Grande and taken power. It was Nino who asked on one of the evenings, "Once we've got control, companero, how are we going to keep it?"

"How do you mean, exactly".

"Well, what do we do about keeping people in line? We can't trust Barbosa's people. The police are corrupt and the judges do what they are told or put their judgements out to tender. And, anyway, most of the lawyers and judges are in Florida now, trying to pass the State Bar Exam so they can rip off the Yanquis like they ripped us off. If we are going to make a revolution, we need courts and judges, but our courts and our judges."

"I understand, companero. It's another of the questions that we need to look at – God knows, there's no lack of them! I've been concentrating on the economy. But, you are right. An early test for us will be how we deal with those who choose not to join us; who think they can oppose us. The people who've welcomed us so warmly will be watching what we do. They'll want action. They'll want justice.

"Why don't you get a group together, Nino," Gaudi went on, "and come up with a plan or a proposal? Call it the 'Justice Group'. In time, I suppose we'll have to come up with some sort of Constitution, so having a go at sorting out what you might call crime and punishment could be part of that."

Nino needed no second invitation. He had seen and been on the wrong end of the old system. They had to change it and change it in a way which really signalled a new start. He put together a group which met in the early morning for an hour while the day's campaign was being organised - while orders were being issued, targets identified, and units were moving out. They sat round a table outside Nino's tent. Besides him, there was Ines Fonseca and her sister Sylvia, an ex-army lawyer named Ricardo Leon who had deserted the moment the campaign was launched, and someone from the union named Bernal Calderon whom Gaudi had proposed - whether to assist or report back to Gaudi, or both, was left unsaid. Usually, one of Nino's staff would lay on a large pot of coffee, a jug of water, and either eggs or fruit depending on what was available, with freshly-made flat bread.

Ricardo Leon tended to take the lead. At the first meeting, he declared,

"Companeros, If we are going to do this right, we have to separate out the usual run-of-the mill petty criminals - the 'pains in the ass' - from those who want to attack us and what we plan to build".

He was passionate about the need to deal with what he called "the wreckers", banging his fist on the table for emphasis. "There must be no mercy. It'll be them or us".

"So what do you propose, Companero Ricardo", Sylvia asked him softly. She rarely spoke except in a whisper.

"Well if there are two kinds of people we have to deal with, we need two kinds of courts. I suppose the first should really be about getting the person to stop messing around and get back on the right path. The second - we're talking about eliminating the threat."

"Eliminating", Sylvia pressed. They all recognised that this was an important moment.

"Yes, eliminating, Companera. Locking them up or shooting them, whichever serves the purpose."

Nino held up his hands as a couple of the others began to get agitated.

"Friends. There you have it. Thank you, Companero Leon. The 'pains in the ass' are easy, but, he asks us how should we deal with those who would destroy us. I am with him. I agree that we must deal with them without flinching. We owe it to those who have got us here and want us to build a new Caribe, one that cannot tolerate enemies within. Companero Leon has started the conversation. Let's work on a blueprint and then take it to Companero Gaudi and the War Council."

* * * * *

Once he had his feet under the table of power as First Minister, Nino set about putting into operation the approach that the Justice Group had thrashed out in those last days of the campaign. For the petty crimes, Ricardo Leon had come up with the idea of Tribunales Populares (People's Courts). Nino had said it was a great idea and a great name.

"This is how I see them working," Nino said. "They've got to be court, classroom and street theatre all rolled into one. There'll be one in each

Barrio and local neighbourhood. We'll hold them in the evenings so people can go after work. We'll keep an eye on anyone who doesn't go – if they're the people's courts we want the people there".

"What about judges", a young assistant in his office had asked.

"Well, what about them? What do think we should do?"

The assistant paused, taken aback by being consulted by the First Minister. "Perhaps we could get people from the Barrio – 3 perhaps."

"Excellent. Thank you. That's what we'll do. And what's your name, please?"

"Gloria, Companero", she replied, blushing deeply.

Nino smiled.

Early on, Nino sat in on one of the new People's Courts to see how it was run and whether any changes were needed. The case involved a Carlos Morales, the son of a taxi-driver according to the charge sheet. The Court met in the open on a steamy Tuesday evening. The afternoon rain had passed through, leaving puddles but no real sense of relief from the oppressive heat. In fact, if anything, it seemed even more humid. A street, the Rincon de Cinco de Mayo, had been blocked off on the edge of the Barrio La Joya and chairs had been put out as if in a cinema or theatre. The trial was scheduled to begin at 7.00pm. Neighbours with children in tow began to appear around 7.30pm. This was their first Tribunal in the Barrio, so it was a new experience. There was much discussion to and fro about what it was all about. Dogs wandered in and out of the chairs, scuffling over scraps of food thrown to them by people as they ate the last of their dinner. Cats curled up on window sills watching through half-closed eyes. Most of those attending were women - the men had opted for the baseball on television. Newspapers and magazines served as fans.

By 8.15pm the panel decided that they could begin – about half of the seats were taken and there were people still arriving. The two men and a woman on the panel seated themselves at a table at one end of the blocked-off street. One of the men, Saul Noriega, the chairman on this occasion, banged a make-shift gavel on the table and called for order. The audience settled down.

"Welcome, companeros, to the first Tribunal Popular in our Barrio. I know most of you here, but, just in case, I'm Saul, Saul Noriega. We're here to see what is acceptable and what is unacceptable in the new Caribe. Will the accused step forward?"

Saul pointed Carlos to the chair at the side of the table. At the back, Josefina, his mother, watched with a mixture of shame, fear and horror. What was going to happen to her boy? He'd got himself mixed up in politics and look where it had landed him. His father, Luis, had virtually disowned him.

It was true that Carlos had been a member of the Alianza and therefore was someone to be watched. But, unbeknown to his mother, because he hadn't told her, the charge that evening had nothing to do with his politics. One evening, after a long and frustrating day working at the shoe shop, instead of going straight home, he went to the ice-cream parlour in the Plaza de Roma.

Saul read out the charge.

"The accused, Companero Morales, took his tray with a tub of vanilla and pistachio ice-cream and a glass of iced water back to a table in the ice-cream parlour and sat under a street light so that he could read his magazine. As he sat there, a young waitress, Amalia Prieto, came over to wipe down his table. When he ignored her, Companera Amalia moved his tray towards him so that she could at least wipe most of the table. In the process she knocked his magazine. The accused looked up. Furious, he put his hands under the tray and knocked it into the air. The glass shattered on the floor and ice-cream went all over the Companera who, understandably, cried out. The accused then swore at her and was about to walk off when he was stopped by two other waiters".

Saul called several witnesses to verify the account. He then asked Carlos if he wished to say anything. He looked down and shook his head.

"Speak up, Companero, please".

Carlos shook his head again and said "No gracias, Señor". His mother was pleased that he'd at least remembered to be polite for once.

"Now, Companero, we have to decide what we should do."

* * * * *

The group that Nino had assembled had agreed early on in their deliberations that, as regards the People's Courts, it wasn't what the accused had done that was most important. It was necessary to set it out but it was only a prelude. It was the next stage that mattered - what the Court should do about it.

They'd argued back and forth about what to do with the guilty – how should they be punished.

"Putting people in prison isn't an option." This was the union member, Calderon. "We're talking about petty crimes and anyway what's the point of putting people in jail in the new society based on the dignity of work. It would just mean that they couldn't be productive workers nor could those who had to guard them."

They all agreed, despite some dissent from Ricardo Leon who was something of a hard-liner.

"What about fines", Leon then asked.

"No way," Ines shouted hotly. "I've seen all those rich society girls constantly getting into hot water for some reason or another and then just paying whatever the fine was, courtesy of Papa. This is while poor families had to go hungry to pay a fine (or buy off the police) just for being too noisy in the street. That's not what we want for the future".

"There won't be rich Papas in our society," Ricardo Leon argued. "And we could make the fine reflect what the accused earns".

They went back and forth for some time. Eventually, they decided not to use fines, at least for the time being.

"We can come back to it," Nino offered, "if we need to. So, now. We've rejected prison and fines. I propose we do the following. Ricardo and I will put together a protocol for the Court's panel to follow in deciding cases. If you agree, companeros, the key must be that the panel must engage with the local people attending the trial and use their imagination to design sanctions that educate rather than just punish offenders."

They all agreed enthusiastically. When Nino produced the protocol, it was signed off by everyone. Then it was printed and distributed.

* * * * *

Saul reminded himself of the protocol and then turned to the audience.

"So, my friends, what should we do with Companero Morales? We need to do something – what he did was wrong - but we need you to guide us. He is part of our community. It should be you who decide. It's now nine-o-clock so let's discuss for a while and then we'll make our decision. That means we should be able to finish by 9.30pm."

Saul saw Nino nod approvingly. Not only had Saul understood the purpose of the exercise but it was also a skilful exercise in leadership. He had drawn them in but also indicated that they would not be there for ever - they'd be home in half an hour or so.

An elderly woman, a friend of Josefina, put her hand up. She was invited to give her name and speak. "I'm Evangelina. You all know me. I live over there", pointing to the corner of the street. "Carlos is a good boy. He work hard. He just had a bad day. We all have 'em," she added, turning to her neighbours who nodded in agreement. "I think all he need is a good telling off. That teach him a lesson".

A young man still in fatigues and beard immediately jumped up. "I'm Anibal Figueroa. I'm from La Fortaleza, but I'm staying here with my aunt in the Barrio."

"Welcome, Anibal", Saul replied. "It's a privilege to have a young fighter amongst us. Go ahead. Give us your view".

"Whether Companero Morales is a good boy or not depends on the facts before the Tribunal. Clearly he is not a good boy because he has behaved badly - he has assaulted the waitress and sworn at her. You", pointing to the panel, "should make an example of him." Anibal sat down amid murmuring.

The arguments went back and forth. The audience had got the bit between their teeth. As 9.30 approached, Saul banged down the gavel.

"Companeros. Thank you. This has been a very good example of what justice in the new Caribe will look like. Some of you have spoken. We and you have heard the views expressed. Now, guided by you, we will decide what to do."

He pulled his chair back and the other two members of the panel huddled around him. While they deliberated, the audience continued to argue, some heatedly. After a few moments Saul banged his gavel again.

"Companero Morales, stand up."

The audience went quiet. Josefina crossed herself and closed her eyes.

"Companero Morales, clearly, even though you work in a shop, you do not seem to understand the demands made on those who serve others, particularly those who wait on tables. You need to have the opportunity to learn and we will give it to you. We believe that a sanction is called for and that a fitting sanction would be to work as a waiter cleaning tables in the ice-cream parlour every evening for two weeks. That will give you a greater insight into the contribution made by other workers and make you a better person".

The audience broke into applause. Josefina realised she had been holding her breath and breathed out. Carlos accepted the penalty. In truth he'd expected much worse.

* * * * *

The other question which had occupied Nino's Justice Group was what they should do about those whom Ricardo Leon called 'wreckers'. Nino had agreed with him when he talked about 'eliminating the threat' from 'enemies within'. In the weeks that followed, Nino and Leon had set about designing another new system – this time to deal with what they began to call 'crimes against the state'.

In the first few days after the rebels had entered the capital, Nino was given the responsibility of dealing with those who openly opposed the revolution – the enemies within. The most prominent had been rounded up and detained. They were dealt with within weeks. It was summary justice at best - the law of the victor. One of the first persons to be dealt with was Captain Alberto Gomes. He had been captured two days after fleeing the airfield where he'd taken Barbosa, his wife and Raul. Within two weeks he was in front of what Nino and Gaudi had agreed should be called Revolutionary Tribunals. Four of these Tribunals had been set up – at a military base in the capital and in three of Caribe's major towns.

Military officers served as judges. The accused could be sent to prison or executed.

Nino made sure that Alberto was dealt with in Puerto Grande where he could chair the panel of judges.

"It's vitally important", he told the group of thirty officers he had selected to sit as judges, "that you know what's expected of you and how to proceed. You should be in no doubt as to the importance of the responsibility you bear and the trust I'm placing in you. The trial of former police captain Gomes can serve as an example."

As a consequence, all thirty of the officers crowded into the room where the trial was held: to watch and learn.

Gomes was brought in. His handcuffs were removed.

"Alberto Gomes", Nino intoned, "you are charged with war crimes. The maximum sentence is execution by firing squad. Do you understand?"

Alberto ignored him. He was not inclined to co-operate with the Tribunal but that did not concern Nino. He called witnesses and questioned them himself - there were no lawyers. After just over an hour, Nino and the two other members of the panel retired for fifteen minutes, giving Alberto time to shake out a Camel for what turned out to be his last smoke. On their return, Nino spoke,

"We find you guilty of all of the charges." Turning to one of the guards, he said, "Take him away".

He was taken out to the parade ground, stood up against a wall and shot.

The officers observing the trial were duly impressed.

Captain Gomes' execution was reported widely and greeted with widespread approval. Many were disappointed, particularly those in the unions, that Raul Salcedo had escaped justice, but there was a feeling that Alberto was the next best thing. If Alberto gave it a thought as he walked the few yards from the courtroom to the parade ground, he probably reflected that Raul had not protected him after all, but then that's what bosses do. They let you take the rap.

Chapter 29

Lydia meets Nino

Lydia busied herself in her apartment. She wasn't sure who would pay the rent now that Raul had left, but decided to cross that bridge when she came to it. For the moment, she watched and waited to see what Gaudi would do with the revolution that unknown to him she'd had such a significant role in bringing about. Mostly she wrote. She had decided to put on paper what she had done - as a record. She didn't plan to give it to anyone, far less to try to publish it, but it served as a kind of therapy.

As she wrote, she could grieve again over the deaths of Ramon and Cesar and her decision to cut herself off from her family. She could describe the successes she had achieved through her collaboration with Cesar and the network. And she could ask what the revolution would bring and what lay ahead for her. As she had said to Circe, she was sure that they would come for her. The only knowledge they had of her was as Raul's partner, supporting Barbosa's tyranny and consorting with those who were now described as the oppressors.

"Yes", she said to herself, one day, "to them I was an oppressor and there's no-one to say otherwise but me. And who would believe an oppressor?"

She was right. They did come for her one morning nearly three months after Gaudi's entry into the capital. It was Nino's doing. He had worked his way through his list of those to be dealt with. She was next. She was the rich, spoiled beauty set up in a fancy apartment paying homage to the court of Barbosa and Salcedo and their vile cronies.

As Nino confided in Gaudi, one evening, "Raul may have escaped but his courtesan won't. We have to make an example of her, Companero. She is Caribe's dishonourable past, not its bright future."

There were two of them, military police in fatigues and boots, shown in by Melba. Lydia had been expecting them, so she had a bag of clothes, toiletries and books already packed.

"Would you permit me to change my clothes?"

They nodded. One looked round her bedroom, checked the window, then stood by the door out of sight while she changed into a pair of old jeans, a bright pink sweater and tennis shoes. As she came out of her room, Melba took her in her arms and held her close. In a whisper, Melba told her, "Be brave, my love". Lydia pushed an envelope into Melba's hands. One of the police tried to take it from her, but she politely asked him not to.

"It's just some notes about where she should go and things which need to be done, plus a bit of money. That's all."

In truth it also contained the journal that she had been working on over the past months. Knowing that they would search the apartment, Lydia was keen to make sure that it would not fall into their hands. Turning to Melba she said, "Go to Consuela. She's expecting you". Then she turned and said to the police. "Shall we go?" One of them carried her bag.

Lydia was taken to the central police station. Her bag was taken from her and put aside. "What do you think this is, Companera, a hotel", the angry-looking policewoman on the desk asked her. Lydia smiled and said she understood, but perhaps she could keep just one book as well as some toiletries and a change of clothes. The policewoman allowed her just the toothbrush and toothpaste and some tampons. Though she pulled a face at being allowed so little, she offered up a silent prayer of 'thank you' to whoever was up there - secreted in the box of tampons was an old torn photograph held together by scotch tape. It was Ramon.

She was fingerprinted and photographed and then led down a flight of stairs into a gloomy corridor lit by an overhead neon light. There were ten cells along one side. Hers was Number 4. As the door clanged shut, she thought back to the moment she had been put in a cell by Captain Gomes' policemen. That was where her life had changed. It was where she'd betrayed Ramon and where she'd promised him that she would get justice for him. Well, the revolution that he'd fought and died for had come to Caribe, Barbosa and Raul had gone and Gomes, who she thought had probably shot Ramon, had himself been shot. That was the plus side. On the other side was the death, most likely the murder, of Cesar and a revolution which was not the one Ramon, Cesar and she had dreamed of. Was that justice for Ramon? She didn't know, but deep down she felt she had failed. Gaudi was just Barbosa with a different vocabulary.

The cell was better than her previous one. It had recently been painted a kind of mushroomy white. There was a bed, a sink, a lavatory with a seat, a small table and chair bolted to the concrete floor, and a window high in one wall through which she could see some sky. It was humid and smelled of sweat, but she could live with that. She sat on the side of the bed and turned her mind to what might happen next.

The immediate answer was that nothing happened. She was allowed out to exercise twice each day which involved walking around the police parade ground. There were no trees and no vegetation, just concrete and a wall which ran around the parade ground till it joined the walls of the station at either side. Beyond the wall she could hear traffic and voices and could see trees but they seemed to belong to another world. They brought her food three times a day – fruit in the morning, bread and watery soup at midday and rice and beans, sometimes with a bit of chicken, in the evening.

Melba visited her on the second day but then no more visits were allowed. Apart from the guard who brought her food, she saw no-one – her only companion her thoughts. She had hoped that they would allow her some writing materials but they refused. She was at least allowed to keep the book that Melba had brought. Magda Gonzalez hoped that Lydia loved the works of Borges as much as she did, so sent a copy of *Ficciones*. Lydia knew it well and dipped in and out of it each day, reading just one or two of the short stories and being carried away on the surreal imagination of the remarkable Argentinian writer.

After ten days she had visitors - Nino with two assistants. They were each dressed in what appeared to be the uniform of the new government - combat fatigues and boots. The guard unlocked the cell and they walked in. Lydia was sitting on the bed, reading. She stood up and greeted them with a 'Buenas dias' but was ignored. There were no pleasantries.

Nino was all brusqueness.

"I am First Minister Nino Acevedo. You, Señorita Lydia Echevarria, are charged with collaboration with the enemy. You will appear before a Revolutionary Tribunal. You will have the opportunity to address the Tribunal before sentence is passed. These two companeros", indicating but not introducing his two colleagues, "will be presenting the case".

They nodded but said nothing.

She began to speak but they had turned on their heels and walked out. The guard quickly locked the door behind them. What, she thought, would she have said if they had not left so abruptly? Well, was it a slip of the tongue when the man Nino said 'before sentence is passed'? She thought not. Ideas of listening to evidence or the presumption of innocence were probably regarded as sentimental weaknesses by the likes of Nino. And another thing, wasn't there a contradiction in accusing her of collaborating with the enemy, when at the time, they were the enemy, rebelling against the established, albeit hated and hateful government?

She smiled to herself. That was the problem with having a proper education and being clever - you saw the holes in the bullies' posturing. It didn't help, of course, because they still had the power. But it gave her the satisfaction of knowing that whatever they might say, she had not done the things she was accused of. She had lived her life trying to do the right thing. Their nonsense was just that - nonsense. Of course, it was nonsense that could well result in them putting a bullet in her breast. But it could not undermine her conviction that she had done the right thing and would continue to do so. Then she remembered that she had betrayed Ramon, albeit to save her father and in the hope that Ramon would not, in fact, be harmed. Her fingers found a strand of hair to twist. Was that doing the right thing? Did all that she did afterwards wipe the slate clean? No, she said to herself, sadly. You are human. You failed. But you need not fail again. You need not let these bullies have their sport.

It was at least a change of surroundings. After a breakfast of an orange and a banana, she had been led upstairs six days after the meeting with Nino, and put in a police car. She washed her sweater most evenings and laid it out to dry over her chair. It was no longer pink but a kind of smudged rose but at least it meant that she looked presentable. Her hair had grown a little so she gathered it in a braid tied with a rubber band that she had cadged off a guard. A policeman sat next to her and another was in the passenger seat. The driver was a middle-aged black man with a thin pencil moustache and balding head. He had previously been a taxi-driver but had answered the call for recruits, particularly from those who had suffered under the old regime, to join the new 'people's police', As he had said to his wife, Josefina, it would make a welcome change to be giving orders instead of being on the receiving end. He was wearing a new police uniform with a name badge which identified him as Officer L. Morales. The faux-gold bracelet which he continued to wear even though it was against regulations completed the story, announcing that his name was Luis.

They drove to the military headquarters in the Campo Militar on the outskirts of the city on the road to San Rafael. Once out of the car, she was led into a building constructed on the cheap from breeze blocks with a corrugated iron roof. Passing through a metal door, she found herself in a waiting area with plastic chairs arranged against the wall. Pride of place on the wall to her left was a picture of the tank entering the Plaza Central festooned with garlands and with Gaudi, Nino and the others clinging to it. On the wall in front of her was a sign reading: Sala del Tribunal

Revolucionario and a list of names under the heading of Jueces (Judges). The first name on the list was Nino Acevedo.

She sat and waited. She was more intrigued than apprehensive about what would happen since the outcome had clearly been decided and it was just a matter of what they decided to do with her. After about half an hour, a soldier came to fetch her. Through a series of corridors painted that particular shade of dirty green associated with public buildings and up a flight of stairs, she found herself in what looked like a conference room. It was almost square with four picture windows looking out onto a baseball field. The floor was rough floorboards stained dark brown. There was a table at one end with three chairs behind it. The national flag of Caribe, horizontal stripes of red and green with a palm tree in the bottom right hand corner, stood in the corner. A solitary metal chair for the accused was to the side and then five rows of chairs facing the table. Eerily, all but two of the chairs were empty.

There was no-one in the room except the same two men who had come with Nino to her cell and were now sitting in the front row. This time they were in what looked like their dress uniform – a smart well-pressed olive-green shirt, olive-green trousers with razor-sharp creases, and highly polished black shoes. Epaulettes on their shirts indicated that they were officers. She amused herself by wondering whether the absence of an audience was because onlookers might be led astray or infected by her and the recital of her misdeeds.

The soldier who brought her in showed her to the metal chair and told her to stand there. He then withdrew. Three men in uniform came in through a side door and took their seats at the table. In the centre of the three was Nino, also sporting his dress uniform. The other judges were dressed similarly. The two men in the front row of chairs had stood when the judges entered. They remained standing. Nino turned to her.

"You may sit".

Lydia nodded and sat down.

"Señorita Echevarria, you are charged before this Revolutionary Tribunal with collaborating with the enemy. Captain Crespo and Lieutenant Fernando will present the case." Nodding to Crespo, he went on, "Please begin."

Crespo remained standing while Fernando sat down.

"I will bring before you, Companero First Minister", Crespo began, "a number of witnesses who will demonstrate the accused's guilt. There are many examples of her collaboration but I will not tire the Tribunal by introducing every one. Instead, I shall concentrate on three principal matters: the defiling of the memory of Companero Ramon Aguirre; the co-habitation with the war criminal Raul Salcedo; and the establishment of the Circulo Latino as a haven for oppressors and conspirators."

Crespo opened the file in front of him and appeared to consult it for a moment.

"As regards Companero Ramon, it is well known that he was a leading figure in the fight against the corrupt Barbosa. The accused befriended him. She thought it was fashionable to consort with someone from what her class regarded as 'the lower orders'. She introduced him to her social group and tried to persuade him to forget the cause. When that did not succeed, she abandoned him like any other plaything. When he was brutally murdered she did not even attend his funeral. She had already moved on."

Crespo sat down and Fernando took over.

"And who did she move on to," he asked rhetorically. "None other than Barbosa's right hand man and principal accessory in his corrupt regime, Raul Salcedo. To the outrage of decent society and to the consternation of her parents, she became Salcedo's courtesan or, since Companero First Minister demands that we speak plainly, his whore. And in that role, the accused gave support and succour to the enemies of the people of Caribe".

Crespo took over again:

"The accused created the Circulo Latino under the guise of fostering culture in our island. But it was a trick. In concert with Salcedo, she diverted funds intended for the education and welfare of fellow-citizens and created a place where disaffected young people and foreigners could support Barbosa and plot against the revolution. Particularly destructive were the so-called 'events' which the accused created and which gave foreigners the opportunity to organise their opposition to the revolution."

The two prosecutors then called their witnesses to establish each of the matters put before the Tribunal. As they were questioned, it appeared to Lydia that they had learned a script which either Crespo or Fernando then took them through. First came the police photographs of those attending Ramon's funeral – it had been under surveillance – to show that she did not attend. Then there followed an odd mix of people. There were the chancers, keen to ingratiate themselves with their new masters; the ne'er-do-wells, happy to say anything if there was a reward attached; the busybodies, for whom the Tribunal offered the state's blessing for the fine arts of gossip; and the people who had taken against her. In this last group were some relatives of Ramon who peddled the line that she had toyed with Ramon only to throw him over. A couple in their Sunday best described the noise created by the parties that she'd held at her apartment and the scandalous goings-on (unspecified but hinted at). Three elderly women who said that they were cleaners described the lavish entertainment provided as part of the 'events' at the Circulo which they had to clean up after – food which would feed hungry families just thrown out, and dozens of empty liquor bottles. One witness who claimed to be a neighbour's maid described in detail how Melba had wept at the mistreatment she received at the hands of the accused and Salcedo.

Unsurprisingly, Lydia didn't recognise any of them.

After all of them had been heard, there was time for a final flourish from Crespo. "On behalf of the people of Caribe, Companero First Minister, I demand that, in the light of all the evidence, the Tribunal should make an example of the accused".

Nino thanked him and Lieutenant Fernando and then turned to her.

"Echevarria, do you have anything to say before the Tribunal announces its decision?"

Lydia smiled and thanked him. "Might I have a glass of water," she asked. "Crespo and Fernando have been speaking for over two hours and I'm afraid I'm very thirsty."

The officer closest to her poured a glass from the jug of water on the table and passed it to Crespo who handed it to her.

"Thank you".

As they had been speaking, she understood how they could see things as they did. It was if there was a looking glass and they were on the other side. From that other side, everything looked the opposite of what she saw (and knew). What they said about Ramon was entirely plausible even if so very wrong and so very cruel. She knew why she had not been to his funeral. But her absence could be interpreted as they had done. She knew why she allowed Raul to set her up in Roosevelt Tower – it was so that she could destroy him and what he stood for. But how could they know if they only saw what appeared to be in front of them? She knew that the 'events' had been a crucial last straw in breaking the regime. But they knew nothing of her links to Cesar and how she brought off the kidnaps. They just saw her consorting with the rich and powerful, drinking Manhattans and Budweiser and eating steaks and pasta.

This was their looking glass world. She had no interest in persuading them that they were wrong nor in defending herself. It would be pointless. So she turned to Nino.

"Thank you, Señor First Minister. I'm grateful to you for giving me the opportunity to address you but I have nothing to say."

"I am not surprised, Señorita. You come from a background of privilege. You have only disdain for your fellow citizens. By addressing us you would have to accept our authority, our legitimacy. You would have to accept that we are the new Caribe. You would have to accept that things have utterly changed. You would have to accept that you are on the wrong side of history. Instead you choose silence because you cannot accept these things, you cannot understand."

She imagined the looking glass again. She wanted to say that it was he who did not understand, but she didn't. There was no point. It was her fate, she reflected, to pay the ultimate price for her dedication to the service of others – she would become a victim, her role unknown, while the ambitious and power-hungry scrambled to the top of the heap. She smiled at the eternal irony – it was in a history class in Boston that she'd come across the French writer Mallet du Pan. He it was who'd said of the French Revolution, "... like Saturn, the Revolution devours its children".

Nino's two colleagues had drawn their chairs close to his, conferring in whispers. After a few minutes, they drew back and Nino ordered her to stand.

"Señorita Echevarria, the Tribunal is grateful to Companeros Crespo and Fernando for setting out the facts so clearly. We are grateful to you for choosing not to waste the Tribunal's time by trying to offer some defence. There is no defence. We find you guilty. We sentence you to five years imprisonment in the state prison on the island of Los Olivos. That will be all. Take her away. The Tribunal is adjourned."

The three judges trooped out. Crespo lit a cigarette and he and Fernando gathered up their papers and began to chat. Neither looked across at her who, even at this moment, looked serene and calm. She did not need a strand of hair to twist. It was over. A soldier came and led her away.

Chapter 30

A package

Conway fell into a routine. The alarm went off at 7.30am. He shaved, washed, and made a cup of tea with the BBC Home Service in the background describing the catastrophes of the day. Then it was a short walk to the greasy spoon in Southend Green for breakfast. Depending on the level of his commitment to losing weight and eating healthy food, he did or did not have the sausage and fried bread with his bacon and eggs. Then it was back to the tiny flat in Glenilla Road to work on the book till lunch at The George – just a sandwich and one pint of Special out of concern for the waistline and the need to avoid falling asleep at his typewriter in the afternoon. More writing till 5.30pm, followed by 5-a-side football twice-a-week in Paddington and healthy walks over Primrose Hill or up to Hampstead Heath on most other evenings unless the weather was really foul. Dinner was usually the time to catch up with friends. There was one woman among them whom he was keen on but it was not clear whether she was equally keen on him. Not knowing spurred him on. Saturdays were for cricket matches – the Globe had a team in the London Newspapers League - and drinks after the match with mates. Sundays were for staying in bed till noon, reading the papers, reading a book and generally doing nothing. It was also the day when he used his kitchen – knocking together things he remembered from home, particularly neck-of-lamb stew and cheese and ham omelettes.

He worked at the dining table which also doubled as his desk. It meant that there was room for his typewriter and the piles of notes and papers which represented the accumulated memory of his time in Caribe. He decided he'd start the book at the point when Harry told him he was being sent to Caribe – he hadn't a clue what the title should be so it was known as 'The Book'. Then it was just a question of knitting together his despatches and the notes he had kept, many of which, for reasons of space in the paper or the need for discretion, had not been published. Now was the chance.

After six weeks Conway was feeling pleased with the progress he was making. He figured he'd be able to complete the first draft in another couple of weeks. Then he would still have two months left before he was due back at the Globe - ample time to improve the draft, get it to an editor, do the proofs and still have time for a fortnight's holiday somewhere abroad in mid-September where it would be warm but the tourists with children would have gone home. He persuaded himself that if he could get the woman he liked to go out with him, things might have progressed far enough by September that she might come on holiday with him - to Venice, perhaps. He knew it was a total fantasy, but, nothing venture ... .

Though he was pleased with how things were going, Conway also realised when he reviewed what he'd written so far that it was only half the story. He was describing the revolution from the perspective of the campaign - fighting and marching its way for months till it reached the capital. The other half of the story was missing - what was happening in other parts of Caribe and, most important, in Puerto Grande. Once he had climbed over the Embassy wall, which he described with some delight, he had only a very partial knowledge of what went on. He heard things from time to time. Atilio had filled him in on what he had been doing as had Teresa, albeit briefly when they spoke after Cesar's death. And, of course, there were his last couple of days holed up with Magda Gonzalez, but, in truth, what he had were snippets. So, the only thing he could do to remain completely honest was to make it clear that his was just one account of the armed struggle. It would be for others to write their accounts to complete the story. It was a regrettable compromise but he couldn't see any other way.

It was a Tuesday morning in the last week of July when he was disturbed in mid-morning. There was someone ringing the front door bell. The flat downstairs was unoccupied at the time, so he plodded down to see who or what it was. It was the postman.

"You Mr," looking down, "Conway? Package for you, mate. Special Delivery. You gotta sign for it".

"Sure. You have a pen?"

"No mate. I thought you people round here would have one".

"Hang on a minute". He ran back up the stairs and came back with a pencil.

"Sorry, mate. Has to be a pen."

"Oh God!" Back up he went and came down this time with a chewed biro.

He signed. Once back in his flat he realised that he hadn't really checked what it was. On examination he saw that the sender was Her Britannic Majesty's Embassy - Puerto Grande, Caribe. A name was typed below - Jeremy Brown.

"Crikey", he muttered to himself. "I must have left an old pair of trousers somewhere and Brown's clearing up, anxious to rid himself of the last trace of his nemesis".

Carefully opening the package, he saw that it contained two separate envelopes and a covering letter. The letter was curt and succinct:

"Dear Conway" (no Tony – he was destined to remain in the dog-house), "I am forwarding these two envelopes at the request of a Miss Circe Garcia" (it dawned on him that he'd never known her family name till then). "She was most insistent that you receive them". Brown's name was typed but there was no signature (he really was in the dog-house). There was a typed post-script which read, "I look forward to the settlement at your very earliest convenience of the invoice that I gave you. From an abundance of caution, I enclose a copy".

He put Brown's letter aside, deciding that his initial judgement that Brown was a twit was right after all. What was inside the two envelopes?

As he opened them he gasped. He could not believe what he had in his hands. He let out a yelp of sheer delight. In the first envelope were about 20 hand-written pages stapled together, with a cover page which read: *Caribe's Revolution 1962-3: The Journal of Circe Garcia*. What was in the second envelope was even more remarkable. He could barely believe his eyes. There were about fifty-odd type-written pages, single-spaced, with a small font-size, on super-thin typing paper. The front cover read: *My Story* by Lydia Echevarria de Colon y Mendieta.

He carefully drew out the papers. This was a treasure trove. Now, after all, he would be able to tell the full story of the revolution, not just the half he'd witnessed. As he leafed through the papers, he soon realised that there was even more in the envelopes than he'd initially thought.

He laid everything out on the table. There were, in fact, four documents, not two. The first was a letter from Circe to him, then her Journal, then Lydia's *Story*, then finally something else - a letter from Lydia to her parents.

Circe had written:

"Dear Tony,

I hope and pray that this package reaches you. Señor Brown promised to send it and I have to trust him.

I know that you wanted to tell the story of what happened in Caribe so I've included my Journal. You may use it. I hope it helps.

I do not have permission to send you Lydia's story or her letter. She entrusted them to Melba. When I visited Magda's house where she now lives, Melba gave them to me, saying that she believed that Lydia's story should be told even if Lydia does not wish it. I do not know what is best, so I leave that decision to you. As for Lydia's letter to her parents, as you can see it is a very private letter. Again, I leave it to you to decide what to do with it. I have tried to discover where her parents are. Melba told me that they had moved to Mexico because they were so unhappy in Caribe and that Lydia was unable to trace them. I think it broke her heart, if she has any heart left that is not already broken.

Tomasito and I are safe and well. He goes to school and is reading well. I paint and do some writing and live on the money Lydia gave me.

I have no word of Lydia. You will have heard that she has been sent to prison in Los Olivos for five years. No-one is allowed to make contact.

I wish you well, Tony.

With fond memories of La Perla and all that followed.

Circe.

Conway was deeply moved. He had grown to love Circe: her resolve, her courage, her practical, no-nonsense attitude, her love for her little brother, and her serious aspect. Her Journal would be a Godsend in filling out the story of what went on in Puerto Grande, especially Cesar's network and the activities at the Circulo.

He was greatly saddened by the news that Lydia had been imprisoned. He had tried to keep up with events in Caribe but had not seen any report of it. He hoped that her *Story* would explain what had happened.

Then he turned to the *Story* and Lydia's letter. Circe had left it to him to decide what to do with them. Well, he would read them and then decide.

First, the letter. It was short:

My beloved Mami and Papi,

How I wish that I was not writing this letter but walking on the beach with you, all holding hands and laughing at one of Papi's bad jokes about quadratic equations.

I hope that you can forgive me for the pain I have caused you. Ramon gave up his life for our little island. I caused his death. I had no choice but to give my life to the cause that he and so many others believed in.

I consorted with the devil – Salcedo – so as to destroy him and Barbosa and all the other criminals. Now they have gone. The price has been too great – the death of our leader Professor Sanchez and my loss of you, the two people who gave me life and whom I love so much. I know that you could not understand what I did but I hope now you will see that it had to be that way.

The new dictators intend to condemn me because they fear me. So be it. I do not seek glory – I do not deserve it. But I do seek your understanding. Please God you will come to know why I did what I did.

I send you my kisses.

Your loving daughter,

Lydia.

He had to sit down for a while. The emotion was almost overwhelming. He was back in Caribe, in the Casa Joaquin the little restaurant where they had lunch and she talked about star signs. It was there that he first saw the passion she felt for what she called her 'little island'. He smiled as he remembered the fool he had made of himself at her party. He recalled his feeling that all was not as it seemed when Raul squeezed Lydia's arm too tightly at that party. And then she had dropped off his radar. He realised that she had been playing a very dangerous game.

He turned to her *Story*. It took him nearly four hours to work through what Lydia had written. As a trained journalist, she knew how to tell a story. She began with her interest in Caribe's welfare and politics as a teenager and the various activities and organisations she'd been involved with. Then she met Ramon.

"It was Ramon," she wrote, "and those around him who introduced me to the need for action if Caribe was to avoid becoming, as he put it, a place for cheap labour, cheap holidays and cheap prostitutes. He was the love of my life, my soul mate, an intellectual, and a natural leader. His death and my involvement in it changed me forever. I had to bring Salcedo down, for what he had done to Ramon but also for being part of Barbosa's corrupt regime".

She explained clear-headedly how she appeared to surrender to Raul. She became a spy, a fifth columnist, working undercover in concert with Cesar. It meant that no-one could know and consequently most would condemn her. He was staggered at her achievements in supplying information and intelligence to Cesar to pass to Gaudi, without the latter ever knowing. He was even more staggered by her decision to launch a series of kidnaps. This was a master stroke and probably marked the beginning of the regime's ultimate collapse.

But for Lydia there was no happy ending. She recognised with tragic clarity that her vision of the revolution had been displaced.

"Cesar is dead and Gaudi and his clique have won. They are the new dictators". She ended her *Story* poignantly – "So, here I sit patiently in my apartment waiting for the knock on the door."

Reading this last sentence, he asked out loud,

"Why didn't she go underground or escape when it was clear that Gaudi's men would come for her?"

Lydia didn't offer a clue. As Conway sat there, he tried to put himself in Lydia's shoes. His thoughts went back and forth. He admitted that there was a danger in constructing overcomplicated explanations – the easy answer was that she'd fought for Caribe and wasn't going to leave, even if she had to do some prison time because the thugs had taken over. But that was too easy, too simple. Lydia was one of the most complicated people he'd ever met. He settled on the conclusion that he didn't know the answer – a desire for punishment because of Ramon's murder coupled with a desire for expiation by destroying Barbosa and Salcedo were the best he could come up with, but it sounded like a bad case of psycho-babble after three pints of beer at the pub.

Whatever her motives, Lydia's *Story* was a gift from the Gods in terms of his book. The question, however, was what was he going to do – was he going to use it? Was he entitled to use it? Circe had left it to him to decide. The first step was to make a cup of tea and sit down to think.

He decided to consider the *Story* first. If he was just concerned with his selfish ambition to write a book which people would read and like and, most important, buy, clearly he had to take advantage of what had landed in his lap, and include Lydia's account. But there was Lydia to consider. Assuming that the book or the serialisations would find their way to Caribe, two factors weighed most heavily with him. First, did Lydia want it to be published? There was no evidence either way. The fact that she had written such a detailed account suggested that she meant it to be read. But by whom? The fact that she hadn't asked Melba to do anything with it suggested that she intended it to remain private – her personal settling of accounts with those she conspired to bring down.

"There you have it, Tony my boy," he said to himself, "a classic case of 'on the one hand this and on the other hand that'".

And then there was a second consideration. Would using it put Lydia in danger? She had already fallen foul of Gaudi's regime it appeared, no doubt because they thought she had colluded with Raul and, thus, with Barbosa. If what she had really done was known, she could, of course, be feted as a hero. But, more likely, her closeness to Cesar and what he stood for would mark her out as a threat. Was it enough that they had already hidden her away in an island prison, or would they feel the need to do more? Once the book appeared, could she become a figure around whom those who felt that the revolution had been stolen from them could rally? That spelled danger for her.

Conway decided to go for a walk. He'd think things through as he made his way up towards Hampstead Heath. It was a pleasant warm evening as he set off. He'd put on tracksuit bottoms, a T shirt and an old pair of trainers - if the spirit moved him he could jog for a while. He went across the Heath to the top of Parliament Hill to look down at the panorama of London set out before him. The sun was reflecting off the dome of St Paul's Cathedral. It was good to be alive and good to be in London. A young, attractive, dark-haired woman walked by and his mind was immediately drawn back to images of Lydia and thoughts of her in some awful Devil's Island prison. His mood became sombre. He trotted down the hill and stopped off at the Roebuck in Pond Street for a pint and a beef sandwich.

The pint helped. He made up his mind. Lydia's *Story* must see the light of day. It was important for the history of the revolution that her account be heard, not least to counter other accounts celebrating Gaudi and his triumph. Yes, it could expose her to further danger, but if he and others worked hard enough to keep the spotlight on Gaudi's regime they would probably be reluctant to do anything more to her. Indeed, they might even let her go, preferring to keep a close eye on her rather than create a martyr.

On the walk back to his flat Conway asked himself about the other problem - Lydia's letter to her parents. It was part of Lydia's story - how she had had to create the impression of turning her back on everything and everyone to get Raul to believe that she belonged to him. It showed the price she was prepared to pay to achieve something for her 'little island'. She had undoubtedly comforted herself with the thought that once the revolution was won, she would be reunited with her parents and things would return to what they had been. It must never have occurred to her for a moment that her parents would be so distressed by losing her that they would abandon Caribe. Even worse, that they would disappear and be untraceable.

He let himself in, climbed the stairs, went into his flat and flopped into a comfortable old chair that his mother had given him when he moved in. Within a couple of minutes he was up again, restless, unable to make his mind up. He phoned Zack who was an old mate from the Globe. Zack could track down anything and anyone. He laid out the challenge:

"Zack, my son, sorry to drag you away from the pub" - loud protests - "but I have an important assignment. Can you see if could find a Señor and Señora Echevarria who moved to somewhere in Mexico from the island of Caribe about a year or so ago?"

"Not in the pub, mate. I'm round Lucy's place, but she's asleep 'cause she was on duty last night. Now, what did you want me to do? Needles and haystacks come to mind. Don't you have anything else?"

"No, I don't, sorry mate. If I did, I could've found them myself, couldn't I, without bothering the Globe's own Sherlock Holmes."

"Well, I have to tell you, my son, that the prospect of finding someone in Mexico when you only have the last name to go on comes close to the prospect of winning the football pools - very remote. I'll tell you what. I'll warm up a contact in the Embassy in Mexico City and get back to you as soon as I can. Now, what was the name again? Spell it out."

The exchange bought Conway some time before he had to make a final decision. He decided that in the meantime he'd include the letter in the book. If Zack found the parents and if they said no, then he could take it out. Otherwise, it would serve as another demonstration of the choices Lydia had felt obliged to make. Admittedly, if the parents ever saw the book without knowing about the letter, they'd be shocked to see it there, but he had no doubt that the shock would quickly turn to understanding and reinforce the love they'd always felt for her.

Now it was just a question of preparing a revised plan for the book so as to incorporate both Circe's and Lydia's accounts. He decided to divide the book into three parts - his despatches and notes, Circe's journal, then

Lydia's *Story*. He smiled to himself. As every schoolboy knew, Cesar's namesake, Julius Caesar, divided Gaul into three parts in his *Gallic War Part I*. Cesar would have been proud of him! Lydia's letter would come at the end of Lydia's *Story*. He would do the translating himself because he was familiar with the context. He could always ask one of the mates he played football with who was from Granada if he was stumped over some word or expression and needed help.

Once he'd settled on the plan it was just a question of knitting everything together. But, there was one question which he still hadn't resolved. How explicit should he be about Cesar's death? Should he talk of his views as suspicions or should he come straight out and accuse Gaudi and Nino of killing Cesar so as to wrest the revolution from him and turn it into something more to their liking? He re-read all his notes and revisited what had happened and what Nino and others had said. He added into the equation what Circe and Lydia had written. He cast aside his doubts. Cesar had been murdered and he would accuse them.

He heard from Zack a few days later.

"Sorry, sunshine. No luck. My contact put the word out but he said there's no real way to check. He said that even in Mexico City the records are rudimentary and outside the capital they veer between poor to non-existent".

"Thanks, anyway, Zack".

So, Lydia's letter to her parents would stay in.

Conway phoned Harry at the Globe on a Monday morning towards the end of August.

"Harry, it's Tony. I have a manuscript for you. Ninety thousand magical words all waiting to amaze and delight".

"Yeah, yeah. About time I heard from you. If you bring it in we can start re-writing it in English and generally getting it in shape. Then I'll let the editor loose on it. Then, you can do the proofs. Then we can sign up the publisher. Then we can agree on what bits we use for serialisation. Then we can plan the launch. Then we can plan the interviews and the book tour. Then you can come back to work because by the time we've done all that, there won't be any time for that holiday you thought you'd sneak past me."

Conway was used to Harry's curmudgeonly banter but this seemed excessive.

"Harry. How about 'Well done and thanks, old boy?'"

"Yeah, well you'll get my thanks when I've seen it. So, shall we say twelve o'clock today? And, have you thought of a title?"

"Yes," he replied, not a little deflated, though recognising that this was what Harry was paid to do. "I think you'll like it, Harry - '*The Theft of a Revolution*'".

"Sounds catchy. You'll probably get sued or shot, or both. See you in a while", and he rang off.

Conway took the Tube to the Aldwych and then hiked down Fleet Street to the Globe. Harry met him outside his office and took the manuscript inside beckoning him to follow. Settling his ample frame into his chair, Harry pulled his glasses off his forehead and looked at what he'd got.

"Looks substantial, son. Leave it with me for a couple of days and then give me a call. If I like it, and notice the 'if' Tony, there'll be plenty to do. Now, bugger off and let me get started."

Conway backed out of the office, contenting himself with "Nice to see you too, Harry", and went down to the third floor to find Zack and thank him. They decided to have an early lunch at El Vino's and catch up on what they'd been doing.

Then it was back to Belsize Park. Sitting at his typewriter, he realised that he needed to add an '*Introduction*'. What emerged was:

'This book could not have been written without the help and kindness of others. Some I cannot name but they know who they are and how grateful I am. Some are dead and I grieve for them and remember them here - especially Atilio the painter and the remarkable Professor Sanchez whom you will meet as you read on. Two women stand out as heroes, though they would reject the description. I dedicate the book to them. One is Circe Garcia, a young woman from the country who showed incredible courage, tenacity and leadership to advance the cause she knew was right. The other is the remarkable Lydia Echevarria. If Professor Sanchez was the father of the revolution, Lydia was his right hand. She never thought of herself, only of those less fortunate, ground down by Caribe's President Barbosa and his henchmen, led by Raul Salcedo. Her reward is imprisonment. Though she did not seek reward this is a cruel fate to endure. Should her parents ever read this book they will be re-united, at least in print, with the daughter who, they will see, loves them dearly.

Finally, I am grateful to the staff of the British Embassy in Caribe and particularly Mr Jeremy Brown for the assistance extended to me which was in the finest traditions of the British Foreign Service.'

He typed it out and put it in an envelope addressed to Harry. Then, he remembered that he needed to correct one very important oversight which had occurred to him as he was coming back on the Tube. He tore open the envelope and added:

"*Harry, I refer quite often in the second half of my section of the book to a Señora Magda Gonzalez. Could your people make sure that she becomes X (no señora), otherwise she'll be in danger. The same applies where Circe and Lydia refer to h*

* * * * *

He was suddenly something of a star. The book was serialised in the Globe and greeted with acclaim. The launch at Foyles attracted a big crowd - he spent nearly two hours signing copies. He was interviewed on the BBC's Home Service and Third Programme and by Cliff Michelmore for Tonight on BBC Television. The Globe ran a centre page biography of him titled, 'From Tipton to Fleet Street to Caribe'. The Guardian carried an interview in the Women's Section, concentrating on the contributions of Circe and Lydia. The Wolverhampton *Express and Star* had the inevitable, "Local Boy Toast of London".

Within weeks, a 'Free Lydia' movement had been set up, supposedly with the encouragement of the Labour Party MP, Michael Foot. Penguin reported a surge in sales of Robert Graves' translation of Suetonius' *Twelve Caesars*. On a visit to his parents' home, Ted his father announced shyly, in the English way, how proud he was of his son. Wendy, his mother, nodded approvingly. They joked about the role that Latin and Suetonius had played in the story, with Ted conceding that studying classics "had turned out alright in the end". Ted and Wendy had just bought a new Jack Russell puppy and Ted said he was minded to name him Suetonius in Tony's honour. Conway suggested it wasn't the best idea because his Dad would look a bit of a prat shouting 'Suetonius' across the local park. Ted saw the point and they settled on Nero for the puppy.

Over the days and weeks, Conway wrestled with how to reach Lydia's parents. At his request, the publishers agreed to advertise the book as widely as possible in Mexico and make sure that copies were available to meet any demand. He also needed to get a copy to Circe (and, if possible, Lydia). He decided he would kill two birds with one stone. He drafted a letter to Jeremy Brown at the Embassy in Puerto Grande. He then asked Harry at the Globe to send the letter, together with the money he owed according to the invoice Brown had sent, plus a dozen copies of the book. One copy was for Brown - could Harry draw his attention to the comment in the Introduction? The other copies were for Circe - would Brown please use his best endeavours to get them to her? If she, in turn, could get one to Lydia, that would be wonderful, but they understood it may not be possible.

* * * * *

'*The Theft of a Revolution*' was not only well received in the UK. It was picked up across the Americas, North and South. Book reviewers praised it as a 'significant piece of writing' complimenting Conway particularly on his skill in weaving together his story with those of two remarkable women. Political commentators in the United States expressed gratitude for reporting a story that would not otherwise have been known - how a revolution was stolen - and urged Congress and the State Department to take appropriate action (whatever that might be).

Even if there was no coverage in the state-controlled media in Caribe, the coverage in the US newspapers which were still on sale there, and on US radio and television stations which Caribinos tuned into, could not be ignored by Gaudi's government. Moreover, copies of the book began to appear despite efforts to prevent them from being imported. Weeks passed and there was no let-up in the questions being asked of him, particularly by elements of the foreign media. Furiously, Gaudi finally decided to give an interview on television to denounce the book and the press reports.

Speaking through an interpreter who took it upon herself to moderate the language somewhat, Gaudi fumed to Walter Cronkite on CBS Evening News, "The book is a work of fiction put about by counter-revolutionaries who want to turn back the clock and hand Caribe back to the Yanqui oppressors and their bankers".

The interview was a catastrophic blunder. People scrabbled to get copies, particularly from the large Caribino community who had settled in Florida and were only too happy to send them if it would fuel the fire of opposition.

"What are the options, Companero", Nino asked Gaudi as they talked across the dinner table a few days after the disastrous interview.

Nino drew deeply on his evil-smelling Royal then continued, "We have to do something. The backlash from that damned book and the Echevarria woman's so-called *Story* can hurt us. The people still love you but we all know how quickly that can change. The people can be fickle."

Gaudi waved the smoke away – he was an ex-smoker, always an inch away from asking for a cigarette as the familiar smell beckoned him to recant and come back to nicotine's intoxicating embrace. He took a swig from his mug of coffee and stared out of the window.

"You are right, Nino. The interview was a mistake". Nino raised his hand as if to indicate that he didn't say that, but he waved the protests away. "Don't worry. I accept that I was wrong. Now we have to repair the damage".

"Look, Companero", Nino said. "Mistake or no mistake, the damned book and our response have thrown a lifeline to those who are still carrying a torch for Cesar and want to challenge what they'll soon be calling our 'regime', if we aren't careful. There's a danger that the Echevarria woman will become some kind of symbol, a rallying point for opposition. We can't do anything about the book except continue to say it's nonsense. But we can do something about her".

Gaudi nodded. "OK. You mentioned options. Let's go through them. First, we could set her free – say that we're releasing her on licence, say it's a gesture to internationalism. There's some kind of international movement led by some crack-pot socialist named Foot in London who's always looking for some noble cause to carry a placard for. We'd have to manage her release very carefully, of course. If we got it right, she could lead us to anyone working against us."

"Second, Nino, we could put her on trial again for further undermining the state by collaborating, this time on a book with, how shall we describe him - 'the English fantasist Conway.'"

Nino smiled.

"We could find her guilty and solve the problem by shooting her, but the danger is that word would get out and she'd become a martyr."

"Or third, we could offer to let her go into exile in Mexico or the USA, if they'd take her."

Nino shook his head. "She wouldn't go".

"No, she undoubtedly wouldn't, but it's an option to be considered. And, fourthly, we could arrange for her to die. Los Olivos isn't exactly a health spa and there's more than enough malaria and yellow fever to go round".

Gaudi leaned back. "Those are the only options I can come up with. Can you think of any other?"

Nino shook his head.

"Well, Nino, which should it be?"

They talked late into the night.

Chapter 31

A room with a view

Lydia sat in the room assigned to her in the prison on the island of Los Olivos. It was pleasant and airy, the slatted windows letting in the afternoon breeze off the sea half a mile away. At this time of day she could smell the salt and picture the waves on the shore. The parakeets hadn't started to chatter yet, so it was relatively peaceful – just the noise of doors clanging and women talking as they worked in the gardens that she could see from her chair. She had on a white outfit – a long-sleeved top, buttoned up the front, white trousers and white shoes. She was training to be a nurse and this was her uniform. The room was where she saw patients who did not need to be hospitalised in the infirmary.

She had been told of Conway's book. Despite what they'd said, she was sure that he had done a good job. They told her that he'd included her *Story*. She didn't know how he had got hold of it, but it didn't matter. Perhaps it was best if it was told, but she could understand that it might make the likes of Nino very angry. They told her that they were reconsidering what to do with her in the light of the further evidence of her collaboration, this time with 'the English fantasist'. She could imagine the options.

So, she sat, waiting to hear what they would do - smelling the sea and thinking of home. She was twisting a strand of hair with her fingers. On a shelf was a small picture frame that one of the women had made for her. It had a photograph in it. She looked at it and smiled. It was Ramon.

Printed in Great Britain
by Amazon